I0602233

# AN IMPOSTER IN WARRIORS CLOTHING

Copyright © 2021 by
Elissa Emory

All rights reserved. No
part of this book may be
reproduced or used in any
manner without written
permission of the
copyright owner except
for the use of quotations
in a book review. For
more information,
address:
contact@ellemaebooks.c
om

FIRST EDITION

www.ellemaebooks.com

*For all the "imposters" out there, keep doing your best and do not let anyone tear you down.*

## Trigger Warning

Before moving forward, please note that the themes in this
book can be dark and trigger some people. The themes can
include but are not limited to; sexual assault, death, gore,
domestic abuse, and violence.
If you need help, please reach out to the resources below.

**National Suicide Prevention Lifeline**
1-800-273-8255
https://suicidepreventionlifeline.org/

**National Domestic Violence Hotline**
1-800-799-7233
https://www.thehotline.org/

# AN IMPOSTER IN WARRIORS CLOTHING

## ELLE MAE

# Chapter One

### Unknown

For all my six-hundred years of life, the mortal realm has always left me with one resounding conclusion: it's a curse.

The mortal world has not changed much in the three hundred years since I last traveled, but now it's filled with much more dangerous players. Seeing *her* here only proved as much. Her now mortal body hid her well, but the unmistakable thrum of magic that seemed to seep out of her did not fool me. Seeing her here gave me a sliver of hope, while she might have been cursed to live here as such… at least she lived once more.

I stayed carefully hidden from view, ensuring no mortals could see me and only hoping that my own kind could not sense me. If they found me here, I would be done before she even remembered my name, but I had to see her one last time before the plan begun. Even with the cemetery littered with mortals, they remained far away from her, almost as if they too could sense what lay beneath her skin. Her brown hair fell across her face slightly, the rest resting itself on the nape of her neck. The black dress she wore came up to her collar bones and hugged her figure slightly, but not enough to draw attention; the dress modest in fashion, appropriate for the mortal occasion. Even as the casket descended, people's eyes were drawn to her.

People only deterred their stares once the casket faded from view and the final prayer was spoken. Their voices flitted across the quiet space in hushed tones, no doubt she could also hear them from where she stood.

"I can't believe she has the nerve to show up here."

"It's a disgrace to see her like this."

"Who gave her the location?"

I kept still, trying to soak her in as much as I could before I was forced to leave. She had tear marks on her face. From the outside, it would look like she had been crying, but I knew better. Her shoulders were hunched forward and shaking slightly, and she brought her hand up to cup her mouth so no sound could escape. When she removed her hand, the people around her recoiled—I couldn't blame them. Seeing her like this… it felt like you were witnessing a monster shed its all too human skin giving you a peek of what it held beneath. Her shell has always been carefully crafted, leaving her insides hidden from the world, but some parts are harder to hide than others, and more often than not, they force themselves to the front.

The story that was given to the rest of the magical world is that she had died suddenly. No other details, no other mess. I was one of the unlucky ones who knew the truth. Staring at her now in this mortal form, I was unsure if I was excited to have her back or if I should have prayed harder to keep her dead.

Without her hand covering herself, her bone-chilling smile stood on display for all to see. Not a moment later, her laugh broke through the silent cemetery.

# Chapter Two

### Vien

I shut the door softly behind me and leaned my back against the hard surface. I sighed loudly and threw my bookbag haphazardly across the room. This had been the third job that I had lost this year due to… my behavior. I'd really came to enjoy my job at the bookstore. Before this, I had an even better job at a publishing agency, but when I had been fired from there, it had been hard to find another one. I thought that a book shop would be the perfect place to lay low while I collected myself. I loved to read, and I really didn't think that trouble would be able to find me there… trouble isn't doing the finding, instead, it seems to come off me in waves.

I let myself slide down the wall and to the hard floor. Luck would have it that this book shop really didn't care about who it hired, but the other employees did. On my first day, the other sales associates whispered behind their hands and refused to answer any of my questions. They confronted me later about my part in Addie's death. They were schoolmates apparently, and they believed the rumors that had been spread. That I had something to do with it. Even after two years, people in this town whispered about how much of a monster I was, how I didn't bat an eyelash at her death, how I had pushed her towards it. Today, when I heard them talking loudly about how Addie killed herself because she caught me in bed with another, let's just say that I was let off easy when I was found smiling over the bleeding body of one of the associates.

I reached for my phone to check the time, but I got distracted. On the screen was the picture of me and Addie. I felt the sides of my mouth curl at the sight of her dimples and soft face. She had a carefree spirit. She saw me as more than the rumors, saw something other than a soulless monster. It had been two years since she died. I knew I had moved on, but I still loved looking at her. I sometimes believed what her family said about me. Before she died, she barely had any will to live, as if someone really did suck the soul out of her. She gave everything and more to me, and when I still wasn't happy, and when she couldn't find any other possible reason for it, she took it upon herself to snuff out the only reason she could think of: herself.

I sighed and decided to change it. The ghost of her smile had been following me around for far too long. As much as her death hurt, I had no reason to keep her picture. I kept it out of guilt, not love… I was unsure if I had ever even loved her or anyone else for that matter. I changed it to a random picture that came with the phone and called it a day. Out with the old, in with the new, I guess.

My life was not perfect, but it did its job. I had a place to live and some food. But now that I don't have a job anymore, I would have to go and apply for something or connect with my old contacts. There was no promise that I would ever be able to get a legal job again with my record, but that was not tonight's worry. Looking around, my eyes were open to how much of a mess I had let this place come to. Laundry laid strewn on the couch, I caught sight of a pair of jeans that I had thought I'd lost long ago, and discarded pairs of socks led from the door into the living room. I had a habit of just tearing them off with my shoes and leaving them there until laundry day came around. The problem was that laundry day was often forgotten by me.

I still had too much dignity left to keep wallowing in self-pity. I tried to hold on to the sliver of happiness the scene of the girl bleeding out today brought me. She deserved it and so did her friend, but I did not have enough time to get to her. At that point, I realized that hurting one person may have gotten me fired, the other would have landed me in jail. I smiled softly and poured myself some whiskey. It burned the back of my throat on its way down, but after so many years of nothing else, I'd learned to rather enjoy the feeling. I walked over to the large sliding glass door and laid my head on the cool glass, letting it chase away the burning sensation I felt creeping up. The sun had set long ago; I'd planned to be home before sunset, but they kept me for longer for questioning.

Looking outside, I admired the dark forest. It had seen better days. Growing up here, I had seen it at its best, but as our seasons got drier and drier, the green leaves turned to brown and the bark became thin and brittle. My mom begged my dad to buy this house as soon as they had the money to; she had a thing for fairy tales and insisted that she dreamed of living in a house surrounded by trees. I know which fairytale it was, she read that book to me many times as a child. We would sit not ten feet from where I stood now and would try to point out shapes in the forest, claiming they were faeries.

A movement caught my eye and I tried to focus on it, but it disappeared faster than I could keep up. Maybe my mom spoke some truth about faeries inhabiting these forests. I chuckled to myself but stopped when I saw it again. From what I could tell, it wasn't an animal but something glowing. I put my drink down and pushed my face closer to the glass. It sped across the forest again making my heart pound with excitement. My hand drifted to the lock on the sliding glass door and I slowly started to open it. The cool winter air hit my face, but the urge to find out if faeries actually existed pushed me forward.

Maybe my own stupidity was what plagued me instead of a curse, but I still felt myself smile as I reached the edge of the forest. I couldn't tell if the pounding in my chest was excitement or just the alcohol impairing my thinking. I made my way into the forest trying to gain another glimpse at whatever glowing light I was certain I'd seen. The air was so cold and crisp that I felt as though I could barely breathe. The thickness of the forest did not help with it either. I felt claustrophobia creep up on me suddenly. I almost stopped and gave up when I didn't see it again, but not a second later, I saw the glow in the corner of my eyes, and I whirled around to face it.

I do not know exactly when the forest had turned into nothing, but in an instant, darkness had swallowed me. No glowing light or thick tree branches, just straight darkness. I could feel my heart pounding, and I tried to turn to go back to my home, but darkness clouded the way back as well.

My breathing became rapid. I no longer felt the giddy excitement fill me but instead regret and anger at my own stupidity. I had left my home, barefoot and not paying attention to the things around me, because I thought I could find the faerie my mom was always so excited about. Stupid, it was utter stupidity. My panic was cut off by what seemed to be a small glow—looking around, it didn't take long for me to find out that the glowing came from within me and blanketed my skin.

"What the—"

Feeling a strong pull in my stomach, the darkness swirled around me, and I felt my body being pushed and pulled in all different ways. The feeling caught me so off guard that I tried to grab anything in my range. To my surprise, I found a tree in the ever-shifting void in front of me. Luckily, I did not eat dinner tonight because if I did, I knew that it would have been all over the floor by now. Before I could even get over the feeling of nausea, I heard war cries in the distance.

The abyss was now gone, and instead, I only saw the green forest, but instead of the darkness that surrounded us, the sun peaked through the trees above me. The forest that surrounded me now had nothing in common with the one back home; the trees were taller, healthier, and thicker. Small, glowing balls of pollen seemed to dance in the breeze. They left a sweet taste in my mouth and felt cleaner than anything my town could produce.

In front of me, I saw a tumbling mess of people coming through the forest. Soldiers fighting to get closer to me, pushing each other and attacking those around them. Weapons were being used, and I saw flashes of light and fire being thrown around. A stream of fire came so close to my face that I barely had time to dodge it.

One of the soldiers came dangerously close to reaching me, and in an instant, his hand burst into flames in front of me and he let out a blood-curdling scream. I stumbled back and tried to distance myself from the people clawing at me.

"Don't run!" someone yelled in the distance, but like hell was I going to listen to that.

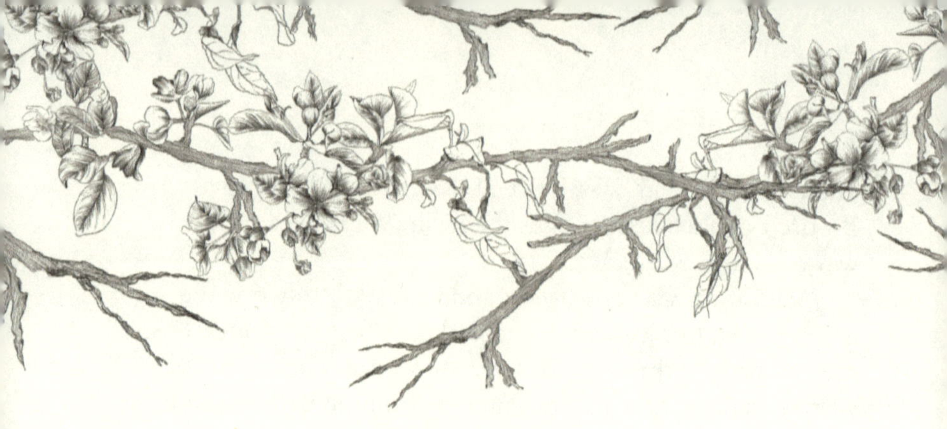

# Chapter Three

Unknown

I felt the ground shake, and a magical signature spiked so largely that even from so far away, it seemed to vibrate throughout my body. She must have entered the door.

I couldn't help myself from smiling and letting out a laugh.

Finally.

Finally, we could start our plans. It had been hundreds of years in the making, and now the day had finally come.

# Chapter Four

## Vien

I turned and started to run. I had no idea where I was or where this forest would lead me, but I didn't have the luxury to take too long to think about it. I started to push myself forward, jumping over fallen trees and trying to dodge the light and fire that was still being thrown through the air. The war cries and screaming behind me persisted as I ran for my life. They were trying to reach me. I tried to run as fast as I could, but my feet were screaming at me to stop. I could feel the skin being torn from them.

Why did I not put slippers on? I cursed my stupidity, but honestly, how would I have known that the glowing faerie light would have led me to a war?

As I weaved through the trees, I could sense that I was gaining traction; the distance between myself and the army of soldiers lengthened, but before I could feel any relief, I saw a man no more than a few feet before me. While he wore the same armor as the others, he had a loose white shirt on that covered his arms but left a bit of his chest exposed. His long blond hair was tied into a delicate ponytail that sat at the nape of his neck and seemed to glow with the forest around us. He was decorated with tattoos, one that went from his mouth all the way down to his chest and joined another that was semi-hidden by his armor. The most shocking though, his eyes were a vibrant purple that seemed to be glowing in the shadows. I skidded to a stop right before him, and he gave me a big smile that showed his perfect white teeth.

"It seems like you may need assistance, m'lady." He bent slightly at the waist and held out a hand to me. His skin was so pale that he seemed to be almost transparent. His beauty was far beyond what I have seen back home. I bet he was some sort of prince.

I shot a glance behind my shoulder and saw that while the battle was still raging, it was further away, and someone stood between the rest of the bloodthirsty soldiers and myself. My heart felt like it stopped for a second and my breath caught in my throat. She was beautiful and frenzied, another person that was without a doubt otherworldly. She was muscular yet slim, but I did not let that fool me. You could tell by her stance that she held some type of power in her. She seemed winded, and you could tell by the dirt and blood on her that she had been fighting. Her hair was short, brushing just the top of her pointed ears, and as black as night. She had an olive complexion and her face too was decorated with tattoos, framing her forehead and the skin around her eyes. Her eyes were even more striking than the man behind me, but they made me recoil in fear. They were blood-red and held so much anger in them. Anger, it seemed, directed at me. She glared at us and bared her teeth, letting out a loud growl. She even had fangs.

I turned back to the man who was still smiling at me. *Nope.*

I ran as fast as I could to my left. Ignoring the cries from both the women and man that I had run away from. My breath was coming out in short huffs and I felt my face begin to burn. I could not stop now. I saw the girl run towards me with an outstretched hand, and I weaved around a tree to dodge her. She stumbled and stared at me in shock.

I did not hesitate. I kept running, but I felt my arm being grabbed behind me. Pain radiated through me, and I turned to face who it could be, but my sight was obstructed by a strong burst of light. I lifted my free hand up to cover my face from the blow, but it never came.

"You can open your eyes now. We are safe," a deep voice spoke from above me. I didn't need to open my eyes to know it was the prince.

I slowly removed my hand from my face and looked around. Gone was the raging war and instead, we were placed right in front of an all-white mansion. It looked like it was plucked from a fairy tale. Everything from the trim on the windows to the green vines running up the sides seemed to give it a story.

The house was surrounded by trees and other greenery, making the house itself seem like it was glowing against the dark green background. Besides us stood two fountains, and beyond those were white rose gardens that seemed the stretch beyond what the eye could see. The path we were on was lined with intricate brickwork that led up to the grand staircase, and that too seemed too elegant to be of this world. Everything was light here. I mean, it literally looked to be almost glowing. I snapped out of my trance and looked at him. He stood there still smiling, and even though I struggled to catch my breath from the run, he seemed unfazed.

He squeezed my hand. With a small jump, I pulled my hand back as though it had been burned and scowled at him. His smile wavered slightly, and his eyes finally showed a bit of emotion, but whatever it was it was gone in an instant. Out of the corner of my eye, I saw what seemed to be guards, similar to the soldiers that were fighting in the forest, shift their stance. Looking around a bit more closely, I saw that there were actually multiple sets of guards all around this area. So, maybe I was not as safe with him as I once thought.

"Who do you think you are?" I hissed and stood guarded, ready to attack at a moment's notice.

"Who do I think I am?" he said between small chuckles, and his smile widened. His tone had a sarcastic drawl. He looked at me intently and started to walk towards me. "Maybe I should be asking you that instead. Who gave you the audacity to run away from me when I was only trying to save your life?"

My eyes narrowed and I felt my heart rate pick back up. With all the guards in the area, there seemed to be little chance of a successful escape. I started to step back until my foot hit the fountain behind us.

"I don't need saving by you," I hissed, trying to take another step to the side, but my foot caught. I would have lost my balance had he not grabbed my waist and pulled me to him. He inhaled deeply and attempted to move hair out of my face, but I smacked away his hand. "What gives you the right to touch me?"

He did not respond, only pulled me back to his chest and let one of his hands cup my face so that I was forced to look at him.

"I have every right to do whatever I want."

A pang of annoyance burst through me, but instead of yelling, I had a better idea of what would work. I gave him my sweetest smile and leaned into his hand; he didn't seem all that surprised by it. Instead, I saw a flash of triumph cross his face. I let myself smile back and lifted my hand to his cheek...

"Thank the gods that be, you found her!"

And forced his nose to meet my forehead with a sickening crunch. He whirled back with a hand clutching his perfect nose, blood trickling through his fingers. I let out a laugh and ran the opposite way of the house.

A pair of strong, unwavering arms stopped me in a matter of seconds. They picked me up just high enough so my feet were off the ground, and I could no longer run. I raged like an animal caught in a trap, growling and swinging my arms back to hit whoever held me.

"Put her down," the prince called out. I turned to look at him, and besides the small blood patch smeared across his face, the rest of his face seemed to have taken no damage. The man behind me put me down but did not move away from me. I stepped back and shot him a glare.

If the other person was a prince, this person had to be a fallen angel. While he may have had the same tattoos as the prince, his hair was a bed of messy black curls that farmed his olive face. He had a stronger jaw, and his cheeks were sharp. His eyes were a pool of onyx, and they left almost no room for the whites of his eyes to show. I shivered just looking into them. Those eyes seemed to reflect at me, and I am not sure I liked what I saw.

Looking back over to the prince, I almost had to do a double-take. Next to him was a carbon copy of the man in front of me. The only difference was he had a smile on his face while the other one seemed to have his scowl tattooed on him.

The prince stalked towards me slowly and I tried to take a step back, but the man next to me put his hand on my back, not allowing me to go any further.

"It's not nice to headbutt your savior, you know."

"Savior my ass," I spit, and the twin behind him growled.

"You should not fight him," the man next to me spoke finally, his voice sharp. I pushed his arm away from me and tried to run again but his hand reached out to grab the collar of my shirt.

"Oh, this time she is feisty." The other twin's voice was higher than the one currently holding me back. I could work with that—easier to distinguish them now.

"We have a spy in our midst, those damn *filth* knew

where she would be." The prince was talking to the twins, but his eyes never left mine. I tried, unsuccessfully, to take a step back. "Would you just stop?"

I threw a punch at him and hit him as hard as I could. "You're only hurting yourself. Stop, and then we can talk." It was the broody one. I stopped and looked over at him. He met my eyes with his own, and I shivered again.

Weighing my options, I relaxed in his grip and he let go of my shirt. Instead of running, I crossed my arms and shifted my stance slightly. I was ready to yell at them once more, but a shooting pain stopped me. I looked down at my feet and realized they were badly hurt and had left blood smeared across the floor.

"For now." I heard the twin next to me sigh. "But can someone please help bandage my feet?"

"I could help you with that, m'lady," the prince spoke softly and gestured to the man at my side. He knelt down and grabbed my foot. His grip gentle, but even though my blood-soaked feet, I could feel how rough his hands were. He lifted them up carefully for the blond man to see. The man, without touching my feet, moved his hand around them, and I saw a light begin to come out of his hand. I gasped when the light touched my skin. It felt warm and made the pain disappear almost instantly. The smile never wiped from his face as he switched to my next foot.

I tried to not let the obvious shock show on my face. When he was done, the twin let my foot go, and I was able to admire his work. Good as new. I wiggled my toes around. This must be how he fixed his face so fast.

"Don't call me m'lady," I grumbled and looked him in the eye.

"Do you not even care what you just witnessed? You are worried about the m'lady part and not even the healing magic?" The one who lifted my feet scoffed. I shot a glance over at him.

"While it is unlikely our foes will come here, I suggest

we go inside to talk. I am sure you have questions."

The prince offered me a hand. This time I just looked at it. His hand was smoother than the twins and looked like it was well taken care of. He pulled it back and stuffed it into his pocket when he realized that I was not going to accept it. He and one of the brothers led me up the staircase and into the mansion. The twin in front seemed to be a very happy-go-lucky person; he was nonstop babbling about things that I did not understand. I looked over my shoulder at the one following us silently. After watching him for a few moments, I concluded that this may be their version of a broody teenager.

"What is your name?" I asked the one behind me, who stiffened immediately.

"Spiris," he replied and I noted the slight difference in voice between him and his twin, Spiris was deeper. I nodded, I would have to try to remember the differences but looking at the ball of excitement that Vitos was I knew it wouldn't be too hard.

"The one that saved you is Baecos, and I am Vitos, the handsome twin if you were wondering." Ah, so that was the annoying one's name.

"I was not," I huffed and continued into the mansion.

The outside of the mansion was beautiful, but nothing could have prepared me for what was waiting on the inside. Everything was in shades of white and gold. Prince or not, this man still had to be made of money. The place oozed riches and royalty, even the trimmings on all the tablecloths seemed to sparkle with gold. I tried not to be distracted by how beautiful this place was, and instead looked to focus on the things around me. There was not much in the main entrance, but the walls were littered with paintings of men and women dressed in clothes that did not seem the norm for back home. There were some tables here and there with white roses and gold vases, but the most breathtaking thing of all was the grand staircase. Of course, also trimmed with gold. I looked down at myself and felt the irrational fear of getting this place dirty, but I quickly shook that off. They took me in here, and if they thought I would be easy, they had another thing coming. I decided the more blood and dirt that would come off my feet and onto this oh-so-perfect mansion, the better.

They led me into a dining room. It looked like they had their branding down pat, white and gold again, but I saw more brown tones here. The windows were open, letting in sunlight and brightening the room even more. Baecos walked over to the dining table and held out a chair for me. I reluctantly let him help me sit and watched as he took the seat right beside me, Vitos beside him, and Spiris stood behind his chair, refusing to sit. Baecos sitting at the head of the table did not get past me. Both Spiris and Vitos had their eyes trained on to him, but Baecos's eyes never left my face.

"We are inside, now speak. What do you want with me?" I shifted in my seat so I looked more relaxed, even though I was far from it.

Baecos gave me another dazzling smile that almost took my breath away. Almost. He was handsome, of course. With a strong jawline, those sparkling eyes, and the tattoos that put it all together, I would be a fool to think anything else.

"I want nothing more than to welcome you, Iniq. It's been a hundred years too long. We have a lot to catch up."

# Chapter Five

### Vien

My body froze. A hundred years? Who does he think he is kidding? I searched their faces for any sign of amusement, but I got nothing. At this point, I was positive that this was not a dream. The handsome men across from me were too real. The table in front of me is too real. The tingling sensation I got from his healing was too real. And most importantly, there was a nagging feeling in the back of my head that told me that this was the truth.

"I asked what you want with me, not what you want to do." The twin named Spiris looked over at me finally. I could not tell if it was pity or sorrow that showed in the black depths of his eyes. Vitos smiled widely and was about to jump in when Baecos put his hand up to silence him.

"Truly, nothing. I want nothing more than to wish you a happy and healthy life within the walls of my kingdom." He waved to the twins.

"That's an obvious lie. Next you're gonna tell me you rule whatever world you took me to?" I waved my hand around gesturing to the environment around us.

"Yes, that is exactly what I was going to tell you." His voice had a hint of playfulness in it. "But I am not the only one, as great as that would be. Vitos and Spiris are a part of my court and help keep the kingdom in order. There are a few other kings but they are not really worth your time."

So, multiple kingdoms and some type of magic. I clicked my tongue. "Who was the woman trying to catch me in the forest? I assume you two are not friends." Vitos laughed loudly at this.

"They are anything but friends." Vitos's hand touched Baecos's arm as he spoke. "She was the person who wanted to take your powers, she is the reason you are staring at us as though we are strangers."

"I think you have the wrong person. Firstly, my name is not Iniq. Secondly, I do not have whatever power you think I do." I pushed my chair back and started to stand up but Vitos grabbed my hand.

"Wait—" He was about to start but I snapped my hand away from him. I almost felt sorry when I saw hurt flash across his face.

"Don't you give me that act, you don't know me, and I do not know you. You essentially kidnapped me. I don't care whatever guise it was under." Vitos's mask of hurt faltered and I saw him begin to smile. When I saw that smile paired with his soulless eyes, it felt like ice water was being poured over me.

"I was trying to be nice to you, isn't that what you stupid humans fall so easily for?" He straightened up and gone was the person who I had first seen running out of the mansion. Instead was a real person, the type of person that seemed to not care for any other living being besides himself.

"You people are the stupid ones if you think that I would fall for your act." I moved toward the door and this time it was Spiris who stopped me from going any further.

"Please stay. I apologize about Vitos, he didn't mean to act like that." His hands were up showing me he was defenseless.

"He did."

"I did."

I shot a glare over at Vitos and he did the same. I could already tell that I would prefer the silent twin. Baecos laughed at our actions but never moved from the chair.

"In truth, it is us who needs you. That is why we brought you here. Not just for your safety, but also for your help."

"Apparently, this *stupid human* wouldn't be able to help you with anything," I spat out at Baecos.

"Vitos, apologize," Baecos demanded. I raised my eyebrows at him. Baecos was obviously not his father.

To my surprise, Vitos only gave him a quick look and then looked at me and bowed deeply. "I apologize for my rudeness."

"Not accepted." I crossed my arms and faced back to Spiris.

"What does he mean by help you?" I asked him, staring intently into his eyes. His hand came up to ruffle his hair as he looked away from me.

"You are—were—a very powerful warrior in your past life," Spiris muttered, still avoiding my gaze.

"And?" My voice was harsh, and I stepped towards him, lessening the space between us.

"And our magic here is failing and your power is the only way to get that magic back," Baecos spoke up from behind me.

"So, you mean a past life. In a past life, I was a warrior that was apparently the only thing saving this world from total destruction. Am I hearing this correctly?"

"I wouldn't say total destruction. We still have some magic, but within the hundred years you were gone, it has only gotten worse." I contemplated returning to my seat as I felt my head spin, but I stood my ground.

"What is this power that you apparently can't achieve without me?"

"You are the only one who can open a certain door,

similar to the one that you came through to enter this world." As Baecos spoke, I distinctly remembered the feeling of my body being torn apart as I came into this *world*. I shuddered. "That door is the only pathway that we have to go to the gods and beg them for an opportunity to get our power back."

I laughed at this. "Even if there were gods, like you said, why would they listen to you?"

"Not us, you. You are blessed by them," Spiris whispered. I tried to whirl back towards him, but I felt the world shift around me.

"You need to rest—the door takes a lot of magic, and in your sealed form, you cannot handle it." Spiris arms had caught me. I tried to push him off, but I was too weak.

"I will take her to her room," Spiris piped in after what felt like hours. I could have sworn Baecos growled.

I felt myself be jostled from Spiris's arms to Baecos's. I could barely keep my eyes open. Every time I tried to open them again, I felt the world spin. I leaned my head against Baecos's chest and felt it rumble as he spoke.

"While you may not remember right now, we have known each other a very long time. We grew up together and have kept a very... close relationship for the last seven hundred years." I scoffed in response, keeping my eyes closed and inhaling his scent. It was clean, like a mix of pine needles and soap.

"I don't care. You are lucky that this door or whatever made me feel this way because if not, I would have slapped you for touching me." He laughed at this.

"Looking forward to it."

"Perv."

I was vaguely aware of him bringing me up the staircase and down what I assumed to be a very long hallway. We stopped and I felt him shift me around so he could open a door. I was able to look around for only a few seconds, but when I did, I was taken aback by how beautiful the room was. There was a big four-poster bed that would have taken up the entire room at home. There was a vanity for makeup and hair in the corner, and I could see the two additional rooms connected. I assumed that one was the bathroom and the other may have been a closet.

"We will get you your own handmaiden and she will help you dress and get ready every day. She will be here tomorrow morning. Until then, would you like me to help you wash?" His tone was playful again.

"I do not need your help, nor do I want it." He set me down gently.

"Please rest well," he said and reached out to brush down my hair. "Tomorrow we will meet for breakfast and we can discuss more. My room is across the hallway."

His tone was nowhere near dangerous, but his last sentence came across as a threat.

"My name is Vien," I whispered and quickly entered the bathroom.

I did not rest for even a second, I went straight to the mirror to see what had happened to me. My pale skin was stained with dirt and even a little blood. I looked like I had been hit by a bus.

I took a shower and went back out into the grand room with a towel wrapped around me. I was exhausted, but I spotted a pair of matching silk sleep clothes waiting for me on the bed. After the shower, I felt more like myself, but there was no way I would just lie down and fall asleep—I was going to escape right now while I still had a chance.

# Chapter Six

## Vien

It did not take long for me to get to work. I had to ditch my dirt and hole-filled clothing that I wore previously and searched the closet for something more comfortable. I would say their clothes were not too different than what I had seen in my own world, just lots of tunics. I dressed in a tunic and some loose pants that tied at the ankles; these would be good for what I needed. I did not find a jacket, but I did find some shoes. Unfortunately, they were flats but tied at the ankle. If I needed to ditch them later, I would.

The world outside was beginning to get dark. I do not know how long I had been in this world, but the darkness was a good sign—it would allow me some coverage while I escaped. I was worried about the guards I'd seen earlier, but I would have to cross that bridge when I came to it.

I wondered if I could escape from the window or if the door would suffice. After looking out the window, I realized that there was no way I would make it down in one piece. I took a deep breath and paused right before my door, listening out for anyone in the hallway outside. When I heard no one, I opened my door and cursed when I heard a soft click.

I looked out into the hallway and was happy to find it empty. I knew it was stupid, but I decided to go the way I assumed we'd come from. I didn't know how big this mansion was and didn't want to risk getting lost. I made sure my footsteps were as quiet as could be and slowly walked the length of the hallway.

I saw a random door in front of me open and out came a person I had never seen before. They bore the same tattoos as the men earlier, but they wore something that I could only assume was this world's maids' attire and held a pile of towels. She paused when she saw me and tilted her head in confusion.

"Are you lost, miss?" she seemed to know that I would be here, so I gave her a small smile.

"Yes, actually, I wanted to get some fresh air. Could you show me the nearest exit into the garden?" My heart pounded when she did not say anything at first, but I felt the tension release when she smiled back.

"I have to drop off these towels on the way, but feel free to join me, miss." She walked back the way I just came and I internally cursed, praying Baecos was not in his room.

She did not speak as we moved down the hallways; she made no sound save the slight ruffling of her dress as she walked. She seemed to know this place like the back of her hand and brought me down a set of corridors, stopping at a set of stairs that paled in comparison to the grand staircase.

"Just go down there, miss, it is the servant's entryway—you should be directly connected to the garden from there." I tried not to run toward the door.

"Thank you…" I paused and she smiled at me.

"You may call me Sol, miss."

"I am Vien." Her brows furrowed when I said this, but I was already down the stairs and opening the door before she could say anything further.

The fresh air hit my face and I smiled at the feeling.

Now was the time.

I closed the door softly behind me and looked around. I did not see any guards in this area, only rose bushes and other small shrubberies. I spotted the forest line and slowly made my way over to it, stopping every time I heard a rustle. I had to be careful but being so close to the forest line made my heart race.

Once I was only a few feet away, I started to run. The forest was very similar to the one that I had arrived in so I had a small hope that I would be able to find myself out of this situation. I panted as my feet hit the moist ground with soft thumps. I felt a smile grace my face. The wind blowing through my hair and running like no tomorrow made me feel giddy, I hadn't felt this free in all the years of my life.

I had my happiness cut short as I heard a yell behind me. "Stop! Please!" I did not stop. I could tell distinctly by the deeper voice that it was Spiris, he seemed to be the realist of them all, but I could not stop now. I felt something creep up on me in the shadows, it was as fast as I was. No, it was faster. It was running beside me in the trees where my eyes could not see, but now, I felt it in front of me.

I came to a halt and felt a body collide painfully with me from behind. I was forced to the ground and my mouth filled with dirt. I spit it out and tried to look up, but a hand kept my face down.

"It's not time, please listen to me." It was Spiris speaking from on top of me but the shadow that I felt was still in front of me. "You know this is not the way yet. I beg you—she doesn't know."

Spiris was never speaking to me, he was speaking to the creature that had chased me through the forest. He was not reaching to catch me but racing to beat whatever was standing before us.

"Then teach her." Before I could decipher whose voice it was, I felt a sharp pain in the back of my head and my world turned to black.

I awoke with a start.

I was no longer in the forest, I was back in my bed, but I was not alone.

I quickly tried to sit up but there was a pounding in my head that stopped me. Next to my bed was a woman, probably younger than myself, and she was reaching her hand out towards me. I slapped her hand away and covered my pounding head.

"Don't you touch me," I hissed at her. She looked slightly hurt by my rejection.

"Come, miss. Let's get you ready for breakfast." She smiled at me while she said this and held out her hand for me. It seemed that she was also not human. She had the same markings as the men I had met previously but her skin was pale like Baecos, and she had blond hair. Her blue eyes shone with concern. She was dressed in a light floor-length dress that hugged her body. The dress itself was very pretty but paired with her, everything would have seemed magical.

"I don't need to do anything for you people." I tried to hiss this out but my throat was aching, and I was in desperate need of water.

"You will need to eat and drink. The move through the doorway must have exhausted you, you have been asleep for almost 12 hours." She reached out towards me again. I did not take it, but I got up myself. I regretted it almost immediately as I flailed and had to hold on to her.

"Sorry," I grumbled, and she only gave me a small smile and led me to the bathroom.

"You can wash up here, I will await you outside and then we can get you down to breakfast. Let me know if you need any help."

My stomach took that time to growl, and I felt my cheeks heat up. I nodded and headed into the bathroom to wash up. That had to be the most I had slept in years, and while my body felt spent, my mind seemed more alert. I was in no rush to make it downstairs, if anything, I was nervous. I didn't want to face the others, I knew they caught me while I was trying to escape, and given the desperation in Spiris voice last night, there were things that even he could not stop.

I walked again to the mirror and had to do a double take, there was something different than last night. What the hell had happened to my hair? I no longer had dark hair all around, instead, half of my hair was pure and the other half was my normal dark color. Looking closely, the blond was coming right out of my root. I smelled my hair, and it didn't have any chemical smell coming from it. I had never dyed my hair before; when I was younger, it had seemed weird not following in the other girls' footsteps and experimenting with my hair, but I never found the appeal. I loved how it looked but I could just never bring myself to do it.

I would ask the maid about this in a bit, but first, I needed to wash. It seemed that someone had changed me last night but had not cleaned the dirt off me after my run through the woods. I threw my clothes to the floor, and when I showered, I made sure to scrub my body thoroughly to get rid of all the dirt. When I got to my scalp, I winced—there was still a bump there from when Spiris had hit me.

After washing, I met the handmaiden outside in the room.

"What is your name?" I asked softly. She was young and most likely innocent; I did not bear a grudge against her.

She was waiting for me near the vanity and gestured for me to sit. As I did, she raked her hands through my hair gently. I still flinched when she reached the sensitive area.

"It is Flayke, and I will be here taking care of you, miss. You must be more careful next time," she whispered to me, and her eyes darted around the empty room. "Running away may not be an option for you, miss. I know it is not a servant's place to say, but I only wish for your safety. You got lucky it was Spiris who found you this time." I shivered at her words.

Against my own nature, I grabbed her hand. "Servant or not, your job does not determine your worth. Thank you for your concern." Her eyes widened and she said nothing as she continued to brush through my hair.

"I was told to dress you in something comfortable today, a dress specifically. Is that okay?" she asked, but I knew that she didn't really have a choice. I didn't want to make her job harder.

"I normally would say no, but for you, I will say yes." She smiled and got to work curling my hair in loose waves. We decided on light make-up, and I was grateful for it. I had never been so pampered. She seemed kind and knew what she was doing.

"Do you know how my hair is like this?" I asked her, holding up a piece of blond, and she pouted.

"It has been like this for as long as I have known you, miss." Something in her voice made me believe that it was longer than this morning.

"How long have you known me for?"

"A few hundred years, miss. I have worked here a long time—you were always very nice to me. I never forgot that." Her voice was soft and almost pained.

"So, people here are immortal?" I asked, and she shot me a forced smile.

"We can die, miss. If we are healthy though and our magic is strong, we can live very long lives. So yes, to some extent," she explained as she squeezed my shoulder slightly.

Flayke walked over to the closet and handed me the dress. It was a very lightweight fabric that hung loosely off my shoulders. It was easy to move around in and felt like almost nothing. The length was also at my ankles, so it would be easy to run in if I so choose to. I tried to pull up the small sleeves so they would cover my shoulders, but the dress was definitely not made to do that. I sighed and chose to just lay my hair over my shoulder instead.

Flayke was waiting for me in the room and smiled as I emerged. She said nothing but took my hand again and led me through the house and to the dining room. When the door opened, I was hit with the most heavenly of smells. Food. My mouth watered. Baecos sat in what I assumed was his normal spot, but the twins were absent. I was led over to his side and took a seat beside him. He looked the same as yesterday but with slightly different clothes, no leather but still regal looking. His purple eyes sparkled and there was a wide grin on his face.

"You look beautiful. Did you get a good rest?" he asked as the other servants filled up my plate and pushed it in front of me. It was filled with food; it had been a while since I actually enjoyed a home-cooked meal. My stomach twisted painfully.

"You should know the answer to that, your goons knocked me out cold last night." His eyes flashed and his lips pushed together tightly.

"It was necessary, you should know better than to escape."

"Know better?" I picked up the butter knife next to me and threw it at my capture. He easily waved it away with his hand and it landed with a clank on the floor.

"Eat," he commanded. There was no joking in his voice and his stare was unforgiving. I straightened out and did as he said.

"What did you do to my hair?" I asked coldly between bites. He just chuckled.

"You are worried about your hair?"

"You seem pissy when I ask any other questions." I saw him grip his glass so tightly I thought it would break.

"Your powers may have started to show up. You are reverting back to the way you were before you died."

Powers? I didn't feel any different.

"What other fun things can I do besides the door thingy?"

Baecos grimaced. "Eat first."

This time, I did not listen to him at first and wanted to see how long until he gave in. I studied his face. The tattoos seemed to fit his face very well, and his lips were twisted into a smirk. His eyes, trained on me, were narrowed, and after meeting his eyes with my own, I felt my heart skip a beat and I looked down. I picked up my fork and started to eat the food in front of me; it took everything in my power to not inhale it. This food was a far cry from the whiskey and ramen I had been eating. I could get used to this.

"I have decided to spend the day with you today and help you get accustomed to my kingdom. I will try to answer as many questions as I can." He paused and took a sip of his drink.

"I guess I should be honored?" My voice dripped with sarcasm and I gave him a little smile of my own. If he really wanted me here, I would make him regret it sooner rather than later.

He did not indulge me with an answer but gestured for me to keep eating. I huffed and finished what was left on my plate.

"Let's go on an adventure, m'lady."

# Chapter Seven

Vien

An adventure indeed, the first stop was the stables. They rode horses here apparently. I, unfortunately, had never really ridden before. Unless, of course, you count the time that my mom had taken me when I was six to learn how to ride. I hated it. That was the first and the last time. And now here I was, face to face with the biggest one I had ever seen in my life, and Baecos wanted me to ride it.

"I am not getting on that," I huffed.

He chuckled and stepped closer to me.

"I assume you cannot ride." His voice was not teasing but it still infuriated me. "You can ride with me. I will help you get on and you just have to hold on."

Before I could open my mouth to talk, he lifted me up and easily plopped me down on the horse. The horse stirred a bit but Baecos calmed it by running his fingers through its mane and whispering softly to it. He flashed me a smile and mounted the horse behind me. He pulled me against his chest and his hand splayed across my stomach. I understood why he wanted this dress now, it easily splayed around the horse, but it also left very little between his skin and mine. His scent infiltrated my senses again, pine needles and soap. I had to admit his scent was nice, but that didn't stop him from being a bastard.

"I don't want to ride a damn horse." Said horse huffed along with me as if to say he didn't want to be ridden. My heart started racing and I held onto the reins tightly. Get yourself together, Vien.

He grabbed hold of the reins in front of me and made a movement, the horse started to move to a small gallop. I sucked in a breath of air as his hands squeezed my hips.

"Stop it."

"Would you rather I let go?" He let go and I felt myself become unsteady.

"Just hold me somewhere else." My own panic-filled voice betrayed me.

"Here?" His hand squeezed my inner thigh.

"You know what I mean, stupid."

"Ouch," his voice feigned hurt. "I get it, I get it." His arm wrapped around my waist now.

The ride was bumpy, and it only made the situation between us worse. Each bump sent us further and further into each other. I knew that he noticed this as well because he would chuckle in my ear and it would send shivers down my spine.

The horse brought us along a dirt path that seemed to go around the property. The mansion was in the distance and we were getting further and further away from it. Leaving the only thing that I knew of this world did not sit right with me.

"Where are the twins?" I asked. I was curious, they hadn't been with us all morning and they were the only other two people that I knew. Baecos stiffened behind me, and then, after a moment, relaxed. He squeezed me against his body before replying.

"Why are you so interested in them?" he said huskily in my ear. I shivered again.

"One of them did tackle me last night." I shot back.

"Ah yes, you are lucky he found you before I did," he

replied simply as I swallowed at his threat. I didn't recognize that voice yesterday, it was harsh and dangerous. Baecos has yet to show me that side.

When we arrived, I was taken aback by how wonderful sight could be. Before us stood the biggest and most beautiful rose garden that could have ever existed. It just simply could not compare to the one I'd ran through last night. This one had all different colors of roses and spanned farther than the eye could see. From atop the horse, I could see tall pillars in the distance and what looked to be the top of a gazebo.

Baecos got off easily, grabbed me by the waist, and lifted me gently off the horse. He again brought me as close as he could while doing so, trying to get a rise out of me. His body and face were so close to mine, his eyes traveled from my own to my lips. His eyes met mine again and I decided to not give him the satisfaction, he obviously knew what he was doing too well.

"I am not sure what relationship you had with my *past self*," I walked around him and headed to the rose garden, but before moving on, I turned my head back to him and gave him another smile, "but I am not the same woman, so do not try that with me."

For a second, I thought that there was anger across his face, but instead, he threw his head back and laughed. He laughed so hard that he had to hold his stomach, and his long blond hair fell into his face. Once he got over whatever secret joke he was laughing at, he wiped the invisible tears from his eyes and walked towards me, putting his hand on my lower back.

"On the contrary, you seem to be the exact same woman." He removed his hand from my back and walked in front of me, gesturing for me to follow.

He led me through the garden and let me get close and examine the flowers. I reached out and touched the ones closest to me. They were purple, their petals almost transparent. They felt as soft as silk between my fingers and they seemed to vibrate at my touch.

"As much as today is for you, I would also like to ask some questions if you feel comfortable," he spoke up from behind me but kept his distance now. He must have realized that his previous ways were not getting him the results he wanted. I nodded and turned my attention back to the rows and rows of flowers.

"What were you doing before you crossed the doorway? In the mortal realm?" His question threw me off.

"I am not sure why it matters to you," I replied and walked further into the garden. "I was doing nothing, I just got home from work and decided to stupidly go on a midnight stroll."

"Will your job notice you are gone?" His question made me freeze.

"That's very serial killer-like. I'll answer yours if you answer mine." I looked back at him and he smirked.

"Go ahead, a question for a question." No retort on the serial killer comment. My heart sped up slightly and an uneasy smile graced my lips.

"Why am I so important to this world? Why can't someone else open the door?"

"I can show you why if you let me." My head snapped around to look at him.

"What do you mean?" He said nothing but only stepped closer to me. He brought his hand up to my face and laid it on my forehead. I started to pull away, but he stopped me.

"Don't." In an instant, I saw scenes play through my head. Children in the street starving, begging for magic from passersby. I saw people fighting and screaming at each other, people dying of a sickness that did not exist in the mortal realm, bodies piled on top of each other, rituals showing them draining people of blood, and then I saw me, but it was not the me I know now. My entire body was decorated with tattoos and my eyes were glowing gold. That person could only be seen as a real warrior. She had no hesitation as she plowed through people and used magic to swiftly kill her enemies. Even watching her now, her movements were quicker than the eye can see; a proficient killer. But I was able to make out one thing, she did it with a smile.

"What did you just do?" I gasped and pulled away from his hand.

"It's a gift. I showed you why you are so important. Magic is a necessity for the people of this world. If you do not have it, you waste away. This is what the gods have taken from us." His voice held some pain in it.

"Why was I killing people?" I whispered, casting my eyes to the floor.

"You were saving the kingdom. People were trying to take others' magic from them and you put a stop to it." I tried to digest this new information, but it didn't right with me.

"Will your work care that you have left?" he asked me again. "A question for a question," he reminded me.

"No, I was fired."

"Any family that would worry?"

"But why me?" I pushed, not answering his question. It rubbed me the wrong way. I didn't know if he decided to build a conscience or if he was trying to cover his tracks.

"Because you need two sets of powers to open the door and only you have them." He brought me further into the garden as we spoke.

"You don't?" We walked side by side into a new section of the garden that had a large pond filled with fish swimming inside it. I watched as they lazily came up to the surface, expecting us to feed them.

"Nope. Any family?"

"Died long ago. How can one have both?"

"Only when you are blessed by the gods can you have both."

He let me think over his words.

"Does that scare you?" he started and waited for me to look up at him.

I shook my head.

The question game went on as we explored the gardens. I enjoyed being able to be outside and walk around, even if it was with a chaperone. My heart sunk when I found out that that I was an orphan here too. I guess it's not a matter of which body, curses could follow you throughout lifetimes. Losing your parents when you are still young is not something I would wish on anyone.

Baecos was happy to recall the time that we grew up together as children. He shared all the adventures we went on as we explored the world around us. But when I asked, he hesitantly explained the woman who was after me in the forest was someone we knew. She was of the demon race apparently. She was described as the worst type of power-hungry person. Someone who had no problem taking advantage of my previous self and tried to use my magic to prolong the life of her kingdom. Her name was Cruor. And his warnings about her were loud and clear: she apparently would stop at nothing to rip my powers away from me, even if that meant my death.

I also learned that this door was originally a tall tale that was passed down by generations and generations of magic users, but with the help of others, I did end up conjuring it. My fate, though, had run too short, and before I could ever reach the gods, I had died. When I pressed about my death, his excuse was that it would be too much for me to handle at this moment. As if I needed a man to tell me what I could and could not handle.

"So, when can I go home?" From his attitude, it was obvious that he did not intend for me to leave without helping them.

"You can leave if you help us with the door," he said noncommittedly.

"You promise that if I get this door to open for you, you will let me go back home?" I got up from the bench we were seated at and looked down at him.

"If you open that door, Vien, I will give you anything and everything you could ever want. The entire world will." I swallowed loudly. Thoughts raced through my mind at a hundred miles per hour.

Anything I wanted.

I wondered the type of power I could achieve by being here. These people obviously needed my help and had already given me more than I had ever had the chance to receive in the mortal realm. It was a selfish thought, but after growing up the way I did, there was no one to rely on except myself. And here this king was willing to give me everything I ever wanted for just saying yes.

My heart was pounding in my chest and I felt a sliver of a long-forgotten emotion go through me. There were risks of course, but the benefits were seeming to outweigh the costs…

I held my hand out to him.

# Chapter Eight

## Unknown

Iniq in her form now had no reason to offer to build the door so quickly. She had no memories of her past life and nothing holding her here. If she demanded we brought her home right now, it would only have been expected. Her unknown motives only made me more suspicious of her, maybe she was not as different as I thought.

I could tell Baecos thought the same. I kept myself covered by the forest that surrounded the property. If I strained, I could hear their conversation. Baecos had most likely sensed my magic, but with Iniq still sealed, it was unlikely she would even know I was here. I did not have the luxury of leaving them alone together. I had to find a hole, find a time where he was unguarded enough for me to take her. Baecos's eyes drifted behind Iniq to my hiding place behind the trees. He sent me a smirk and it took everything in my power not to conjure a bow and arrow and send it through his head... like it would even reach him, I'd be dead before it made contact. I was already lucky enough that he did not call me out for being the traitor that told Cruor of her arrival. I was pushing my luck.

His hand clasped hers firmly and he shook on her word.

"It's a deal." Iniq's voice did not waver but her

demeanor changed slightly. Gone was the crass behavior, and in its place came narrowed eyes and a bone chilling smile. I had to force myself to breathe; I took a step towards them but stopped when I saw Iniq's smile drop and she lost her balance.

Baecos easily grabbed her, but his eyes shot towards mine again. He had a smile of his own.

# Chapter Nine

### Vien

"Can you hear me?" It was Baecos's voice. The world started to come back to me, and I saw Baecos's face above mine.

"What happened?" I asked as my hand gripped my pounding head.

"You fainted after you shook my hand. Are you okay?"

"I am fine, it's just a headache," I lied. "Can we go back?"

He looked as though he knew I was lying but did not push me on it. Without a word, he came up to me, and with a flash of light, we were back in my room.

"You did that before," I said, looking to him for answers.

"Yes, and you will be able to too once your powers are back."

"Then what was the point of riding that horse?" I growled. I knew he did it to get a rise out of me but instead, he just shrugged with a smirk.

"I wanted to show you the grounds, of course."

I huffed. I was not sure if I could put up with him.

I did not tell Baecos that when I fainted, I actually saw a memory, one that I assumed was Iniq's. I only knew it was hers because she seemed to be joking with both Baecos and

Cruor, and I could never imagine doing that. When the memories came, it was painful, and I could tell my body was fighting against them. The memories were fuzzy, and they came in small snippets giving me little context. The only thing I could make out was "door" and "danger". I couldn't decipher anything else, so I just asked to rest and Baecos didn't bother me any further.

The rest of the day went by uneventful. We ate lunch with the twins, whatever work they were doing seemed to be concluded. After our conversation yesterday, Vitos had dropped the energetic act and had become openly hostile to me. I preferred it this way. Baecos and Spiris didn't admit they were using me, but Vitos outright didn't care about anything.

Baecos had told them that I agreed to help open the door on the condition that I could leave after. The news was met with silence, no one seemed to have expected me to agree—hell, I didn't expect myself to agree. It was stupid, but after the first escape attempt, I needed to be smarter, and I had to admit that I was curious to see where this journey would take me. Baecos happily offered, more like ordered, the twins to train me. I did not get what he meant, but when I saw Vitos's eyes light up, I knew that I would be in trouble.

"You really think a flabby little human like you can open a door to the gods?" Vitos growled. He was pulling on my arm painfully and showing me the training grounds. "You were undoubtedly one of the most powerful people in our world. It is disgusting to see you so weak."

"If I was the most powerful, how did I die so easy?" I growled and pulled my arm away from him.

"I said one of, and your death was anything but easy." Vitos was about to go on, but his eyes caught something from behind me and he stopped. I didn't have to look to know it was Baecos.

Baecos and Spiris were watching from afar. Baecos

shot Spiris a look and that was when I heard Spiris speak up for the first time that day.

"You need to build up your strength before you can even think of building up your magic. Magic lives in your body, the stronger the magic, the stronger your body needs to be." Spiris's tone was bored but his eyes were sharp.

"Why don't you come and fight me instead? I deserve a little payback after yesterday!" I kicked some dirt in his direction.

"That would be no fun," Vitos chuckled, his arms weaved themselves in front of his chest and his feet slid apart.

"You will start the training today." Baecos's voice boomed across the training grounds and I made an obscene gesture at him.

"That will be a hundred extra push-ups." I could feel the glee coming out of Vitos's voice.

When Vitos told me fighting Spiris would be no fun, I found out that it was only to preserve his own sadistic thrill that he got out of destroying my body. In the mortal world, I was not someone who worked out, so what he put me through was nothing short of hell. A thousand and one pushups, a thousand sit-ups, and running for ten miles. When I did not complete a task correctly, he would throw his magic at me and I would have to dodge it. The only leniency he gave me was allowing me to vomit in peace after I couldn't handle the running.

I could only stop when the sun started to set.  I collapsed on the cold earth not caring who saw or how dirty I got.

"You are a sadistic little fuck," I spit at Vitos.

"I am anything but little." He smirked down at me but made no move to help me up.

"Tomorrow you will start the full regime, this is where we will add on to your magic as well." It was Spiris who spoke this time. I thought he had left long ago. He held out a hand to pick me up, but I slapped it away.

"I should have left you all to die."

***

I spent the rest of the day in the library reading a romance novel. I was lucky to find this room, it was far away from my own room and you could only find it if you weaved through a few narrow hallways and up a flight of stairs. I had to admit that I only really found this place because I got lost and didn't want to ask anyone for help.

I shifted uncomfortably in my chair while still trying to remain in the world of this novel. The training had made my muscles ache and it felt like a workout to even hold this book. As I turned the page, I heard the door open and shut softly. Sometimes a maid would come in here to clean but I knew by the way the air shifted that it was Baecos, so I waited for him to come find me. It was not long before I saw a blond head of hair peek its way around the bookshelves.

"I felt you in here, but I didn't believe it." He took the open chair next to me and rested his chin on his palm, still staring at me.

"What's there not to believe?" I turned my page, no longer concentrating on the words.

"You're right, you were always a book worm. I should have known that the only time you'd be out was to read." He gave me a small smile, but I refused to return one.

I let the silence fill the room and tried to get back into the story. It was about a merchant's daughter that fell in love with a king's guard. I was about to give up on the book. It was too fluffy, just straight romance and no hardships until the guard loses his magic and is thrown out of his position. It seemed that even in these times, the loss of magic plagued everyone. When the guard described the loss of his magic, he felt like it was his life force being drained of him, like he lost himself and could barely remember who he was or what he was to become.

"Why do I not experience sickness with the loss of my magic?" I peered over to Baecos; his eyes were still on me.

"Because you still have your magic, it is just unattainable for now." His eyes wandered over to the open window, the breeze brushed across his face causing his hair to move slightly. "You just need a little push and some practice to get it started. Others who have their magic, once they start to lose it… it is almost impossible to get it back."

"Almost?" He nodded and his eyes slowly met mine. I felt them pierce through me and I had the audacity to blush. Regardless of what happened, he still looked like a king, and it would make anyone do a double take. But looking at him now was different, this had to be the most relaxed I have seen him, before this he always seemed to stand so tall and strong, but now he was slouched and his posture was casual. The golden light reflected in his eyes and gave his face a flushed look. If I had any artistic ability, I would dream to paint something like this. I felt like I was seeing something that no one else could. Like a secret of some kind.

"Yes, there are small rituals that we magicians can do to replenish some magic. My kingdom and people, Ullusants, are light, so we obviously gain our power from the most powerful thing in this world." His hand gestured to the open window and out to the now almost set sun.

"What kind of ritual do they do?" My book was in my lap now, the romance between the merchant's daughter and the guard long forgotten.

"Many, none that you need to concern yourself with." I shifted slightly, trying to ignore the pain that radiated through my body.

"Is this training really necessary?" I asked after another moment of silence. The sun was now fully set, and the library was only lit by a few lamps making it hard to see. Baecos's face was covered in shadows.

"Yes, but the faster you train, the faster you can go home." He stood up and held out a hand for me. "It is dark, you most likely cannot finish your book and your body must be hurting. Let's go eat and rest." His face only showed the hint of a smile.

I took his hand and let him lead me out of the library. I left my book back on the seat. I would be back later to finish the story.

# Chapter Ten



After being thrown about ten feet, I hit the ground with a harsh thud and slid until I collided with the bottom of a tree. My whole body hurt. I tried to get up, but my back screamed against it.

You would think after all that time spent torturing me yesterday, they would have given up. Vitos had decided that I needed to work on my fighting skills all of a sudden, and paired with my already aching body, it was hard to even run away.

Vitos stalked towards where I was, and I saw his right leg coming out towards me. I rolled away, and he narrowly missed my head. I crawled up to a standing position and he was already coming at me. I dodged a fist that went flying through the air but his other one caught me in the stomach.

"Hit me," Vitos growled. "It's like playing with a dead animal, you just sit there and take it." I felt blood pool in my mouth, and I spat it in his face. He was caught so off guard that I was able to swing my fist directly into that smug face. It met with a satisfying crunch.

Vitos grabbed his nose and I saw that I'd hit hard enough to make it bleed. "You little..."

"You told me to hit you, now you can't take it?" I smirked at him and held my hands up.

"Vitos," Baecos growled from behind him. In an

instant, the hunter stance Vitos was in was lost. "That is enough physical training today, Spiris will help you with the rest. Vitos, make yourself scarce."

Vitos said nothing and skipped away from us with a flash of light.

I looked over and saw Spiris waiting for me on the other side of the training ground. A scowl still sat on his face, but when he saw me, he gestured for me to come over. I obliged and Baecos followed.

"I will teach you how to call upon your magic. Give me your hand," Spiris instructed.

I gave my hand to him and he put his in mine, the difference between mine and his made me self-conscious. I was caked in dirt and there was some blood still left on my hand, but he was perfectly clean. His hand started to glow with a soft light; it tickled and made me giggle. Spiris gave me an incredulous look and I stopped myself.

"It tickled." I heard Baecos sigh from behind me.

"When you feel this, do you feel something else in your skin trying to get free?" Spiris voice was still unamused. I concentrated on the warmth his hand was radiating and then to my own hand. Sure enough, it felt almost like tiny bugs were filling the space beneath my skin, moving around trying to find a way out.

"How do I get it out?" I asked.

"You command it to." I rolled my eyes at his response but sent a silent command, and to my surprise, my magic started showing immediately, but it was different than Spiris's.

It was much darker than the others' magic. Theirs was a burst of gold life, but when mine showed up, it was a cloud of swirling black fog. The black fog covered my hand and swirled around my palm. There were some small gold flecks that reflected the light in the small clearing. When looking closer, I realized that just like the stars at night, there was gold glitter swirling around in the fog.

And then it was gone.

"She will need a lot more practice," Baecos said behind me. I jumped at how close he was.

"Don't get that close to me."

"You probably won't be able to do this on your own for a while," Spiris continued, ignoring me, "you will most likely have to rely on another's magic to call yours to the surface."

I nodded at him and stared at my hand. I wonder what I could do when I could finally call to my own magic?

"That is enough for today. You should go clean up—I am sure you are tired." Baecos's presence did not move from behind me.

"No door today? That was barely any magic training," I grumbled.

"Not yet," Spiris answered and started walking back home.

I sighed and turned back towards the mansion without saying another word. Baecos's hand rested softly on my back and his voice was a low whisper in my ear.

"You have all the time in the world, there is no rush. You need to rest." I shivered at the feeling of his hand trailing up my back.

I shook him off and followed Spiris into the mansion.

***

Maybe Baecos's library visits would turn into a habit.

When he came this time, I did not speak to him, I just let him take his seat beside me. The sun was still high in the sky, and we ended much earlier today meaning I was able to finish my previous book and start another. The last book was satisfying enough, the guard died in the end and the merchant's daughter went on to take over her father's business. She even named her kid after the guard.

"You read fast," Baecos commented. I turned the page. I was still not happy about the training. If I ever got my powers back, Vitos would be the first to go. I reveled in planning his untimely death.

"Is your book enjoyable?" Baecos's voice snapped me out of my daydream. His eyes were narrowed and there was a small smile that graced his lips. "You were smiling, that's all."

I let out a small laugh. "Yes, very enjoyable."

I closed my book and rested it back on my lap, drinking in his form. Again, he was something to marvel at. His hair was a bit messier today and fell in his face, it seemed silkily smooth and I longed to touch it.

"How did you become king?" His hand came to his mouth and his finger rested there thoughtfully.

"The same way others do—the power has to pass over at some point. The power of a king is tied to their kingdom. If you are powerful, your kingdom will thrive." I crossed my arms and leaned back.

"Does power stay within the family?"

"Usually," he mused. "Have you grown sick of the mortal world already? You seem comfortable here."

I stifled. I was comfortable here; I was taken care of, and it was easy to lose myself in this place. I was fed well, I was able to read, I even had a better time sleeping here.

"I still plan to leave once the door is open," I said decidedly.

"We will see won't we." His voice was playful, and he shot me a wink that made me blush. He stood up, but before he left, he came over to me, tucked my hair behind my ear, and leaned down. "I'm excited to see what's in store for us."

It was a dangerous game he was playing, but my heart sped up at the thought.

***

Another day, another training session. Luckily, Vitos settled for strength training rather than a beat down today, but with my body being so sore from last time, it was much harder to keep up. After just a short time running, I felt like I would vomit. I had to stop with my hands on my knees and catch my breath in order to stop myself. I saw Vitos prepare his magic from the corner of my eye and I took off again.

Yes, his death would be slow.

"Still so disappointing," Vitos's voice rang out after I started my pushups. My arms were burning and with the previous training still causing my muscles to ache, I found my arms giving out faster than he would have liked. Vitos's hand grabbed my hair and roughly yanked my head back. I refused to groan at the pain. I met his eyes and gave him a death glare, he only smiled at this. I could see a plan formulating behind those black eyes of his. Him and Spiris were so different. Vitos's blood lust knew no bounds, he was vindictive, sadistic, and I wouldn't be surprised if he was a killer, but Spiris seemed like he just wanted to be alone.

"I don't have to put up with this shit from you." I was ready to spit in his face again, but he dropped my hair and pushed my face into the ground with his foot. I tried to lift it back up but he put too much weight on his foot. I felt my nose begin to ache and dirt sting my eyes.

"But you do, you agreed to open the door to help this world. Or I could just send you over to that demon. I heard that she has a thing for pathetic things like you. Maybe since you don't have any powers yet, she would just keep you as her own personal slave." Vitos's shoe ground into the back of my head, forcing me deeper into the ground. Dirt was filling my mouth, and it was becoming hard to breathe.

Rage filled me; I was so *goddamn useless.*

"Vitos," Spiris called from the distance, "Baecos told you to quit it."

Ah yes, Baecos. He was nowhere to be seen today, leaving me with these two. Vitos finally let up, and I sat up gasping for air and trying to spit the dirt out of my mouth. The rage built up and I was ready to pounce, but when I looked at him, I felt my blood boil even more; he was standing there with his arms crossed, and he just looked so *bored.*

"You are a literal psychopath. I'm gonna fucking kill you, you bastard!" I growled and threw a nearby rock as hard as I could at his head. His eyes widened and he dodged the rock. It barely missed his face and collided right into the tree behind him, but it didn't stop there. No, the rock seemed to dig itself into the tree, almost so deep that it came out through the other side. My jaw dropped and Spiris let out a whistle.

"Vitos, I don't think you can mess with her for much longer," Spiris said with a smirk.

Vitos grumbled and skipped away, leaving just Spiris and me.

"Do you want to freshen up first? Today will take longer than yesterday," he explained, and I nodded. A little decency was refreshing. He held out a hand to me, and this time I took it. Instead of pulling me up, he skipped us to my room. "Let me know when you are ready." And he was gone again.

I sighed and cleaned myself up in the bathroom. The hot water felt good on my body, but it still ached. There were bruises all over my stomach, arms, and back... all from where Vitos had hit me. Some of the edges were yellowing, but the majority were still fresh and tender. I contemplated asking Baecos for help healing them, but I shot the idea out of my head as quickly as it came. I was not afraid of it. I was excited actually, of the prospects that came with his hands so close to my skin. I felt pain radiate through me as I washed the dirt off my back. Vitos will pay one day.

Spiris was waiting for me outside my room looking at Baecos's door.

"Thanks," I muttered, nudging his arm slightly. "For stopping him." Spiris rubbed the back of his neck, obviously uncomfortable with the praise.

"I only stopped him from killing you, not hurting you." I shrugged. I wouldn't fight him on that. My eyes traveled to Baecos's door. I hadn't heard from him all day.

"Where did he go?" I asked, gesturing to the door in front of mine.

"There is a ritual he must do every fortnight that requires him to be away for some time." I raised my eyebrow at him. "It means we are low on magic and must replenish."

"A ritual? He mentioned something like that before. Something about taking power from the sun?" Spiris just shook his head at me.

"Among other things."

He held out his hand to me signaling that it was time for us to continue our lesson. and without hesitation, I took it. In a flash of light, we were gone. Then, we were in a small clearing in a forest that looked similar to the one I first arrived in. The air was so clean—I inhaled deeply savoring the feeling. It was sweet against my tongue, and I couldn't help but let myself smile at the magic in the air.

"Have we been here before?" I asked Spiris, looking over the many small plants that littered the clearing. From small white flowers to large pink ones, this clearing was home to all kinds of beautiful plants. I was tempted to take some to my room for decoration.

"Not in this lifetime." I was snapped out of my musings and my eyes lazily drifted over to his. They were already watching my face intently. His curls were tied up in a loose bun that still left some out to frame his face; he was already ready for our lesson it seemed. I tried to reach for any memory of us together in this clearing, but they would not come. His eyes were sharp, it's like they dared me to breach the subject, to utter the question that was forming on my tongue. I lost the nerve to ask anything else.

"Oh." I did not know anything else to say. What was unspoken was still in the air. *I had come here with him in my last lifetime.* I wondered briefly if they were close as well.

I watched as Spiris walked to the middle and sat down on the grass. He gestured for me to sit before him. You would think someone as big as him would look cramped and out of place among all the nature here, but his shoulders were slumped and his hands caressed the flowers near him—he was comfortable here, at home. I let myself smile at the picture in front of me.

"Why here of all places?" He did not look up at me but closed his eyes and breathed in deeply. He seemed to be in some type of meditative state. I sat and watched as his chest rose and then fell silently, not daring to interrupt him.

"This is a private place that I enjoy when I need time to think. I thought you may enjoy this," he spoke out after a few minutes of silence and met my eyes. I looked around at the scenery and nodded. It was quiet and tranquil, it felt like we were hidden away from everyone.

"I do, better than a beat down for sure." He sighed and rubbed his hand through his hair pulling at the ends softly. He was not cold-blooded, I could tell, the beat downs must have been getting to him as well. It is not easy watching someone get beat within an inch of their life.

"I know that it is likely that no one else will say this," he paused and met my eyes, "but I am extremely grateful that you agreed to help us. I know that it may not seem like it from the others, but you are and will be the only hope that we have. So, thank you."

My mouth opened and then snapped shut. I didn't

know how to respond. When was the last time someone had ever said they were grateful for me? Not Addie, a family member, a friend, or hell, even a manager had ever uttered those words.

We started the same as yesterday. He fed magic into my hand and I commanded the rest to appear. This time though, he gave me a more powerful dose and it allowed my magic to expand almost all the way up my arm. While we were holding the magic, I decided to see if I could pry some information out of him.

"Can you tell me a bit about Iniq's parents?" I asked. Spiris sighed and gave me a tired look. He ran his hand through his hair again and I was able to see his face better, his cheeks were a bit flushed.

"They were from different kingdoms. Your mom was from this one, the light, and your dad was from the dark." His voice wavered slightly.

"Is that why I can have both sets of powers?"

"No, it is only those chosen who can. People can have parents with different powers, but they always show up with one or the other." His sentences were short and clipped. I could tell he was getting annoyed, but I decided to keep pushing anyway.

"Why would the gods do that?" His magic reached up to my shoulder now and I commanded my magic to do the same.

"I wouldn't question them. When you open the door, you can ask." I huffed and looked away.

Up until now, my arm had felt warm and tingly, but it took a sharp turn, growing hotter and hotter, but there was no pain. If anything, it felt good. It wafted across my entire body and up to my face. I felt my cheeks flush and the warmth spread to my… *oh*. His magic snapped back into him quickly and he stood up and put some distance between us. I thought I heard him mutter something along the lines of *Baecos is going to kill me.'*

"I am sorry, I was not paying attention to my magic." His hand came up to his neck where his blush had reached, and he rubbed the skin there, looking sheepish.

"What happened? It felt… different." I shifted uncomfortably.

"You can choose the intent of your magic. If you want someone to feel pain, they will… if you want them to feel something else, they can as well." He cleared his throat and his eyes met mine briefly.

"But I didn't put intent in mine."

"You did unknowingly, and it was a struggle to keep my magic at bay. I slipped at the end." I groaned loudly. I was turning him on without even knowing it. I looked at my hands as I felt myself blush. The gods must have had a blast building this type of magic.

"Why didn't you tell me?!" I picked up a rock and threw it at him.

"I didn't want to embarrass you!" He dodged as I threw more rocks at him.

"Are you not a teacher?! Aren't you supposed to teach?" My embarrassment may have been what fueled what happened next, but when I saw the rock leave my hand, it was no longer just a rock; my magic was covering it. Spiris's eyes widened, and I watched as the rock barely skimmed his face and exploded into the tree behind him.

"You and your damn rocks," Spiris muttered, holding his singed cheek.

"Sorry," I muttered and looked away from him.

"A lot of magic is about intent," he explained, his blush disappearing slightly. "Even just commanding it to the surface of your skin, you need to have the intent to do so. Using it as a weapon? Intent. Skipping? Intent. Healing? Intent. Remember that as your magic grows."

I rolled my eyes at him and nodded. "Okay, intent, I get it."

His mini lecture seemed to dissipate the embarrassment that was between us, but that didn't stop me from watching him. Not because he was attractive, because he was, but I felt that there was something bigger here between my past self and him. He was always watching me. During breakfast, he would meet my eyes often and engage in conversation. He was always searching, probably for whatever was left of Iniq.

The next lesson was on feeling magical signatures. Entering this world, it was very obvious that things hung in the air. Plants even felt like they were breathing and vibrated under your touch. It was all magic he explained to me.

"Every living thing has magic." He picked up a white flower and handed it to me. "Do you feel the magic coming off of it?"

I let my fingers brush across the petals softly and sure enough, there was a small vibration coming from inside the flower.

"Close your eyes and get used to the feeling." I nodded and did as he said. I focused on the small amount of magic that the flower had; it was waning slowly though, dying out.

"The flower cannot use magic as we can. It lacks intent." He gave me another bigger flower and took the dead one away. I felt the magical signature of this one, but it seemed much bigger than the other one. It was not just on the flower itself, but it surrounded it like a veil. "Magic is all about giving and taking. You give your magic to achieve a desired result. Magic comes from within, in our blood, so we can easily replenish it. But once it is gone, it cannot come back." The bigger flower died in my hand too.

"What about the door?" I asked with my eyes still closed. This time, his hands brushed mine and had them lay palms facing up. "What will it take?"

"Just a lot of magic," he answered, and I felt him lift his palms from mine. "Focus on the feeling between our hands."

I knew his magic already, so it was much easier to feel it again. My thoughts returned to the feeling he gave me earlier, but I stifled it. I felt the magic surround him much like it did the bigger flower. It was covering him like a veil, and it brushed against my hands. I could feel it lightly tickling my fingers. Spiris tested it by moving further and further away. After feeling his magic, it was much easier to find him; even if my eyes were closed, his magic would always brush against the corner of my mind—it was warm. I enjoyed this time with him, but as the sun started to fade, we knew that we had spent too much time away from the mansion. I had to admit, Spiris might have been my favorite, but he was still on my shit list for knocking me unconscious the other day.

***

When we got back, Baecos and Vitos were waiting in the dining room for us and dinner was ready. But as soon as we reached the doorway, I could feel the difference in the air, it was staggering. The woods were calm and quiet... the magic there was sweet, but the house was filled with something darker and more intoxicating. I recognized right away that the source was Baecos. Like Spiris's magic was warm, Baecos was overpowering and had him infused with it. As soon as we walked in, Baecos looked at me and back at Spiris and bared his teeth. The magic shifted and it felt dangerous, my heart pounded against my chest and I felt the corners of my lips twitch. The feeling almost got to be too unbearable. I stepped back without thinking but Spiris's hand pushed my lower back. Baecos's eyes narrowed at the movement.

"Don't run, not now," Spiris whispered next to me and he walked in to take his seat. I sat down, not looking Baecos in the eyes.

56

No one moved. Even the servants in the room seemed to sense something dangerous floating around. I gulped and tried to calm myself.

"The air feels different," I commented and watched Spiris stiffen across from me. "Is it from the ritual?" A servant dropped a plate and it shattered loudly across the floor. Everyone stopped to look at her while she cleaned it up.

"I see you learned a lot today," Baecos commented with a sharp edge to his voice, his eyes being the only ones not watching the girl clean up the broken glass on the floor. Instead, they focused on me.

"Yes, I did."

"Did you know, Vien," Vitos spoke up, "that when your magic is strong enough, you can sense when people's magic gets entangled?" My eyes shifted to Spiris, but he refused to look at me, he simply continued eating.

*Baecos is going to kill me.*

It was easy to understand what happened. I swallowed and tried to eat my food as well. Baecos must have felt our magic together.

While eating, I found my mind drifting back to the air around Baecos, the magic around him was intoxicating. I felt drawn to it, and all I wanted to do was run my hand through the thick air that surrounded him. I felt the power licking at my skin even when I tried to focus on the food in front of me like it was enticing me to take notice instead of ignoring it. After I was done, Baecos interrupted the silence.

"I will walk you up to your room, Vien," Baecos insisted. I knew that right now may not be the time to argue with him.

He followed me out the room and up the stairs.

"I apologize for earlier," Baecos said, stopping me and grabbing my hands. "I did not mean to scare you."

"You did not *scare me*," I lied to him and tried to pull

my hands away, but he kept a tight hold.

"Oh?" he asked, getting closer to me. "Then what was that in the dining room?"

My heart pounded loudly in my chest.

"So, the air around you is because of the ritual?" I asked, and he narrowed his eyes when he realized what I was doing.

"Why don't you admit that I can scare you?" His eyes were searching, and they dropped down to my lips. I bit them self-consciously but did not let him affect me.

"Like you could, you looked like a harmless puppy dog," I hissed at him and tried to move forward.

"Don't you walk away from me," he growled and pushed me into the adjacent wall while holding my hands above my head. "I was *displeased* when I had felt how much and what type of magic filled the two of you."

"You asked him to train me, that is your doing. And what I do with Spiris in my spare time, magic or not," I narrowed my eyes and got closer to his face, intent on making sure the words I said next were understood, "does. Not. Concern. You."

I felt him snap as soon as the words were out of my mouth. He started to glow, and I felt his magic explode around us. It was mixing with the already intoxicating air around him, and I felt my subconscious begging to be bathed in this power. It didn't stop at just the surface of my skin; his powers sank deep into me and ignited the same feeling that I had felt in the clearing earlier.

He was baring his teeth at me, and he was so close to my face that his hair brushed against my cheeks. I flushed and tried to kick him off, but he only caught my leg and forced it to wrap around his waist. This magic moved beyond what I felt with Spiris too quickly, with just the magic alone, I already felt my head spin.

"Stop it," I tried to growl back at him, but it came out weakly. My eyes began to water, and I felt shame fill me.

"This is what real magic feels like, Vien," he whispered, his hot breath wafting across my face. His voice caused my stomach to tighten and I felt heat pool within me. "Is this what you felt with him? Hm?" He leaned his face down so he was just inches from me. His scent was overpowering now, and my eyes stayed on his lips. I watched as they turned up into a smirk. "I asked him to train you, not seduce you."

So, he was jealous?

"This is also your spare time, is it not?" he teased and burrowed his face into my neck.

I couldn't help myself; I moved my neck to the side to allow him more room. He chuckled and started to lick down the length of my neck to my collar bone.

I shivered against him. I became all too aware of his body against mine, the magic by now had me begging for any type of touch. Thoughts of where his hands could go filled my head. This was too much for me.

As if he read my mind, a hand freed itself and started to make its way down my front... His mouth was now back to sucking on my neck. His hand continued, and against my better judgment, I spread my legs wider for him. He growled at this invitation but his magic all of a sudden snapped back into him, and it gave me clarity of mind.

Oh my god. I was mortified. What did he just do to me? I felt blinding rage flash through me, and I pushed him off me. He seemed to enjoy this. His eyes were wild, and a smirk graced his full lips. His tongue darted out to lick his lips. I ignored how the gesture made me feel and my hand connect with his face causing a loud crack to echo across the hallway. For good measure, I kicked him and stormed down to my room.

"Pigs, all of you."

"If you want more tonight, you know where to find me," he teased, and I slammed the door in response.

When I went to the library that night, Baecos did not follow me.

# Chapter Eleven



After the incident, I threw myself into my training. Progress came fast and easier than expected. Every morning I would train with Vitos, and in the afternoon I would meet with Spiris to grow my magic. I saw myself become stronger, the strength training hurt less, and I could go farther for longer and could keep up with Vitos more now. However, I was still never able to take him down.

After hours upon hours of training and calling forth my magic, I was able to call on it without Spiris's help. It was a big step, and while I was filled with pride when I first called it forth without his help, I did not miss the small panic that flashed across his eyes when I showed him what I could do. Today though, instead of practicing calling my magic, he decided it was time to work on the door.

"You have to call from your core, clear your mind, and watch the door appear in front of you."

"You act like you have done this before." I huffed as sweat poured down my face.

"I have, but not for your door."

I scoffed. It's not *mine*.

"You've been to the human realm?" I asked, giving him a disbelieving look. I could not imagine someone like Spiris stepping foot in the mortal world. He'd stand out like a sore thumb.

"Just continue." I raised my eyebrow at this, but he refused to explain any further.

I called to the magic inside me and commanded it to come to the surface. From there, I tried to imagine it flowing across the floor in front of me and twisting itself into something solid. My breath started coming out in short pants as I felt my magic strain against me. I heard Spiris take a sharp breath and my eyes snapped open, before me was not a door by any means, but I saw my magic gathering like a cloud on the floor and there seemed to be something solid laying on the ground. Seeing the change made me lose my concentration and the magic snapped back into me, taking the cloud with it.

Spiris walked over to the spot where the door once was and picked up something from the ground. He flipped it over in his hand and then handed it to me. He dropped what looked like a black lava rock in my hand. Looking more closely at it, I could tell that it was my magic in a physical form, it had sparkles across it just like my magic did when it appeared.

"This is also the material that we use to make our weapons out of. Think of this process if you ever need to make one." I refrained from asking him why I would need to make one if I was safely tucked away in the mansion.

Instead, I just nodded and marveled at the stone in my hand. I made this with my own magic, and I could do so much more if given the time. I was strangely proud of myself.

"You did good," Spiris whispered and rested his hand down on my head and smoothed the top of my hair down. I don't know why the gesture made my eyes sting, but I struggled to keep the tears out of them. I looked away from him and down at the rock in my hand.

"I don't need your praise."

"You never did." He chuckled and removed his hand from my head. I smiled.

I could now feel magic without trying so hard. It was astounding to see everything that held magic, even some of the house plants around the mansion held so much power in them. But with the progress came some issues. I could feel Baecos's power more now, on some days I felt it waft through my room, beckoning me to follow it. I asked Spiris about it, but he just shrugged and said that powerful magic attracts people. Sometimes when I slept I felt a burst in power wake me, but I didn't dare to venture out and see what was happening. After the last time, I was not sure what I would like to see.

Baecos stopped by the library every now and then, but he rarely stayed for long. His power seemed to have dulled a bit, but it was still distracting. Whenever he came in, my eyes were drawn to it, and instead of reading, I just basked in the feeling of it. I longed to reach out and touch it with my own magic and see how it would react. On a night where I felt ballsy, I flirted with the idea of asking him to extend his magic to me once more, but I backed down after weighing the consequences.

This afternoon, I nagged Spiris to have us walk back through the forest instead of skipping. He looked reluctant but agreed anyway. I was thankful, even though I was tired after the training my sore muscles begged to be worked, and I knew a nice walk in the forest would do just the trick.

"How do you even stay so fit? I haven't seen you train once while I've been here," I said and poked his muscular arm.

"I get up early," was his gruff response. "If I didn't, I probably wouldn't be able to stop Vitos from killing you." I scoffed at this.

"One day, the tables will turn." I shot him a smile and winked at him, picking up my pace and weaving through the trees. I let my fingers brush across the bark of the trees enjoying the feeling of the magic tickling my own.

As we walked further and further, I was stopped when I saw something fall almost directly in front of me. I gasped and tried to look at what came out of the canopy above.

"Spiris! Come look!" On the forest ground in front of me was a creature no bigger than a common mouse. The skin was pure white, but if you looked closely at the human-shaped hands, they had black on the very tips. There was black hair messily surrounding its head, and its face looked to be twisted in pain. The biggest thing that put it apart from a human, besides its size, were the black as night wings that jutted out of its back—they were almost bigger than its body.

"That's a faerie, don't touch it." I shot him a look.

"It's hurt! You just want to leave it here?"

"You don't want to get on their bad side, they could make your life a living hell. They are not dangerous, just annoying." His eyes narrowed and he shook his head at me.

"You're annoying too." I shot back and gently picked its small body up, holding it against my own. I heard Spiris groan.

"You will have to ask Baecos to heal it, and if you can even keep it."

And that is exactly what brought me to the current situation. It was long after dinner, the mansion was quiet, and the sky was dark. With the faerie still asleep in my hands, I stood face to face with the door across from me, knowing that Baecos was in there. There was a small light coming from underneath his door and I could feel his magic crawling beneath it. I took a deep breath and crossed the hallway, but before I could knock on the door, I heard a muffled sound from within.

"Feel free to come in, Vien," Baecos called out. I shifted nervously and opened the door. His room was just as big as mine but with less feminine colors; it was actually much darker than the rest of his mansion. I could not make out everything as the sun had already set, but from what I can tell, this suited him far more than the rest of the mansion.

Baecos was sitting against the window opposite the door I had just came through. He was looking out the window, but when I stepped in, his eyes drifted towards mine. His hair was fully down and covered some of his broad bare shoulders. I had never seen his hair down before, and just like in the library, I wanted to run my hands through it. It didn't help that he was shirtless. He was less muscular than Vitos and Spiris, but he was chiseled nonetheless. His tattoos still showed in the small amount of moonlight that peeked through the windows. His eyes bore into me, and the moment in the hallway flashed through my mind.

"I need help." I cleared my throat and showed him the faerie in my hands. His eyes widened slightly.

"Did you seriously bring a faerie into this house?"

"They are hurt, can you heal them?" I asked and stepped closer to him. He ran a hand over his face and groaned.

"I can't believe you even found one." He patted the area next to him, and I took a seat and watched as he looked over the faerie in my hands. "It looks like it overworked itself. You better hope this one is merciful." I gulped and watched closely as his hand hovered over the faerie and glowed.

Slowly, the faerie opened their eyes and I sucked in a breath when I saw that they were bright red, and instead of normal pupils, their eyes had slits. The faerie sat up and started to stretch. They cast a look at Baecos but seemed to find him uninteresting.

"Are you okay?" I cooed towards the creature. Their nonexistent eyebrows raised, and it sounded like it tried to speak but I couldn't understand the language it used.

"She asks why you saved her," Baecos translated for

me.

"You understand that?" He just shrugged at this. A man of many talents apparently.

"Because I didn't want you to die."

The faerie waited for Baecos's translation. The language sounded high pitch and Baecos seemed to speak it quickly. The faerie nodded at him and she flew up to my face and planted a kiss right on my cheek. I giggled and the faerie gave me a smile showing its rows of sharp teeth. In an instant, the faerie left in a puff of black smoke.

"Maybe the gods really are on your side," Baecos whispered, and his fingers brushed where the faerie had just kissed me, leaving a tingling feeling. "The faerie just bonded with you. She will be forever attached to you, in this life and next." I lifted my hand up to where his fingers were, and when I brushed his fingers with my own, his breath caught.

"Please don't tell me there is a mark," I joked, but he did not laugh. "Oh no, is it big?"

"No," his voice was husky. "It looks like a small star, barely noticeable."

Now that we were alone, it was hard to keep my eyes off his bare chest. I felt his magic come off him in waves; it toyed with my skin, teasing it slightly.

"Thank you." My own voice came out harder than I expected.

"You do not need to thank me, it was the least I could do."

Looking at him now, I felt as though I needed to tell him about the memories I had been seeing. As I trained myself and felt magic flow through me, it had been easier to remember some memories that Iniq had of her life in the world. There weren't any answers hidden in them, but I did see Baecos, albeit he was much younger. Even in his younger years, he looked like a carbon copy of himself. I knew they grew up together, but seeing it play through my mind was something much different. I felt his magic—and my own—and they were much different than they were now. The magic was pure and unbridled with hurt and anger, different from what I felt coming out of Baecos now. I basked in the purity of his magic back then; it was light in all sense of the word, but now it was intoxicating and dangerous. The memories ranged from buying fruit in a nearby city to playing in the forest. There were times where we practiced magic together, and I smiled when I saw his face light up with excitement. We were learning together back then, but now I had a lot of catching up to do.

I decided it may not be best to tell Baecos about the memories. I did not want him to get the wrong idea and assume that I would be more inclined to stay because I saw more of him.

"I made some progress today." I dug in my pants pocket and brought out the rock that I had formed today. "It is not much, and I still need Spiris to help most of the time, but it is something."

Baecos took the rock and looked it over carefully. "Something indeed." His lips pursed and he handed the rock back to me.

I placed it back in my pocket and made my way back to my room but Baecos's voice stopped me before I had shut his door.

"Please do not make a habit out of bringing faeries home, I will not heal the next one." I swallowed and shut the door gently.

***

The only excitement that came out of training was that I had somehow convinced Baecos to heal my sore muscles. Between our normal library visits and the healing session, I was able to spend more time with him. Every time I did, I felt like whatever mask he had on was slipping inch by inch.

Baecos had found me after a particularly grueling fight with Vitos and put a hold on the magic training for the day. He gave me one look and motioned for me to follow him into the house and into the hallway that separated our rooms.

"I have a seating area that can be used while I heal you, or I could go into yours." His eyes narrowed and a smirk graced his lips.

"I am surprised you even asked this time," I scoffed and gestured to his door, signaling that I would rather go to his. I was far from trusting him but thought it may give me some clues as to who he was.

As we entered his room, I was given a better view and could make out everything that I had missed last time. While the floors were white marble and the walls were also white, there were dark black rugs laid about the room, and even his four-poster bed that seemed to be able to hold a family was dressed in black silk sheets.

I gulped. Maybe his bedroom wasn't the right choice.

Instead of making a sexually suggestive comment like I expected him to, he pointed me to the sitting area he was talking about. It was in the corner of his room right by one of the large windows; there were two large, dark red, leather sofas decorated with pillows and even a blanket.

A room for a king.

"Lay down on your stomach, we will start with your back." I nodded and did as he said.

"Don't try anything," I warned and let the leather of the sofa cool my suddenly warm cheek.

"Backs aren't my thing but…" I didn't have to look at him to know his eyes were trailing down my form. I shivered. "If I wanted to do *that,* I would have asked you to take your clothes off."

He had a point, but that didn't stop me from trying to take the pillow nearest to me and throw it back at his face. His chuckle was warm and filled the empty space between us.

"Just heal me." He murmured something under his breath, but I soon felt the healing warmth of his hands dance across my shoulders. Before my muscles relaxed, they all tightened painfully. I let out a hiss.

"Apologies… I can't just speed up the healing process so it may still hurt sometimes." I snorted but didn't overlook his apology.

"Do I have the ability to heal?" I asked as his hands drifted to my lower back.

"If you practice."

"I don't… feel much different than you," I said and moved my head to the side so I could watch him work. He was on his knees and his body was leaned over mine, his hair fell slightly in his face.

"We are very different, I assure you."

"I mean… my power. The only thing I have heard that you can't do is build the door, and that I haven't even been able to confirm."

I watched as his lips pursed then relaxed. "Is this a trust thing?"

"Yes and no, just, I don't feel like this all-power warrior you have made it out to be. I heard I was a mix of light and dark, but I have yet to really see where our magic differs."

"There are many ways that we do. I am not privy to all the powers that the Dark Kingdom holds, but there is one that I know for sure."

I raised my eyebrow to him, but instead of continuing, he paused, and then his hands stopped their movement. "Sit up." His voice was different this time, it was a smooth as honey, and before I knew it, my body moved by itself and I was in a sitting position. I couldn't even focus on anything else. It was like all I could think of was the overwhelming need to sit up.

"What was that?" I asked and my fists balled at my

side. He grabbed one of my legs and started to heal those as well.

"Part of my power," he said simply.

"Mind control?"

"I wouldn't call it that." He moved on to the next leg, but this time his hand lightly massaged the area as well. I almost moaned at the feeling. "The light is like a sliver of hope. Once I use my power on someone, I focus on bringing that light to the forefront of their mind so they cannot think of anything else. It's not really mind control if one part of you wants it, I just make you focus on that one part."

"It works on everyone?" His eyes met mine as he spoke.

"No, just those who have more darkness than light in them. I can only guess that if you were sitting, you may have felt more at ease, you may not have been consciously thinking of it. It's not always guaranteed to work, especially if you are strong of mind."

"Are you saying I am weak-minded?" I hissed at him but didn't stop him as he moved to my arm next.

He just winked at me.

"And how does my power work with this?"

"Yours, or at least part of it, is the opposite. You can surround the mind in darkness. Make them relive their worst moments. Make them become those moments. And then if you see that small sliver of light, you can yank it to the front making them believe it's the only way."

*I watched as Addie's face became shrouded in darkness. Her tearful expression changed to one void of emotion.*

*"You realize it now too, right?" My voice rang across her darkened apartment. The sun had set long ago but I had not arrived until just moments before. Addie wanted to talk, she called me in tears while I was on my way back home begging me to come to her apartment. I knew it was a bad idea, we broke up a week ago. I should have stayed away; it was my choice anyway. I just needed to*

*move on. We had been together for years at this point, and she still kept me from her parents. "That you're just a coward. I can't be seen with you in public, I can't know your friends or your family. I am alone, Addie, our secret meetings don't count. I need someone to build a life with, someone who recognizes me."*

*"I'm a coward," she echoed back to me.*

*"The biggest. I was willing to give my whole life to you, and you couldn't even do that." I felt anger well up in my chest, it was warm and left my skin tingling. Part of me wanted to snap Addie out of her trance-like state, but I reminded myself that she wasn't my problem anymore. I gave her an ultimatum. She has to tell her parents, or we were over. I wanted to build a life with her, and I was hurt by the fact that she seemed to not feel the same.*

*"Give my whole life for you," she echoed again. I let out a breath and fisted my hand through my hair. I watched as her expression changed to one of understanding.*

*"You get it now. Then there is nothing else to discuss." I started to leave, but just before I did, I turned to face her. "Don't call me again."*

*She looked at me then, tears were gone, and in their place was a chilling smile.*

*She was dead not an hour later.*

"You sound knowledgeable," I commented and tried to push the memory away, but my voice cracked and my throat closed.

I knew it was my fault, but knowing this…

"Just speaking from experience. This is why you are so powerful. My power has limitations… yours does not." I said nothing but just nodded. He sighed and grabbed my hands with both of his.

"Is there something you remembered?" I couldn't meet his eyes. I felt a new wave of guilt take over me. I knew that I wouldn't care if it was anyone else, really… maybe some part of me did love Addie more than I originally thought. "It happened to me once," he started and squeezed my hands, "I accidentally killed one of my teachers when I was younger." My eyes met his now and I saw his brows pull together. He wasn't worried, no, he understood. "The offspring of kings tend to have more power, and I came into mine at an early age. He was new to this and while we were sparring… I went too far. My father was proud, but even after I became king, I made sure his family were taken care of."

My eyes widened. He had no reason to lie about this nor did his facial expression give anything away. While I may not trust him, I understood this, and I knew that he would understand my situation too.

"I think I used my power when I was in the mortal realm," I started and he nodded at me, encouraging me to continue. "I used it on my ex-girlfriend and it obviously worked because she killed herself not an hour later."

"That's what happens when you have power, sometimes it slips and you hurt the people you love the most."

The words tingled my tongue and made my heart speed up. My whole life had been a struggle to prove myself and stand on my own, even with Addie I felt like I was trying to climb to the surface so her and those around her knew that I was significant enough to be remembered… but then she refused to even acknowledge me in public. I steeled my resolve then; if anything were to change out of my experience, it would be that I would not let another Addie happen. I would work here if not to complete the door, then at least to understand myself and finally be able to claw my way to the surface, to make people remember me.

"I want that power back," I said after I cleared my throat. I saw Baecos put on a small smile of his own.

"You will get it one day, after all, the door needs you at your best to open it."

There was a pause.

"So… women huh?" he asked playfully. I huffed and

stalked towards the door.

"Don't fetishize it you pervert."

***

The next day, I threw myself even harder into training. Vitos didn't give two shits but Spiris raised his eyebrow at my new demeanor. When he asked me, I just pushed harder and shrugged him off.

Baecos joined us for magic training that day.

"What do we owe the pleasure?" I jabbed with a small smirk on my face. Baecos returned it with one of his own. Out the corner of my eye, I saw Spiris shift slightly.

"I want to show you what happens when I try to build the door." He spread his hands out in front of himself, palms faced downwards.

"Baecos are you sure—" Spiris was cut off by Baecos's glare.

I saw a door different from the one I had seen previously; it actually wasn't a door at all. Just a black pit that seemed to suck in the light around it.

"This is the door to the mortal realm," he responded and then placed his hands in his pocket. He walked closer to me and pointed his chin to it. "You could run now and probably make it back."

"Vien, you shouldn't," Spiris chided, "our world is dying. You know that Baecos," his voice was pleading.

My heart pounded as I looked into the depths of the door. I could go back right now. I could join the mortal world as if nothing happened. I could search for another job and live in my parents' cold and lonely house. I could go back to the town of the people who called me a monster.

Or… my eyes shifted to Baecos. His own eyes were twinkling. His face of understanding yesterday flitted through my mind.

Have power.

Or I could be here, with these people I barely knew, in the world of make-believe and lies. But I could have power. My heart sped up even faster; I remembered the tingling feeling that the magic left. I remembered seeing the faces of these surprised men every time I did something new. I enjoyed surprising them. I knew that if I could continue to grow, I would never be forgotten or overlooked by anyone ever again.

"If you choose to stay here from now on," Baecos continued, "then recognize it was of your own volition. You are not a prisoner. You are not here against your will. You are here for yourself."

I shot him a smile.

"I will leave once I feel like I have gained enough power. But up until then, I will be here of my own accord." Baecos waved the door away and then turned to walk away from us.

"We will see about that." He was gone in a flash.

"You are playing a dangerous game," Spiris growled, but I ignored him. I was too busy wondering what it would actually be like after I opened the door.

***

Spiris was right, I was playing a dangerous game. It wasn't long until a familiar itch crept up on me. It was the kind of itch you got when things were… too quiet. The feeling of wanting to jump out of your skin, the feeling of wanting to start a fight with someone just because you could.

The training with Vitos was as horrible as ever, but he never surprised me, it seemed his intellect only went so far. At night I would spend time with Baecos in the library. I got more used to his magic so it was more bearable now, but it was obvious what he was doing. He would engage me in conversation, flirt a little, then leave. I started flirting back but only to see if I could get a rise out of him, but he seemed to enjoy it and always responded with that damn smirk. The itch was in full force when I woke up that morning, I needed to do something anything other than what I was here to do. I sighed as I got ready for my training. I was bored again. I was absolutely bored out of my mind. The magic had lost its charm and the people around me seemed to not help with any of it. In my mortal life, this was one thing that always had me on edge. I would get bored too easily and throw whatever I was doing away in search of something new. Relationships were no exception to this rule.

The door was coming along. At this point, I had started to construct the entire bottom of the door, but for the last three days, I hadn't gotten any further than that. No matter how hard I tried, it never changed the outcome.

"Why won't it move?" I slammed my fist into the earth.

"It may not be a physical block," Spiris explained as he threw the now solid rock into the pile on the other side of the field. "Magic is tied to our emotions more than anything else. If you are experiencing a block, you may have to look further inside yourself."

Look further inside? I scoffed and ran my hand through my hair. I knew what was holding me back, there was nothing exciting to hold my attention anymore. Much to Spiris's dismay, I walked away from training early that day. I decided that it was time to go out and find something more exciting.

The sun was fully set now, and darkness overtook the grounds. There was a small chill in the air, but I welcomed it, the never-changing perfect weather was even boring at this point. Not once had I seen it rain here, nor had it been cold enough to even wear anything heavier than a long-sleeved shirt. I decided to walk back to the rose garden where Baecos had first brought me; it was quiet and out of the way. The first time I came here at night, I basked in the beauty of the plants. Their magic was better seen at night, and it left them to glow in the dark, but now I paid no mind to this. I walked silently and quickly, hoping that none of the guards would catch me. Maybe if I didn't find anyone outside, I would attempt to escape again. I smiled at the thought.

In the distance near the gazebo, I heard voices talking, and I slowly stalked over to them and hid behind a pillar. They were in a circle gathered around what looked like a cauldron of boiling liquid, but there was no fire underneath, so it had to have been heated by magic. Their voices were hushed but I could make out that they were talking in a different language. They went around the circle; each person would say their part and they would drop something into the cauldron. I smiled as I watched, so this was the ritual that I've heard of. I moved around the pillar and silently walked up to the group, one girl spotted me instantly and she jumped slightly. This caused the others to look at me and they all looked like they were about to be hanged. I smiled at the thought, I was not that bloodthirsty, but it did keep the boredom away.

"Miss you scared us—you were so silent." It was Flayke. I hadn't recognized her in the dark distance.

"What are you doing?" I asked and walked closer to them. I let my hand drift along the side of the cauldron.

"We are doing a replenishing ritual. It will help us bring out some magic." Indeed, it seemed now that the cauldron had a magic signature of its own.

"How do you get magic... out of that? Do you drink it?" The other women laughed at my ignorance but Flayke shushed them.

"We leave it out in the sunlight for a fortnight and cover it with a special cloth during the night to keep the light in. And yes, we drink it." I nodded.

"Should we ask her?" one of the unnamed girls whispered and Flayke shot them a look.

"Ask what?" I spoke up, curiosity getting the better of me.

"Don't worry about it, miss, sorry to disturb your walk." The other girl huffed at her response.

"It won't hurt, Flayke." One the of girls walked near me and reached out to grab my hand, I pulled it back swiftly. "We would like to ask if you could give us some of your magic. Rumor has it you have more than even some of the kings."

Before I could begin to refuse, I felt a surge of power come from behind me. It was the same intoxicating feeling that I had felt two weeks ago. The magic was now licking at my heels and making its way up my neck. I stiffened and saw the others do the same.

"This better not be what I think it is," Baecos's voice rumbled from behind me. I heard his footsteps behind us. "Rituals are forbidden on my grounds. Did you forget?" His tone was sharp and commanding as a king should be. My heart started to race, and I knew the perfect ploy to stir things up.

"This was my idea." My voice was slow and deliberate—testing—but refused to face him. Flayke shot me a panicked look. "I made these servants teach me how to do this ritual."

Baecos made a clicking noise behind me. "And now why would you need any more magic?" I felt him get closer to me and the magic swiftly surrounded my body. This time though, the magic was ice cold.

"Not for me, to help the kingdom." I felt his hand clamp down on my shoulder and I jumped. "And I was bored," I admitted, still refusing to meet his face. My body welcomed the invasion of magic that leaked through my shoulder. He wasn't even calling on it, just his magic signature alone made me giddy, it felt like a drug.

"Leave us, take that *thing* with you," Baecos growled, and immediately the servants left our sight. "Now what am I to do with you?" He circled around me, and when he came into sight, he looked much different than before. His eyes were dark, and his face was twisted into its own grin. I shivered when his eyes met mine.

"That's a million-dollar question, isn't it?" I only hoped he didn't notice the quiver in my voice.

"Are you really that stupid to test me in this state?" The hand that was still on my shoulder squeezed me painfully. "From the look on your face, it seems like that is exactly what you hope to accomplish."

The air changed and instead of coldness, there was heat. I felt the electricity nip at my skin, and I shivered as it wafted across my skin teasingly.

"Maybe I am just a little bored," I admitted. "If I knew giving my magic out would incite such a response, I would have given it away to the entire kingdom." I narrowed my eyes at him, testing him.

His hand gripped my chin roughly and he brought my face closer to his. A breath got caught in my throat, and looking at him now, I felt myself turn to jelly.

"They are unworthy of the gift you were about to bestow on them." My eye caught his lips and I saw them change to a smirk. He knew the effect he had on me, and I could tell he was up to no good. I shivered at the thought of his hands over my body, they were so persistent last time and *precise*—he knew what he was doing.

"Should we finish what we started last time?" he growled, and with a flash of light, we skipped into his room. Before I could register what happened, he had me backed into a wall. I swallowed loudly. I tried to squirm away, but he held my face with his hands.

"Are you scared?" The tip of his nose traveled the

length of my face and down to my neck, stopping just over the pulsing vein there. The pounding of my heart was rarely ever due to being frightened. I found some sick pleasure in danger; he had to know that by now, didn't he? If I didn't, I wouldn't have come here, nor would I have let him touch me like this. Some part of me begged for it after being alone for so long, but I would never let him know that.

"Why? Do you have a thing for scaring people before you bed them?" I hissed at him, and I felt his tongue lick the side of my neck.

"You were never scared to begin with, from the start you wanted this. I just wanted you to admit it." I knew he had seen right through me; a sense of sick triumph ran through me. At least someone really saw me now.

"You can't just act like this every time you go through that damn ritual." I yelped as his teeth bit into my neck.

"Then tell me to stop." I opened my mouth to tell him exactly that, but no sound came out. "As soon as you tell me to stop, I will." He pushed open my legs with his own as I groaned.

*You're playing a dangerous game.*

I knew I was, but I couldn't stop myself from feeling the excitement of being touched again. Ever since Addie had died, it had been hard to shake my reputation off long enough to even get any type of human touch. I wasn't sure if Baecos was exactly human, but his touch and magic ignited a fire in me that I had lost long ago.

There were two crossroads ahead of me, and it became clearer and clearer which one I wanted as his hands trailed my body. I swallowed loudly as he paused and watched my face, waiting for permission.

"You haven't even really kissed me yet," I teased breathlessly. His lips twisted into a smile and I felt his magic pull back ever so slightly.

"I can do way more than that." His lips were now mere

centimeters away from mine. I felt the pull to close the space between us, but I hesitated. "But remember that you chose this."

Is this really what I wanted?

"Just kissing," I warned, trailing my hand up into his long hair and gripping it roughly once more.

"For now," he agreed and crushed his lips to mine.

The kiss was full of need, and at that moment, it was hard to imagine that I would have ever wanted anything else. His lips were so soft against mine, but the kisses he left were anything but delicate. Each one felt like it was awakening a fire deep inside me. I foolishly worried that maybe it was his magic burning me up from the inside out. I knew that with every flick of his tongue I was circling deeper and deeper into him—his kisses could easily become addictive.

Maybe this is why this was so dangerous.

His teeth sank lightly into my bottom lip and I let out a small noise. He pulled himself away from me only to laugh and get a good look at me. I watched as his eyes slowly rolled over my form and his thumb brushed across my now swollen lips. His own hair was very disheveled and there was a slight pink tint to his lips and skin. I felt a small sense of satisfaction at seeing how I messed up his kingly appearance.

"Just kissing," he reminded.

# Chapter Twelve

## Vien

Baecos was absent from breakfast the next day, and for that I was grateful, but Vitos continued to be anything but pleasant. Sitting down across from Spiris, I spotted Vitos wearing a shit-eating grin. He was in the middle of eating, but when I entered, he perked up and his eyes never left my face.

"It was bound to happen sometime," his voice carried across the table.

"Charming as ever I see." I focused on my food instead of falling for his jabs.

"I mean, there are three handsome men here. I am just surprised that Baecos got in your pants before Spiris did." I heard Spiris choke on his food and I felt my face flush with heat.

"He didn't get in my pants," I hissed. "Mind your own business."

"I dunno Spiris, maybe if you begged, she would spread her legs for you too." I grabbed the knife on the table and threw it in his direction, he had to skip in order to dodge it. His voice came from right by my ear. "Today's training will be fun."

When Vitos found something fun, it meant that he would be inflicting pain somehow. He was waiting for me to finish stretching, eyeing me like I was a mouse and he just so happened to be a cat.

He seemed to get bored of watching me and he decided to run at me head-on. At this point I was used to his attacks, there was a power difference of course, but he was easily taunted. When he got close enough, I saw his hand wind back like he was going to punch me—I smiled at this, he was so predictable.

I sidestepped his punch and put some space between us by rolling away. He quickly turned around, expecting me to be in the space beside him, but I was already running in the opposite direction.

"Why are you running?" His voice was smug, but not for long. I spied Spiris across the field and shot him a smile. I could finally show him what I had been practicing when the sun went down. I called to my magic and forced it to create the image I saw in my head. In an instant, I felt the weight of a bow and arrow fill the empty space in my hands. It was the same material as the rocks that made the door, making it heavier than its usual mortal counterpart, but I had been practicing.

In between the training at night, I had been working on conjuring my magic to be something other than the door. I assumed that if I could understand my magic more and actually use it for other things, it may help me with the creation of the door. It was hard work; I had only succeeded for the first time a few nights prior and never used it before. Using it here and now was nothing more than a shot in the dark. I felt giddy that it actually worked, and I felt even giddier realizing that the arrows would soon be lodged into Vitos body.

Vitos had caught up to me; I felt his magic behind me. I tried to dodge but his fist crashed into my shoulder, causing me to lose balance. Instead of falling straight to the floor, I rolled away from him, wincing as his punch started to ache. I let my instincts pull me along; I was on one knee and I loaded the arrow into the bow, and without hesitation,

I fired it directly at Vitos's chest. He barely had time to dodge it. It flew past him and even seemed to cut off a part of his dark hair.

I didn't wait for him to recover. I conjured another arrow and readied it again, focusing on his shocked frame. His eyes caught mine and they were wide with panic. I sent him a smile.

I fired another. He dodged right, cursing at me while holding his now wounded shoulder.

And another. He dived left and tried to keep standing, but I saw him falter.

And another. The last one was unavoidable, it sunk straight into his right thigh. He dropped to his knee and howled in pain. I quickly got up and ran towards him. He looked at me with bared teeth, but I had already loaded my arrow. This time it was pointed at his head.

I let go.

"Vien, no!" Spiris called, but I did not care. I watched as Vitos moved his head to the side, but he wasn't fast enough. It tore through part of the skin in his temple and no doubt took out some hair along with it.

I did not see his next move, but in an instant, the Vitos in front of me was gone and a body collided with mine causing us both to fall to the floor.

"You play dirty." It was Vitos. His blood was dripping down his face and onto mine. His hand was around my throat, and he started to squeeze. I tried to claw at his face, but I couldn't reach him.

I let out a breathless laugh. "You're weak," I spat. I heard Spiris calling for us, but my magic was failing me, and my senses were beginning to dull. I wondered briefly what my next life would be like, but the thought got cut off by the feeling of memories bursting through my brain.

Memories started to flash before my eyes, not my own, Iniq's. I had seen this frenzied blooded look on Vitos's face before. His eyes were wide, and his lips were twisted up into a sadistic smile. Sometimes he was laughing, other times he was just there watching my pain. There were thousands of these memories, but all of them though had one thing in common: Vitos was causing me pain. It was always in the same place though, a dark and wet dungeon.

Gone were the memories and back was Vitos's face. He was triumphant this time. I wish I killed him. There was a sudden rumbling in me, it flooded my ears, and I felt the pressure build inside me. Something wanted out, and it wanted out now. Before I could even think to let it out, it forcefully burst through my body and expanded outward quickly. Magic felt like it was covering my whole body, and now I could feel it crawling up Vitos's. Vitos's smile stopped, and his hand left my throat like he had been burned. I watched him as he held his hand to his chest. He was cursing, aging, and tried to shake his hand around as if that would stop the pain. It *was* burned. His whole hand looked to be burned to a crisp; there was no more of his tan skin left, it was all just charred black skin.

Spiris came to my side and helped me sit up. I coughed and gasped for air.

"You are a sick being," I spat. He looked like he was about to say something, but he skipped away.

Spiris rubbed circles in my back until my breathing was normal again.

"It took you long enough to step in." His hand dropped from my back.

"It was necessary." I gave him a questioning look, but he did not respond. Did he know what I just saw?

"That was not the first time," I stated and looked into his eyes. His eyes widened and he looked down. "Was he the one to kill me?" I grabbed his shirt and brought his face close to mine. "Answer me."

"No, it was not him." He still did not look at my face.

"Tell me why I remember him hurting me."

"I… I cannot, Vien." He finally looked at me, his eyes were pained. "I'm sorry, truly."

I pushed him away from me and stood up. I would not be conjuring the door today.

***

I did not leave my room for the rest of the day. My boredom was certainly diminished, but seeing Vitos's smug face over mine ignited a new type of frustration and even just a little bit of fear. He was different in the memories, more calculating and seemingly more dangerous. I'd had my fun recently playing with him and Baecos, but seeing him like this made me rethink whether this journey was worth it.

I played around with my magic while I was deep in thought. I practiced making various types of weapons and then having them disappear. So far, I had made a sword, a dagger, and the arrow I had used to hurt Vitos earlier. After the incident with him, I felt my senses on high alert. I was looking over my shoulder every few seconds. The mansion was relatively quiet but even the slightest noise made me jump. Vitos was definitely a sore loser and I expected him to come at me full force. I welcomed the fight.

I decided that I needed to arm myself in case I did not have time to call upon my magic in the future. I created a set of throwing daggers and hid one under my pillow. The other I wanted to keep on my person, so I grabbed a cloth from the closet and tied it tightly on my leg. I slipped the dagger there for safekeeping—it would be easy to reach if I continued to wear dresses. I would have to ask Flayke in the morning to find me a proper harness. Speaking of Flayke, she hadn't mentioned last night to me. Whether it was because of embarrassment or fear I did not know, but she came in and did her duties just like any other day.

Night came quickly without anyone looking for me. I

couldn't help but fall asleep. After the training and self-practice of my magic today, I felt exhausted. I slowly drifted off to sleep only to be awoken by the sound of someone moving in my room not long after.

My eyes snapped open and I quickly grabbed the knife that lay hidden under my pillow. I heard the intruder move closer to my bed and I threw the dagger towards them. The dagger hit the wall with a thump and the lights turned on. Before registering the change, my hand had already gripped the one on my thigh and pulled it from the cloth holder I'd made.

"Hold on!" It was Baecos. His hands were held up in the air and he was standing just a few feet away from me. "It's just me."

I sighed and set my dagger down on the bed, noticing that I had cut my thigh with the dagger by accident. I cursed and undid the cloth. Baecos sat down next to me on the bed and his hands hovered over the wound. He started healing it immediately.

"Why do you even have this silly little thing?" he sighed, and his brows were pulled together.

"It's not silly. This wouldn't have happened if you knocked like a normal person," I hissed and pushed his hands away from my thigh. I did not need a repeat of yesterday, especially with the newfound memories.

"I came because I heard that you had gotten back some memories." I cursed Spiris. Of course he would sell me out.

"I did." I crossed my arms and leaned back onto my bed. "You had forgotten to mention that Vitos has tried to kill me multiple times in my past life."

Baecos sighed and pushed a hand through his hair.

"He never tried to kill you," he explained. "It was like your relationship now. Sparing and such."

"That is the biggest lie. A dungeon is not sparring."

"You could say he got... carried away. But Spiris and I were always there to stop it."

I laughed humorlessly. Did he really think I believed this?

His hand reached out and squeezed my own. He had the audacity to look down and act like a...

"Please believe me," he whispered, his gaze meeting mine again.

I shook my head. Like hell I would.

"Keep that bastard away from me. If you don't, I will not hesitate to kill him." Baecos's mouth turned upwards at the corners.

"Did you remember anything else?"

I paused. I did, but given his lie right now, there was no way that I would give him any more information.

"No. Unfortunately, it seems my magic is working on instinct." I settled for a half-truth.

He sighed and nodded. I think it was a sigh of relief.

I finally brought up the courage to ask him about the relationship he had with my past self. He walked me through their whole younger life together as friends, filling in the gaps. As he grew, Baecos admitted that he came to fall for Iniq and tried to court her many times throughout their friendship, but they never built anything solid. They had experimented, he called it, in their early years, but besides that, they just remained good friends until the day she died. He did not spare the details when he talked about those said experiments. It made my mind travel to the previous night.

"Why do you act like that? Last night... was it the ritual?"

The air became heavy. "Yes, it causes the magic to be ten times stronger than normal, and it has effects on a person's... mood. Usually, I'm able to get a hold of myself, but last night, I found myself unable to. Even now, I am struggling." I shivered as his hand moved its way up my thigh. It would be so easy to fall into this routine with him I realized. His hand stopped and he sucked in a breath, I looked at his hand and my heart stopped.

There was a feather tattooed on my skin. I had never seen this before, but my hand came up to cover the one on my shoulder.

"Do you have any more of these?" I nodded and pulled the sleeve of my nightgown down to show him my shoulder.

"This one has been with me for most of my life, though, the one on my thigh is new." His hand reached out to touch the one on my shoulder, but when he did, it felt like he shocked me. I pulled away from him. "What the hell was that?"

He shrugged at this. "Have you looked at your back lately?"

I raised my eyebrow at him. "Why is that important?" He shook his head and gestured for me to turn around. I did and he slowly peeled back my night gown.

"Your seal is weakening," he explained, and I shivered as his delicate fingers traced something on my back. He pulled me up and brought me to look in the vanity mirror. What I saw first was not my back, but us together. His hands were pulling my hair out of the way, his fingers lightly brushing across my skin, my nightdress off my shoulders, and his face was close to my own. My eyes met his through the mirror, and he gave me a smile and ran his hands down my shoulder and over the skin of my back.

I gasped when I saw the markings there. I had two large wings tattooed on my back with feathers that were as dark as night. I had seen these in some of the memories of Iniq but barely more than a glance. Most of the wings were covered by my clothes, but what I could see took my breath away. The wings were so intricate that I wouldn't have been surprised if they lifted right off my back.

"The wings are seen as a rite of passage," he explained as he traced some of the feathers. "They are so huge that I am surprised you didn't notice."

"Why do these ones allow you to touch them and not the other one?" He rested his chin on my shoulder and sighed.

"I guess that one is just a bit more temperamental." He brushed his fingers across it again and I felt the shock.

"Tattoos do not have emotions," I grumbled against him, but enjoyed the warmth and secretly inhaled his scent.

"No, but your magic does, and tattoos are connected to your magic." I rolled my eyes at him. He would forever be difficult. I pushed him away and fixed my nightgown. The absence of his warmth was not easily forgotten.

"It is time for bed, please see yourself out."

He smiled, and in an instant, the room was dark again.

"Goodnight, Vien."

# Chapter Thirteen

## Vien

The next day I was awoken by Flayke earlier than necessary and with shouting.

"Come one, miss! The king specifically requested that you be up early and meet him downstairs!"

I groaned and turned around. I was still not a morning person. She clapped and threw the covers off me. I groaned again but forced myself up.

"You have only a few minutes, miss!" I grumbled and went to the bathroom to clean myself up. After a shower, Flayke practically threw me into the vanity chair and started pulling at my hair. Instead of the loose waves she normally did, she braided my hair so that it was up and elegantly wrapped around my face. She left some curls to frame my face and started to put on some light makeup. During my training days, she had stopped putting makeup on me as she saw how it was wiped away in mere minutes.

After she was done, she pulled me to the closest and handed me something that looked like a white dress. I almost pushed it away, but she insisted. Much to my excitement, I realized it was not a dress, but instead like a fancy jumper. The jumper had flowy sleeves that were cut down vertically, so it showed my arms. It had a deep V-neck that was embroidered with gold beads and it had wide flowy pant legs. Overall, I looked much like I belonged to the

Kingdom of Light. The only thing that stood out was that it showed my entire back tattoo. Memories of the previous night flitted through my mind.

*A rite of passage.*

I scoffed at the thought, I wondered what Iniq had done to receive these. Maybe her first kill?

Before Flayke ushered me out of the room, I made sure to pull her aside and ask that she have a dagger holder made for me. I was more than a little shocked when she happily agreed, but I remembered she knew my past self and I could only guess at what she must have seen her do.

"Wait, miss," she called as I was leaving, I turned to her and she gave me a dazzling smile. "You look beautiful today." I felt my cheeks burn and I uttered a thank you before leaving.

I met Baecos downstairs and as usual, he looked like royalty. His hair was tied loosely back as it always was, but instead of his normal attire, he wore an open-neck button-up that showed his chest markings, fitted riding pants, and a long coat sat on his shoulders. He really looked like a king here, shit-eating grin and all. The only thing missing was a crown.

"Where are we going dressed so fancy?" I teased, flicking the elegant coat that graced his shoulders. The fabric was thick and trimmed with gold, no doubt having cost more than my parents' house. His eyes lit up and a smile graced his full lips.

"We are going into a nearby city," he answered smoothly.

"A city?" I asked, my voice raising an octave.

"What is so surprising about that?" He let out a laugh. "Did you think I ruled a kingdom with no people?"

I flushed. "No, it's just I never thought you would actually let me leave the grounds."

Baecos just shook his head and led me outside the

mansion. Outside, a carriage awaited us. A carriage, really?

"If you try to run," he said softly and helped me board the carriage, "I will catch you before you reach the forest. But we should be past that now, right?" His voice was still cheerful even with the threat laced into his words. He placed a gentle kiss on my knuckles before closing the door. My heart skipped a beat at the threat and a devious thought entered my mind: maybe I could try to run. He joined me not a second later with a smile still on his face. It did not falter when he saw my own smug smile.

"I told you to keep this *thing* away from me," I growled, ready to pounce on Vitos. Baecos and his smile faltered.

"Oh, come on, Vien," Vitos teased and tried to reach out to touch my arm, but I pulled away. "Maybe I like women who shoot me with arrows."

"I wouldn't put it past him," Baecos shrugged nonchalantly.

Vitos let out a laugh and playfully kicked at him. Baecos smiled with him. I raised my eyebrows at them, but they ignored it.

"What about Spiris, is he coming?" I asked. Baecos's eyes flashed but he kept a cool exterior.

"No, he is not, why do you ask Vien?"

"Because he is the only one out of you three that is a real friend," I finished with a smirk. Neither Vitos nor Baecos smiled at that. Baecos clenched his fist and signaled for the coach to head out.

"Why is he suddenly your friend, Vien?" It was Vitos who spoke up. His face was dark, and his eyes were hard.

"Why does it even bother you?" I let the venom seep through my words. "Or is your anger towards me really only because I am taking your brother away?"

"If anything, it is Baecos that should be bothered." I saw a mischievous glint in his eyes. "You two spend an awful a lot of alone time together, he has even moved up to friend status now. But Baecos here, he got you writhing and

moaning underneath him while his rank remains the same."
I felt my face heat up.

"You don't know shit," I growled at him. His eyes lit up and he leaned closer to me.

"Don't act like no one can see how much of a whore you are, Vien." He laughed again. "I bet if I did not join today that just the feeling of Baecos's magic filling you up would cause you to beg for hi-"

Baecos cut in with a large growl. Vitos stopped and centered himself. He looked like a kid who had gotten in trouble.

"As entertaining as this is, I would prefer if you kept your mouth shut on matters that don't concern you, Vitos." The air became thick with volatile magic, a sudden change from the light airy mood they were just in. My breath caught in my throat and I felt a cold sweat come over me.

"I apologize, my lord." I think my eyebrows raised to my hairline. My lord? Did Baecos just play the rank card? I caught his eye and he looked at me and winked. I frowned and looked out the window.

I hated it here.

***

After a very silent and awkward ride, Baecos cleared his throat.

"We have arrived at Solis."

The city was breathtaking, of course. What else was there to expect when you were in the kingdom of light? The buildings were quaint, and none of them rose more than a few floors, but like the mansion, things seemed to be glowing and kept in pristine condition. As our carriage made its way through the town, people stopped and stared. I guessed a visit from the king was not common. Watching so many people go about their daily lives made me feel so small in comparison. What was I really doing here? Imposter seemed to be branded on my face for all to see.

"Try not to talk to them," Vitos's snide voice cut through my trance.

"It is because they may know your previous life," Baecos explained. "It is better to not let them know what has become of you."

"Do they know about the door?" I asked, horrified that they may view me as some kind of savior.

"Of course not, they would not be privy to such information," Vitos scoffed.

It took all my might to not try to blow this carriage up with him.

The carriage stopped and the door was opened. Baecos left first, then Vitos, and then me. It was not hard to hear the excitement stirring in the crowd that had now formed around us. Much of the excitement was directed at the king, but I met the eyes of a few people who in turn frowned at me.

"Please my lord I beg of you!"

# Chapter Fourteen



I ran through the maze as fast as I could trying to get the meeting spot before time ran out. I was beyond late and I knew it was too risky for her to wait too long, but she needed to know what was going on. We were so close. Mere weeks away from when we would see our plan come to fruition. We had been working on this for over sixty years now, and it was too late to turn back.

I emerged at the meeting spot, but it was empty, no demon in sight. I cursed and kicked a rock that was lying on the ground next to me.

"I was about to be spotted, you're lucky you have been able to keep up this mirage for so long, or else the guards would have seen me." I watched as the demon stepped through the maze wall. I let out a sigh as soon as I saw her. She wore a cloak to hide whatever she could of herself, but I could easily see her blood-red eyes shining through the shadows.

"She is more herself than expected. She doesn't realize it but I see how she acts when she thinks no one is watching." I saw the demon flinch. "Does this worry you?" In all honesty, I may have been projecting my worry onto her, after watching Iniq for so long, I was afraid that the blood lust would overtake her before we could save her.

"No, she will still be the same Iniq, regardless." I saw her shift uncomfortably and I looked over my shoulder for extra measure, but I had yet to feel a guard's magical presence yet.

"He may be manipulating her. They have been together more intimately—once she remembers, I am not sure what she will do."

"She is a manipulator herself, keep her on the right track and all should go according to plan." Cruor sighed and tapped her foot anxiously. "Has she remembered anything worth noting?"

"She remembers what Vitos did to her but nothing else as of yet."

"Get her to trust you, if our plan fails, you are our last chance." I ran my hand roughly on the back of my neck. "I have waited too long. I must go back."

"Wait, just… while the old Iniq is in there, I feel that this one is more dangerous. She lacks the foresight and knowledge of this world, anything you and I would run away from, she runs to. Over the last few weeks, I have seen a dangerous habit start to form, taunting Baecos after he has done the ritual and purposefully pushing the boundaries on everything. She is growing restless with us."

Cruor laughed without humor. "You must not have known her well back then. I would say that before she was broken, that she was much more of a demon than myself, that combined with her power is what made everyone want her… and fear her."

I saw her quickly run back through the wall and not a moment too late, I felt a guard's magical signature in the maze. I sighed and quickly left the area, giving a small nod towards the guard as I left, who eyed me warily. I needed to be more careful.

*There is a spy in our midsts.*

Damn right there was, and Baecos looked right at me

as he said it. It was the one thing I refused to tell Cruor, not like it would matter. I would be stuck here until I got both of us out. I had the chance long ago to steal her away and bring her right to Cruor when I visited her in the human world over two years ago, but seeing her with that smile on her face made me hesitate. I had only heard of what she was capable of, never fully seen. Would it be cowardly to say I was glad?

I thought back to Cruor's motives. I only prayed that she knew what she was doing. Iniq's powers were second to only the High Kings'. One misstep and there was no going back. Especially if that person had no memories of you two together, I worried that Iniq could very well destroy us all if she really wanted to.

I sent another prayer, hoping that whenever she decided to open the door that no more of her kind slip back into this world. I shivered at the thought.

# Chapter Fifteen

Vien

I turned around to face the shrill voice that cut through the crowd's murmurs. I saw a young boy no more than twelve hanging onto Baecos's pant leg.

"Our parents have already died, and our magic is failing as well. Please!" I watched as the boy's tears fell to the ground and sobs racked his small frame. Just a few steps behind him was another small boy who looked starved.

Was this what the loss of magic has done to these people?

Baecos's face was stone cold, and he didn't even have to gesture for Vitos to come, who was already at his side removing the boy from his leg. The boy kicked and screamed, and I saw Vitos raise his arm as if to smack him.

From the instant I saw his hand raise, I was already in front of it and ready to take the blow. Before it could hit my face though, I reached out and smacked his hand away with my own. The loud noise seemed to silence the crowd, even the boy's sobs seized.

"Let it go," Baecos murmured, and Vitos lowered his arm. Shooting me a nasty glace, he motioned for the boy to let go of the king's leg. This time there was no fuss.

"I am sorry, miss." The boy's voice was small and

dejected. I turned to face him and laid my hand gently on his head. His eyes widened and he flinched at the contact.

"There is nothing for you to be sorry for," I whispered and ruffled his already messy hair. He gave me a small sad smile and walked over to his companion. Kids were always my soft spot, adults be damned, but I remember what it felt like to be that young and have no one bat an eyelash at you. Baecos cleared his throat and I followed him through the city, trying not to spare another look at the two boys.

I tried to speak but Baecos held up a hand to stop me.

"Not here." I frowned but nodded my agreement. A smug look graced Vitos lips; he wore this expression like a professional.

Vitos seemed to relish in the attention he was getting from the people around us. Every time someone would stare, he would wave or send them a wink. His act disgusted me. I could only see the wolf hiding under sheep's clothing, I vowed that I would never be so stupid again. We stopped in front of a windowless shop, the only indicator of what they sold was the signage in front that was shaped like a dress. The shop was small and had an air about it that screamed royalty. Just like the mansion, everything in there was bathed in white and gold tones. Even the young women at the counter looked primed and ready to go to a ball.

"It is an honor to receive you, my lord." She was fidgeting as Baecos looked her over.

"The pleasure is all mine, young lady," he said with a soft smile. "I have a gala coming up and I would like you to fit this lady for it." I almost rolled my eyes at this. A gala? What was he playing at?

The girl looked me over and motioned for me to follow. I narrowed my eyes at Baecos and he sent me a wink. I returned the sentiment with a vulgar gesture that caused Vitos's eyes to light up. In the backroom, she had me undress and then worked on taking my measurements. And just like that, it was done.

The small woman ran over to Baecos with a receipt and he gestured for Vitos to pay.

"I would like something elegant, but the fabric should be light. Let's have it show off her tattoos," Baecos told the girl.

She nodded and was about to speak but Vitos interrupted her. "Please keep the change. We will need this by the fifth of next month." She nodded, and we left the shop without another world.

Without speaking, we headed to another shop. The shop window was filled with varying sizes of jewels and diamonds. I could only guess what we were getting there. Another young Ullusant met us at the shop, but this one seemed to recognize me. Her face became hard and she focused her attention on her king.

"Thank you for stopping by my lord." She bowed at the waist. "How can I help you?"

"We have something in the back waiting for us, would you be a doll and go get it?" It was Vitos who spoke. She flushed and did as he asked. She came back out with a thin dark box. Baecos took it from her and walked over to me.

"Please take a look to see if you like it." I raised my brow at this but opened it anyway. Nice was an understatement. Most of the necklaces were white diamonds but in the middle was a very large yellow one that outshone the rest. How could I not like it? I swallowed loudly and plastered a smile on my face.

"It's nice," I muttered, handing it back to him. The woman's face held a look of utter horror; it was almost laughable.

Vitos paid the woman and we were on our way back to the carriage. I looked for the boys again, but they were nowhere to be seen. This time, Vitos had decided to ride with the coach and leave me alone with Baecos in the back.

"Can you call yourself a king if you do not care for your people?" I crossed my arms over my chest.

He sighed and knocked on the wall of the carriage. Vitos opened the door with a questioning look. "Go give them some of your magic."

"Are you serious?" Vitos's voice rose and he bared his teeth at me. "Because she said so?"

"No, because I said so." Baecos eyes flashed and Vitos got the hint to do as he was told. "Skip home, we are leaving."

Vitos shut the door harshly and I watched him stalk his way back into town. The carriage lurched forward, and we were off again.

"So, you decided for us to play dress up and then go shopping." He let out a chuckle at this.

"Were you displeased?" I shifted uncomfortably.

"Yes," I answered truthfully. "And what is this about a gala?"

"We have one a few times a year. This was in celebration of my birthday coincidentally, and I would be honored if you would accompany me as my date."

"It looks like you already decided for me," I grumbled and watched the town disappear behind us. I felt him move from his side of the carriage to beside me. I refused to meet his face, but when he put his hand on my thigh and poured magic into me, I had no choice.

"Would you please do me the utmost honor of being my date?" His eyes were smoldering, and I felt his magic travel up my leg. I licked my lips and watched his eyes widen at the sight.

"I guess I have nothing better to do." I cleared my throat and his hand moved up my thigh. So close, dangerously close.

"I'll make it worth it," he whispered, and one of his hands cupped my face. "Maybe after this, I can move up to friend as well." His face was mere inches from mine. I could feel his breath wafting across my face. His tongue darted out and licked my lips.

"Acquaintance at most."

He tsked at my answer and his hand went from my thigh to my hip, to my bare back. I shivered at the skin-to-skin contact; his magic left hot spots on my skin, slowly warming me up. His hand toyed with my zipper and I tried to catch his hand with mine, but he caught it and brought it to his face. With moves like this, I didn't think that just kissing would cut it.

He smiled and brought two of my fingers into his mouth. I stifled a groan as I felt him suck on my fingers, his tongue dancing across the sensitive tips, and I felt my brows furrow. I was too busy watching his tongue dance across my fingers to realize that he had undone my zipper and the jumper was falling off my shoulders.

I gasped and tried to cover myself, but he growled and pulled the top of my jumper clean off, exposing me.

"The window," I hissed and moved my arm up to my chest, but he swiped it away. His eyes were transfixed on my now exposed chest and I watched his tongue lick his own lips. That stupid tongue.

"I was thinking of how delicious you look in that outfit and I just wanted to try for myself. I have to admit though, Vitos put the idea in my head. Something like this in a carriage? How scandalous." His eyes never left my chest as he spoke, as if he were talking to my breasts and not me. I felt a small burst of satisfaction knowing I plagued his mind.

He positioned himself so that instead of being in the seat next to me, he was on the floor. He spread my legs and positioned himself between them. He was so tall that even kneeling we were almost face to face. Almost.

"One thing you should never forget..." He dropped his head down and his tongue circled my erect nipple. "...is that as king, I will only kneel for you." He took my whole nipple in his mouth and I arched into the warmth of his mouth.

He easily tugged the rest of my jumper off while he was

busy with my nipples. I was left just in my small panties and shoes. He slowly tugged on my underwear and slipped them off one leg, never breaking eye contact. He took one of my legs and rested it on his shoulders. I tangled my hand in his long hair, prepared for what was coming, and he chuckled.

"Eager, are we?"

I growled at him, but before I could answer, his lips and tongue were already working through my wetness. Throwing my head back, it was easy to lose myself in the feeling of his magic and tongue working me. I tugged on his hair, bringing him closer.

I bucked my hips and felt his fingers play at my entrance. Slowly he entered a single digit.

"Is this friend status yet?" He pumped his finger just once. I tried to move my hips against him but he gipped them so I couldn't.

I shot him a look and he moved it in me, teasing me. "Not yet."

He smirked and pulled out his finger only to add another one and plunge it deep inside me. I threw my head back and moaned. He slowly started pumping in and out of me.

"Faster," I growled. The same smirk never left his face and his eyes never left mine. He slowed even more.

"You know what I want to hear." He brought his mouth down to my clit and started sucking. I could feel the vibrations of his magic ride through me.

"Fine! A friend, you can be a friend." As soon as the words left my mouth, he was pumping in and out of me bringing me closer and closer to oblivion.

With one deep thrust, I let go around his fingers. With his magic still running wildly inside me, I needed more. I lowered my leg from his shoulder and pushed him to the ground of the rocky carriage, he did not object and let me climb on top of him. I slowly undid the zipper to his pants and reached in, feeling his full length.

"I didn't plan for our first time together to be inside of a moving carriage." His voice was hoarse, but it didn't deter me. I could think of nothing more than to quench this insane need that I had running through me. I felt like my body had a mind of its own, it was almost trance-like. I felt him trying to speak to me again, but I was already trying to pull his pants down.

"Vien, stop." His magic snapped back into him and I felt the haze of my mind clear. I saw myself fully naked on top of him, ready to take it further than I had planned to. Shame rose in me so fast that I felt like I was hit with a truck full of it.

"I don't know—" He stopped me with his hand and started to pull his pants back up.

"It was the magic. It can do that if we are not careful. I was not and I apologize for that." He helped me put my clothes back on and I refused to look up at him. He lifted my chin so our eyes met and gave me a small kiss on the lips. "We have time for that later."

When we arrived back at the mansion, it was Vitos who opened the door for us.

"So… friends, right?" I kicked him as hard as I could in the chest. Sending him flying a few feet was satisfying enough for me.

# Chapter Sixteen

## Vien

Something must have changed in Baecos because instead of finding me in the library at night, he chose to take me out more. I don't know if it was because he trusted me or perhaps because he saw how bored I was. My training shifted only slightly; Vitos still tried to train me in the mornings, but I began walking away from him and instead spent more time on opening the door. I made only slight progress. I shifted my focus, and instead of trying to make the door solid from the ground up, I just tried creating the shape of the door and slow hardening it.

"Always such a hard worker."

I was sitting down on the grass floor in the training arena trying not to puke my guts out. I knew the voice was Baecos, but I was too focused on making the door harden. The door in front of me was much bigger than I had imagined previously. It spanned about twenty feet high and was pitch black. There were intricate engravings of a language that I could not understand wrapping its way around the frame. The picture of the door always showed up in my mind as I called for it, but it was never my own creation. Instead, it was always the same pitch-black door. The more I looked at it though, the more it seemed that this door was not going to be easy to open.

With my concentration breaking just slightly, the door shimmered and vanished from sight. I stood up slowly and looked over toward Baecos. His eyes were transfixed on me and not the glittering mess that the door once was.

"Are we going somewhere?" I asked as I walked over to him, trying to push away my nausea.

"You will see when we get there," he replied and held out his hand. I rolled my eyes and cast a glance at Spiris. He was still sitting against a tree and motioned for me to go ahead. I frowned at his gesture. It had been hard to communicate with him lately. He seemed short with me and just overall unwilling to communicate.

I sighed and gave Baecos my hand.

When we arrived, you could say that I was more than a little shocked to be in another forest. I looked to Baecos, but he was already following a trail that had a steep incline. I cursed and ran after him.

"Did you and Spiris have a falling out?" Baecos asked as he moved expertly between the trees.

"Why would we?" I huffed and tried to keep up with his pace. Baecos looked back at me but said nothing else.

The hike was longer than expected. I quickly became out of breath. I still had no idea where we were, but the air started to become thick and my chest started to burn. The walk was mostly silent but Baecos would call out every once in a while to make sure I was keeping up. I had never seen him train before either, so I was surprised to see how fit he was when climbing this mountain.

After about forty minutes of hiking, Baecos stopped abruptly and spun around to face me. The twinkle was still there but he was also sweating, and his long blond hair stuck to his face. I was struck by how disheveled he looked, not once had I seen him work hard enough to even produce any sweat. I stopped hiking and waited for him to speak. He grabbed my hand, leading me out of the tree line and into a clearing.

"This is my most valued spot in my kingdom," he admitted. I let out a small gasp when I realized what he was showing me. From this area, you could see almost the entire kingdom. He brought me to the edge and pointed out his mansion and Solis. I clung to him when I realized how close we were to the edge, but I was still in awe of how vast and beautiful the land around us was.

I looked up at him, but he was already watching me.

"The land is so big. I never would have guessed this was all yours."

"This is the one place where I can go where no one can bother me. I come here to remind myself of my priorities." He swept his arm, gesturing to his land. "After I come here, I always leave feeling much better, I hope that this place can serve as that for you too."

He met my eyes again. There was an openness to his expression; it was unguarded, and not even a smirk was plastered on his face like it usually was. His face was just showing pure honest emotions.

"Did you bring me here so you can remind me of my own priorities?"

"I brought you here because I questioned my own." He wiped the sweat off his face and his eyes raked over the land before us. "I have worked for years on end to secure a magic source for my people, but recently, I felt like giving up."

"Why would you give it up? Isn't that what the door is for?" I asked as I watched him contemplate my words.

"The door is only a small part of what we need to accomplish." His eyes drifted towards mine and I shuddered at the intensity. "We have a much bigger task at hand."

"You have a much bigger task, not we. If you don't want the door, I could always leave," I offered, and he chuckled at me but didn't respond. I let the silence build until something clicked in my mind.

"Why couldn't we just skip here?" I said with a twinge of annoyance.

"The journey here is what makes it so worth it." He laughed and skipped us back to the mansion.

That night I was finally able to visit the library again. I decided that it was time that I did a little digging into what this door entailed. The talk with Baecos today panicked me, he obviously had other things that he was planning on doing. If I could get the door open sooner rather than later, maybe I could get out of here before the gala.

After searching, I found an English book named *Stories from Beyond: Magical Doorways*. I smiled and brought it over to my reading chair ready to dig in. I quickly skimmed the book and found the table of contents.

*Table of Contents*

1.    *Cross Barrier Doorways*

2.    *Wall Breaker Doorways*

3.    *Mortal Realm Doorways*

4.    *Other World Doorways*

The chapter on mortal doorways made me pause. Could going home be so easy? I know I told Baecos that I would stay here until the door was complete, but I still marked it in my head for later. I flipped to that chapter first, but it was only filled with stories and many warnings for those who do try to conjure it. The stories all had a theme: those who go, don't come back. Spiris had mentioned once that he had opened the door but never said if he had actually crossed over, and I was here as well so it was obvious that people could come back.

I moved on to the one labeled Other World. Without putting too much thought into it, I realized that it was about the realm of the gods or whatever the others had been spewing.

*The Other World was built for one reason; to divide the common folk and their High Kings. After living among us for so long, the High Kings were tired of the fighting and tired of the dangers that came with living among us. They banded together to create a safe haven for themselves and their blood relatives. Before leaving, they made sure that this door would only be able to be opened by those worthy, those like them. The High Kings put two requirements on the door:*

> *1.  You had to be the descendants of parents that had two or more different types of magic flowing through their veins AND be able to harness both.*
>
> *2.  You had to be deemed worthy by them. Every infant that is born with multiple types of magic flowing through them will be watched closely by the High Kings, and if they deem you fit to join them in their kingdom, they will allow you to call upon the door.*

*No one in history has been able to open this door besides the High Kings themselves, nor does anyone know the type of world that lies beyond. Ever since the High Kings vanished, they have not reappeared; it is rumored that those who can open the door are decedents of High Kings themselves that were cast into this realm as a test to see if they are truly worthy of the honor bestowed upon them.*

My mind was whirling as I put the book down on my lap. I felt a headache start to blossom behind my temples. I knew nothing more of how to easily conjure the door but only that there was a lot that no one here had bothered mentioning to me. Not only did they know that I was somehow worthy of opening the door, but that they had no idea what was behind there, and these gods were really High Kings or whatever they called them. As if he knew I was thinking about him, Baecos appeared in the library with his usual smile.

"Miss me yet?" he teased and took his seat across from me. This time he had brought a cup of tea with him to sip while I read.

"Could I conjure a door to the mortal realm if I really wanted to?" His teacup stopped at his lips. I could see his wheels turning, he was debating what to tell me.

"If you really wanted to," he replied and took another sip of his tea.

"How?" I saw his eyes narrow at me, sizing me up.

"We agreed you would conjure the door to the gods first." I knew this was coming. I smiled and held up the book I was reading. His eyes followed my gesture.

"But they aren't really gods, are they?" His eyes widened, and he put down his teacup so fast that I thought it would break against the glass table. "They are *High Kings*."

"That may be what their common name is, but they are in every truth of the word *gods*." He stressed the words heavily. "They created this realm and their own—"

"The Other World," I interrupted, and he huffed.

"Yes, the Other World. Did your book tell you that they were the ones that created the magic the flows through us? Did it tell you that with the snap of their fingers they can destroy all our magic? Do not think that because you are *chosen* that you cannot lose their favor. Do not doubt them." His voice was low and panicked, almost as if he were afraid of the all-seeing gods to hear.

"Oh, I would never doubt them—just you." I gave him a pointed look and rested my head on my hands, trying to look bored. "Why would you not explain this to me?"

"Why would we?" It was his turn to sit back and began sipping his tea again nonchalantly. "Won't you just leave after you open it?"

I grumbled. He was right, if I kept that up, there was no reason for them to waste breath on explaining these things to me.

"Curiosity killed the cat." I caught Baecos's eye and

he sent me a wink.

# Chapter Seventeen

Vien

"I don't know what you are talking about," Spiris growled as he walked into the clearing. He took his signature place in the middle and laid on his side, his head resting comfortably on his arm.

"I mean, you have been standoffish for at least a week!" I plopped down next to him, staring at the sky as well.

"Have not," he grumbled and motioned for me to get started on the door.

"I don't want to build the door goddamn it! I want us to talk! For real!" I felt my eyes water as he looked over me with another bored expression.

"What do you want to talk about?" I shook my head in frustration and trained my eyes on my clenched hands.

"You know that you are the only person I actually like here, and you are acting as if you don't even want to talk to me."

"If I am the only person you like, what about Baecos?" His voice was sharp.

"What about him?" I hissed back.

"I know that you are sleeping with him." I let out a humorless laugh. "So, you find fucking him funny?"

I crawled towards Spiris and watched as his eyes

widened as I neared. I kept a small smirk on my face and ran my nose across his cheek. I felt him suck in a sharp intake of air. He was trembling slightly. I inhaled his scent. He always smelt like flowers.

"Are you jealous?" I whispered against his ear. I trailed my hand from his arm to his neck and cupped his cheek. I decided to test out my magic and commanded it to pool on my hand. His eyes widened and he slapped my hand away from his face.

"Don't you try to manipulate me like that." I felt like he had slapped me right in the face. I swallowed and sat back on my heels. I recalled back when I was with Addie. I remember how I would manipulate her into doing whatever I wanted. I was a shitty person back then. I thought I was over that after she had died, but it seemed that old habits die hard. It was also hard not to forget how Baecos's magic felt when it invaded my senses.

"I am sorry, I wasn't thinking. I was upset." He sighed and shook his head.

"I am just concerned." He put his hand over mine. "Promise me you will not get swept away in him. Promise me that you will remember your goal." His words humbled me more than I thought possible.

"What even is my goal? I don't even want to build this damn door." My voice was barely above a whisper.

"Freedom. It is freedom."

We choose to walk through the forest on the way back again. Spiris's words rang through my head and they left some uncomfortable feelings in their wake. I started to doubt my own intentions regarding my work here. I internally scoffed, what I was doing here was far from work. I stayed because the feeling of my heart beating in my chest, the excitement that I got from this world, was far more than I ever got in the mortal realm. My thoughts drifted to Addie again, I wondered briefly what our life together would have been like. She was too good for that world.

"What are you thinking about?" Spiris's voice cut through my musings. The air had lifted between us leaving us room to talk and laugh as we once were.

"My ex-girlfriend," I admitted.

"Do you miss her?" Spiris slowed his pace.

"Sometimes. She died a long time ago. I would say I miss her company more than anything. The mortal realm could get lonely at times." I gave him a long look. "I bet you get that feeling here too." He nodded.

"Did you love her?" There was no falter in his voice, just pure curiosity.

"No, I don't think I did." I never admitted it out loud before but there it was.

"How did she die?" I sighed, not sure if I wanted to answer this question.

"She killed herself." My eyes drifted over to Spiris, watching his reaction, but he held firm. "My power… it slipped, and I pushed her to do it."

Spiris walked over to me and put his hand on my head, bending slightly so our faces were the same height. "Never blame yourself for someone else taking their life. Even if your power awakened it, it also meant that she was already thinking about it. That is their choice. Respect it." I gave him a sad smile.

Respect the choice of suicide? Her family's tear-stained faces over her freshly-plotted grave filled my mind. Her mother could not stop screaming. From when we found the body to when they buried her, she never stopped screaming.

I was about to speak but Spiris lifted his hand and made a silencing gesture to me. His dark eyes darted around the area around us. I strained my hearing and heard some rustling, but nothing more. I reached out with my senses and felt magical signatures close by. It would seem that this walk always brought some type of situation upon us. We continued to walk silently through the forest and stopped when we saw them fully come into view. I felt my heart rate speed up again; I felt a giddy sense of mischief fill me. There was no more than five and they seemed to be deep inside a ritual.

Spiris grabbed my hand and motioned for me to quietly move around them, but I couldn't let this chance slip away. I may or may not have accidentally snapped a twig underneath my boots. Spiris shot me a glare so deep I thought he was going to burn holes right through my skull. I gave him a smile. This time I did not recognize anyone in the crowd, but they seemed to recognize me. They all bowed at the waist and one younger man started to walk towards us.

"My lady, we are so glad to receive you." He bowed again and Spiris growled at him. His eyes glanced over to him, but he continued to move closer. He reached out his hand and grabbed mine inhaling a sharp breath. "You can feel the magic radiating off of her."

He was cute. I cocked my head as his lips brushed across my knuckles, there was a small smile there. "Isn't this forbidden on these grounds?" I turned toward Spiris and he stiffened but nodded. I spared a glance at the rest of the man's group and they were all wide-eyed, save for one. There was a younger girl towards the back of the group, and she looked to be contemplating something.

"I beg you!" I stiffened as I watched her bow deeply into the ground. She was small and her black hair was in ringlets around her face. "Please spare some magic." The orphans in Solis flitted across my mind. I saw no resemblance between their situation and hers, none of these people seemed to hold the same sickness they did. All the people gathered seemed healthy, and their magical signatures may not have been strong, but they were steady.

"You are obviously not lacking in any." It was Spiris who spoke up this time.

"Says the people who have an unlimited amount of magic." The man in front of me spat on the ground at my feet. My mind flashed to the memory I saw of Iniq's magic failing. I wouldn't call it unlimited. Still, this was something I had been curious to try ever since that night in the gardens. I shuddered at the thought, the feeling of Baecos's magic surrounding me… the punishment. It took all I had to stop the giggle from bubbling up inside me.

"How do I do it?" My voice was steady and strong as I spoke. I not only saw Spiris's anger flash across his face, but I felt it in his magic. He stepped closer to me, his front flush with my back, his lips just centimeters away from my ear.

"Don't you dare." His voice was dangerous, I smiled. I'd wondered if he had the same temperament that Baecos had and my mind went to a place of desperate touches and hot kisses. I quickly shook the thoughts away. I knew that if I wasted any time he would skip us out of here. I took a meaningful step forward, enough to get out of his grasp.

"Just imagine it leaving your body, rolling off of it," the girl piped up. Spiris hissed at her and pulled on my hand hard. I quickly did as they said and commanded my magic to my hand. The group around us hungrily watched as it pooled in my palm. I imagined it turning into a ball and rolling off my hand and off my body. I was not surprised when my magic obeyed. The man in front of me dived for it before it hit the floor, but I was unable to see the end result. Spiris skipped us away before I could see the magic hit the ground.

"You have a death wish," Spiris growled and led me up the stairs of the mansion. "No self-preservation tactics. You will literally be the death of me."

"It was just a little bit. I have a lot of it apparently," I mumbled and tried not to trip over my own two feet.

"You have to tell Baecos." We were going up the stairs at that point, and I stopped him in his tracks, pulling hard on the hand that was leading me.

"Like hell I do. This is my magic." Spiris's eyes snapped to me. They were wide and frenzied.

"Your magic and everything else in this kingdom belong to him until he says so."

Even though I had a feeling this would be the consequence, it didn't stop the white-hot anger from boiling inside me. I belonged to no one; they may have been keeping me here until I could open the door, but I would still always be my own person with my own will.

Spiris practically had to drag me up the stairs and to Baecos's room. We were fighting and struggling the whole way there. Spiris stopped only to knock on the door which was opened almost immediately. Baecos was standing in front of us and motioned silently for Spiris to come in.

"She gave away her magic to some common people in the woods," Spiris explained, not looking Baecos in the eyes. Baecos nostrils flared and his eyes narrowed. He went straight up to Spiris and slapped him right across the face so hard that he almost lost his balance.

"Bae—" I started, but when his eyes met mine, my voice disappeared.

"Why did you not stop her?" His voice was far from yelling, but it silenced the room, nonetheless. "Is it not your job to *teach her*?"

"It is my lord." Spiris got down on his knees and bowed. "I am ready to be punished but came right away to tell you with her so she can see this… *lesson*."

I flinched at what he implied. Baecos let out a dark laugh, and he walked away from Spiris and came towards my frozen body.

"You would teach her at the expense of yourself… I will take care of this lesson." Baecos's hand smoothed my hair down then cupped my cheek. I felt my heart speed up. This was not a side of him I was accustomed to. I knew it existed but to see the change… it made me weary.

"My lord please punish me in—" Baecos was back to his body in a second and Spiris was cut off with a kick to the face. Spiris's head and body jerked back and fell, and he cupped where Baecos had just kicked. I felt guilt fill me. I wanted the punishment. I did not want Spiris to have to go through it.

"I will punish whoever I want. Now leave." Spiris skipped away in silence.

Baecos pushed me towards his bed and sat me down on it. He grabbed his desk chair and put it in front of me so he was facing me.

"Why did you hurt him like that?" I asked meekly.

He didn't reply right away, but he moved his chair closer to the bed, so close that our knees touched. His hand reached out to touch my leg. I was wearing loose cloth pants today so the warmth of his hand could easily be felt through my clothes. I jumped at the contact.

"Why have you yet to learn how important your magic is?" His hand lit up and I felt it start to warm my leg. It did not take long for it to travel upwards. I shifted uncomfortably. Even just this little bit of magic made heat pool in my stomach. "Tell me, what do you feel when my magic touches you?"

"You know what it makes me feel," I growled and tried to move his hand, but he kept it there and increased the amount of magic he was pouring into me. I snapped my legs together and balled my fist. The heat moved from my stomach straight down to my sensitive core. "You are getting away from the point."

"I think I am just getting to it actually." His other hand cupped my face, forcing me to look into his eyes. My blush intensified as I caught his hungry eyes. I couldn't reply at first. I could only focus on how his hand moved from my knee to my thigh. I shivered again; I wasn't sure that I could stop anything this time. I wasn't even sure if I wanted to.

After I didn't answer, he fed magic through the hand

on my face as well. I moaned at the feeling and opened my legs for him. I felt like my body was on fire. I started to feel myself become wet and my core ached. His face got so close to mine that our lips almost touched. His tongue flicked out and he licked my lips. I opened my mouth for him, but he pulled away with a smirk. His hand inched closer and closer to my aching core, but he stopped just shy of it and gripped my thigh.

"If I had found those commoners before Spiris had told me, let's just say that this would not be the type of punishment you would be getting." I heard his threat loud and clear. I don't know what sick part of me was coming through, but his words only intensified what I felt. His magic flared again, and I almost came undone. "Say it, say what this makes you feel."

"It makes me want you. Every single time you use your magic on me, even if it's just a little, I lose control of whatever sense that I have and the only thing that I can think about is your hands on me." After the words were out of my mouth, his expression turned dark and he pushed me back on the bed. I gasped but made no move to leave. I watched from the bed as he slowly took off his shirt and threw it to the ground.

His chest and stomach were toned, and his tattoos covered most of his chest and parts of his stomach. They moved easily with his muscles. My eyes trailed down his body and stopped right at his pants. Even through his leather pants, I could tell that he was hard. I didn't have much time to look as he was on top of me in an instant. His lips crashed to mine in a haste. I gladly matched his needy tempo. My legs spread beneath him and he thrust against me. I groaned as I felt his body move against mine.

I fisted my hands in his hair and moaned against him. He growled in response and moved to my neck. I felt him suck and lick the sensitive skin on my neck. I wrapped my legs around him in an effort to increase the friction between us. His hand moved to cup my breast and I arched against his hand.

I needed more than this. He seemed to sense this as well and began to remove my shirt. I lifted my arms up and he threw it across the room. He looked down at me. I was left breathless and just in a bra, and his hair was like a wild halo around him.

"Take it off," he commanded and went to sit back down on his chair. I ignored whatever feeling of self-consciousness I had and obeyed. With his magic and body leaving me, I found myself desperate to get it back. As I took off my bra, he sucked in a breath and his eyes raked hungrily over my exposed chest. He said nothing but patted his lap. I stood up and slowly sauntered over to him. I was about to climb on top of him, but he held up a hand.

"Take your pants off." His eyes remained hungry, but a smirk graced his pink lips. I swallowed and slowly pulled down my pants and kicked them to the side. I was left there clad in nothing but my small blue underwear, and the fabric was so light that I knew he could see my wetness. His eyes narrowed to my throbbing core and I tried to cover it, but he growled and I put my hands back by my side. He brought his eyes back up to mine and motioned for me to climb on top of him. I obeyed him, and as I did, I was sure now that this wasn't really a punishment at all.

Once I was situated on top, he pulled me close to his chest. From the position here, I had to look down at him, but he didn't meet my eyes. Instead, he was focused solely on my breasts. My nipples were perky and ached with desire. The look of pure desire on his face made me flush and I felt it in my core. His pink tongue slowly came out to lick one of my nipples, and I moaned and arched my back against it. His magic started seeping into me again, and I felt myself warm. He took my whole nipple in my mouth and started sucking. I writhed against him and thrust my hand into his hair trying to bring his face closer to the soft flesh.

His other hand came around my front and brushed against my wetness, rubbing circles through my underwear. I felt him smile against my nipple right before he bit it. I threw my head back and his fingers finally slipped into my underwear.

"We haven't even gotten to the fun part yet, Vien," he said and pulled away to look me in the eyes. As he did so, he removed his fingers from my wetness and looked at them for a short time. He smirked again and put his two fingers near my mouth. I could feel my own wetness against my lips.

"Open," he growled. I didn't even think twice and opened my mouth to allow entrance to him. "Suck them clean." I began to suck. I tasted myself on him. It was sweet and it mixed with the salt from his fingers. He looked at me with hooded eyes as I sucked on his long fingers, letting out a moan and removing his fingers from my mouth. They glistened with spit and he put them in his own mouth. I shuddered at the sheer eroticism of it all.

"Stop teasing me," I groaned and rubbed my wetness against his leather pants. He only chuckled.

"What are you saying, Vien?" His arms moved away from me and to the arms of his chair. "Did you really think I would just give you everything? You forget that this is a punishment."

I growled at him and climbed off. I had no want for these games. I could easily find someone else to help with the ache. I quickly bent down and picked up my pants, heading towards the door. This was not a punishment; it was a game, and I did not want to be toyed with a moment longer. My hand reached for the door, but before I could open it, he pushed me roughly against it and held me there. I dropped my clothes and put my hands against the wall to brace myself.

"I didn't say you could leave yet," he growled in my ear and bit down. He kicked my legs apart. "You continue to disobey me. Maybe you need a better lesson?" I gasped as he ripped away my underwear with ease and attacked my wetness there. There was no gentleness, his fingers plunged straight into me.

"You do not own me," I groaned out between pants. He laughed and only pumped harder.

I moaned against him and bucked my hips. I felt my stomach coil. I would not last long if he kept this up. I felt his magic enter me again and I couldn't contain myself. He added a finger inside me.

"You are so wrong," he growled against me. "Come for me." That was all it took and I came in his hand. I slumped against the door and he kissed my neck. My knees were weak. If he were not holding me up, I would have fallen.

"Next time, I won't let you come," he growled, turning me around, nipping at my swollen lips.

# Chapter Eighteen



Baecos did not let me go so easily after that. While he allowed us out of the room, he would periodically reach his magic out to me, reminding me of his presence.

"Isn't tomorrow the ritual again?" My voice broke the silence that had fallen between us.

Baecos decided that we needed a walk outside, and we were now back in the garden. The same one that he first took me to in this world and the same one where I had come face to face with him after the ritual.

"Yes, it is. I would suggest staying out of trouble, I may not be as lenient tomorrow." While his voice was serious, his face had a smile that showed he was imagining the possibilities. I shivered.

Silence fell between us again. I struggled to find things to say to him, unlike with Spiris. Talking with Spiris came naturally, I found myself multiple times revealing parts of myself—and my past one—that I did not think of previously. But with Baecos, I had to force it. Without his magic flowing through me or starting a conversation at his own will, I found myself becoming silent.

"What about the upcoming gala?" I asked, pressing for any kind of conversation. His hand trailed up my arms leaving a tingling sensation.

"What about it?"

"How should I prepare?"

"Just be yourself. It's my birthday anyway, not like many people will pay attention to you." I blushed at his words. Of course, he was right.

"Do they know who I… was?" I met his eyes and I saw understanding in his face.

"Yes, unfortunately, most of them do." I frowned at this. "They know better than to comment on this." Another flash of magic and his hand squeezed my arm.

Silence again. I shifted uncomfortably as he brushed my arm again sending another wave of magic through me. Images of Addie filled my mind suddenly. This type of relationship was not one that I wanted or was ready for from Baecos. While I enjoyed the outings and the attention, I didn't want anything else to come with it. Instead of being tied to Addie for the rest of my life, I would now, or at least for the time being, be tied to him. It was a suffocating feeling.

"We don't have to pretend."

Baecos's smile dropped as I said this, and he made sure to carefully guard his expressions thereafter. His gentle squeeze turned hard.

"Who is pretending?" His voice was dangerously low again, and I felt my heart rate pick up.

"Us. You take me out to places like I am more than just a *fuck buddy*." My voice was cold. I felt no pain at this, but I was tired of keeping up whatever charade this was. "You don't have to take me out, buy me expensive gala gifts, or take me on long walks in the garden. Our interactions are forced, surely you can tell that?"

Meeting his eyes once more, I was worried that I had hurt his feelings.

"Do you want more?"

I laughed at his response. "God no." His eyebrows raised. "I am okay with whatever we have going on as long as we don't fool ourselves. I am here to build the door and leave. This," I gestured between us, "will not stop me from leaving."

Baecos surprised me by smirking. "We can go along with whatever you would like to make this out to be. But have you ever thought that maybe you would want to stay once you have completed the door?"

A soft wind brushed across my face and I paled at his response. I had not thought of it, but would it be because of him that I would stay? Spiris quickly flashed through my mind.

"Like hell I would."

# Chapter Nineteen

## Unknown

It took everything I had in me not to jump over these garden walls and tear Baecos limb to limb. I watched as he brushed his magic-filled hand against Iniq's face again, pulling her in for a kiss. I growled at the act and watched as Baecos's eyes opened and caught mine, and as if to make me even angrier, his hands started roaming her body, pumping more magic into her. She moaned at the pleasure of his touch.

If it were just sex, I wouldn't give two shits about what Iniq was doing but watching him manipulate her using his magic infuriated me. A little voice whispered to me in the back of my mind...

*She enjoys being manipulated like this. Look at her, she goes running to it every time.*

I watched in disgust as his hand trailed up her skirt, all the while his eyes were on me.

After being unable to sleep for hours, I left my room to go to the kitchen for some tea. I stared out the large window at the guards who were doing their rotating shifts. I silently wished that the gala was sooner, that this would all be over sooner.

"I didn't know you were a midnight snacker," Iniq's

voice rang out through the silence of the kitchen. My eyes drifted over to her, and I watched her glide over in her sleep gown. Hardly appropriate, it left little to the imagination, but I was never one to comment on her state of dress.

"Just some tea. Couldn't sleep." I watched her as she slowly poured her own cup of tea from the kettle I had used; she had a small smile on her face. I wish she could smile like this forever. Innocent smile, playful. Her eyes drifted towards mine, they were full of light. She seemed to always be scheming… her actions never surprised me.

That's a lie, they always did, but I got used to standing on my toes around her.

"A man of little words," she teased and leaned against the counter nearest to me. She drank her tea slowly, savoring the flavor. I let my eyes drift around her form as she was distracted; her long legs were bare and seemed smooth to the touch. I had a chance to touch them, to be with her the way I wanted to last time, but I didn't want to take advantage of the situation. I remembered how she ran her nose across my face in the clearing. It took all my control to not grab her right there.

"Why are you up so late?" I really hoped she would not say it was because of Baecos.

"Nightmares." I raised an eyebrow at this. What nightmares could she have in this body? Maybe she remembered something? "I usually don't have them. This one was weird though. I felt something calling to me *or someone* but I couldn't make out anything."

I nodded at her and let her sit in silence.

"Could you teach me how to make a door to the human world?" Her question caught me so off guard that I swallowed my tea too fast and started choking. She panicked and came to pat my back softly. After clearing my throat a few times, I straightened myself and faced her again. Her eyes had a glint in them again. I felt around for any magical signatures but felt none other than the guards outside. I internally sighed at this; she really did have a death wish.

"Wasn't your brush with Baecos enough?" My voice came out harsher than I intended. "Next time he won't be so lenient. You are pushing your luck… and mine." I saw her face changed to a pout.

"I am willing to accept the punishment." I shook my head, running my hand roughly through my hair. She would really be the death of me, I just knew it. She really wanted to ruin all that I had fought and prepared for. I looked at her and felt my face harden. Everything up until now I had done for her. Seeing her last time was too much and I could not help but try to fight for this shell of a person. Now seeing her here, fully intact, I couldn't help but keep a soft spot for her.

"It's not you that will get punishment, Vien." I put my hand on her shoulder softly, ignoring the way my magic reached out to her when our skin connected. "The reason we came directly to Baecos today was to save the others from punishment. I didn't know he would turn it on you. I fully accepted that I was to be punished for it." Realization dawned on her face and her small hand came up to touch mine. I knew it must be bruising by now. "Are you hurt?"

I saw her blush slightly and she removed her hand from my face. "No, I am fine." I felt a pang of regret as she backed away out of my reach.

*I bet you* get that feeling here too. She was too right.

***

The next morning, I decided to confront my brother. It was long before anyone else in the mansion rose, but I knew where he would be. I walked down to the training grounds. He was already working up a sweat practicing his jabs with a sword he built from his magic. He sensed me and stopped to send me a smirk.

"Look what the cat dragged in." He dropped his sword and placed his hands behind his head stretching. "It's been a while since you joined me for practice. Something happen with your *bitch*?"

I growled at him but forced myself to calm down. I needed something from him.

"Have you been denying Baecos?" I couldn't look at him when I spoke. I knew of their relationship—it was no secret—but I couldn't imagine the two together. Ever since they started, I saw a shift in my brother. He was once caring, but now all I saw was anger and hate.

I didn't have to look at him to know the anger the spread across his face, his magic was thick with it. "You have come to insult me. If you wanted to fuck her, I am sure you could just ask." He walked over towards me and slapped his hand down on my shoulder. After searching my eyes for a moment, he spoke again. "It is not I who has been doing the denying. He's too enamored with that *whore*." His eyes were angry, but I could see through them there was pain there too. Baecos was pushing him away in favor of Iniq. I wondered briefly if my eyes showed the same emotion.

"*Please,*" I started, and his face leaned back with wide eyes, "you know as well as I do that this is a slippery slope, the ritual is tonight. It's dangerous for us all."

"Just replace him with yourself, easy fix." He was daring me.

"You know that would just make him angry. I still want to live."

Vitos looked down and let go of my shoulder. He conjured a bow and arrow in his hand and began practicing without looking in my direction. I had only pleaded to him once before, I hoped he knew that this was serious.

"You know he doesn't give a damn about the door,

right?" His voice was hollow, void of emotion, his eyes watching the target across the field not meeting my own. I knew this was him hearing my request.

"I know." I was about to skip back to the castle, but I shot one more look at him.

"I don't know why you'd think that I'd help her." An arrow soared through the air hitting the bullseyes across the field. "I enjoy watching her pain."

"It's not just helping her. It's helping yourself. What happens when you lose Baecos's favor?" The next arrow missed as his eyes met mine again.

"I would never," he spat, his stance daring me to come at him.

"I know you don't enjoy it as much as you pretend you do." It was a shot in the dark, I wasn't even fully sure of my words.

"You're wrong." He was back shooting arrows, ignoring my presence. He shot four more arrows before speaking again. "He knows what you are doing. I can't guarantee he won't see through it." I felt a spark of hope start deep inside me.

"Thank you," I whispered, but I was unsure if he heard me.

"Don't forget, we are not on the same side here. I will do what he asks of me without question."

I nodded stiffly and left the training ground.

# Chapter Twenty



A week had passed, and the night of the ritual went by without a hitch. Part of me was disappointed that Baecos ignored me that night but I knew it was probably for the best. Spiris was right, I had been pushing my luck, but that didn't mean I would choose to forgo Baecos's company. I would just have to be more careful about it.

After a few days, I had resigned myself to staying in Baecos's room. After our honest talk about what was going on between us, I didn't feel the need to hide the fact that I wanted to seek out his company. Baecos was the easiest choice. Actually, Spiris was because I trusted him more… but I didn't like the way his eyes saw me. I knew they saw more than the others. It was easier this way, albeit more dangerous, there was no chance of us falling for each other.

If the others had noticed the new sleeping arrangements, they didn't mention anything about it. The silence from Vitos surprised me but I knew from the glint in his eyes that his hatred hadn't disappeared. His silence bothered me more than usual that morning, so much so that I decided to ask him to fight.

It was a crisp morning, and I was already beat up after more than an hour of sparing. I was on a knee trying to catch my breath after Vitos had kneed my stomach so hard

I was sure I was going to puke up my breakfast. Sweat was pouring down my face and I was covered in dirt. My fingers brushed across the weapon I had hidden under my skirt. Flayke had finally gotten me the holster that I had asked for, it was leather and fit comfortably around my thigh… maybe this was the real reason I felt safe to provoke Vitos.

I felt him stalk over to me, his magic was always surrounding him, but instead of pleasure, it always brought pain. His magic was different from what I ever expected someone from the kingdom of light to have, it was always sticky and thick with malice. He stopped right in front of me and grabbed me by the hair, forcing me up. I let out a groan and looked him in the eyes. He was smiling and his eyes shone with excitement.

"You think that because you are his whore now that I'll go easy on you?" he spat. I winced as he gripped my hair tighter. I knew it bothered him; he just needed a little bit of goading.

"I knew it bothered you." I felt my lips twist into a smile, and I pulled out my dagger, thrusting it towards his stomach. He cursed and jumped back just narrowly missing a hit.

His eyes darkened and the smile fell off his face. In the blink of an eye, he slammed me against the tree and his hands were constricting my throat. He moved too fast for me to see but I held strong on to my dagger and slashed it at his forearm. Unluckily for me, this did not make him loosen his grip. I thrashed against him and tried to slash him again, but the tightening of his hand made me lose my grip on my weapon and it dropped to the ground.

I tried to pull my magic, but it flickered and refused to make itself known. Vitos eyes were erratic and his mouth was in a permanent snarl.

"Vitos." Spiris's voice was rough. "That is enough."

Vitos's grip relaxed and he let me fall to my feet.

"She just needs to catch her breath," he snarled and

looked down at his bloody arms. "I didn't see you worrying about me when she was stabbing me or shooting me with arrows."

Spiris was at my side rubbing my back while I coughed and tried to breathe through the burn in my throat.

"He's right, I asked for this fight." I patted Spiris on the arm and brushed off the dirt on my clothes. "Let's try the door again today."

Spiris did not comment until I was already drenched in sweat after trying to build the door. I could see the door; it was almost becoming solid instead of the projection it was previously. I saw it becoming more real. I tried to hold my concentration as I stepped closer to the door and reached out to touch it. It was shockingly cool and had the consistency of glass.

"Why are you doing this with him?" My concentration was broken. I watched as the door shattered into a million shimmery pieces in front of me.

"Why not?" I watched as he crossed his arm over his chest, a defensive gesture.

"You have seen how he has acted after the… *ritual.*" He looked down at his feet. "If you could only remember, you would know that he is not the man you think he is."

"Then tell me what I am forgetting," I responded, and Spiris's eyes snapped up to mine. "There are no feelings involved here, he is helping me scratch an itch."

"You could have chosen anyone, why the most dangerous man here?"

"Like you?" I shot at Spiris, and he crossed the space between us putting his hands on my arms. My anger was lost suddenly when I met his eyes. "It's just until the door is open. I will leave afterward."

"Did you really think that this game you are playing will make him want to let you go?" He lifted his hand up to cup my face. His eyes were searching my face and I felt my heart flutter. His face was so close to mine. If he kissed me, I wasn't sure I would object.

Baecos's words swam through my head, it snapped me out of my trance.

*But have you ever thought that maybe you would want to stay once you completed the door?*

"Why does everyone all of a sudden care? It doesn't matter what he wants." I felt my irritation spike, this was my life, and everyone here seemed so bent on controlling it.

"No, it's me, *I care*. I always have, and when I see you freely giving yourself to that *bastard,* it makes my blood boil." I raised an eyebrow at him.

"Doesn't your loyalty lie with him?"

Spiris eyes became hard and he let out a breath of air that he was holding. He was thinking over his next words very carefully.

"It has always lied with you."

I felt my vision swim and I felt my consciousness move further and further away from my physical body. It was a memory. The previous ones have come much easier but this one was making my head hurt and my stomach flip.

*It was another dark dungeon. I felt the coldness seep through my bones and the world became much darker. I was vaguely aware of someone sitting next to me, hands were on my arms wrapping something around them. I looked over at the person and saw Spiris's tear-stricken face. His eyes had dark circles under them, and his skin looked pale.*

*I looked down at what he was doing. His hands were lightly dressing my arm with gauze. The gauze seemed to not be doing much… blood had already soaked through most of it and covered his hands. Looking back up at his face, I saw that there was also blood smeared across his face.*

*Spiris whispered repeated apologies, crying as he did so.*

*"This is not your fault, it is mine," Iniq's voice spoke out. It sounded hollow and void of life. I felt a throat ache from her as she tried to speak… she must not have had water for days.*

*"If I was stronger, I could get you out of this." He finished wrapping my arm and I cupped his face trying to wipe his tears away.*

*"You being here with me is more than enough." Spiris grabbed her hand and gave it a small kiss.*

*"If you had only been fully mated, she would have been able to find you by now." I could tell Spiris was trying to fill his voice with hate but it wavered. After all, if she came, he would be saved from this hell as well.*

*"Please, let's not talk about her," Iniq whispered. I could feel her eyes fill with tears.*

*"It's been a year, Iniq." Iniq looked away from Spiris. "How could she let you go through all this pain?"*

*"She doesn't know." Iniq's voice was barely above a whisper.*

The memories though didn't stop there. I remembered hundreds if not thousands of times where I was in that same dungeon. I was bruised and bloodied but Spiris was always there to nurse me. When I came to, I was still staring at Spiris, but my back was to the grass and his face was above mine. As I opened my eyes, I saw him let out a deep breath. I carefully reached up to cup his cheek like in the memories, he looked surprised, but he leaned into it.

"I remember." I acted as if I was wiping tears away from his face and his eyes widened. "The dungeon. Why was I there?"

Spiris eyebrows were pushed together and his eyes closed.

"You were taken. And your magic was drained from you." My breath caught in my throat. "That was a time very close to your death. I failed you in that life, I will not do the same here. I ask that you please trust me." He grabbed my hand again and brought it to his mouth, his lips brushing across my knuckles.

"Will you leave with me when this is over?" Spiris dark eyes looked over my face, questioning, checking if I was really offering. I could see the questions and emotions floating through his dark eyes.

"When this is over, I will follow you anywhere."

I smiled back up at Spiris, he returned it softly.

***

The next time I was hit with a memory from Iniq, I was in Baecos's bed. It was after a long day of training. I had been putting my all into training trying to find a way to open the door and get both Spiris and I out of this world. It left my magic sore and my body tired. Every time I tried to call to my magic, I felt it expand painfully.

From his bed, I could see Baecos reading over some documents on his desk, there was a stack of them, and he painfully read through each of them and I saw him sign or write on them occasionally. I never really understood what he was looking at or what his job even entailed, but it was so interesting to watch him work. His eyebrows were always pulled together and his lips pursed. As I was about to speak up, my vision blurred, and I let the memory take me away.

*Iniq was laying on the bed as well but instead of Baecos sitting across from her, I saw a familiar cropped dark hair.*

*"How bad is it?" Iniq asked, and I saw Cruor's shoulders sink.*

*"The demons here have been trying their best to supply magic but over half of the magicians in the kingdom are affected."*

*"Are the demons experiencing a loss in power too?" Iniq sat up slowly and stretched her muscles, Cruor was still focused on the papers in front of her.*

*"No, and if it continues this way, they should be able to sustain the people if everyone gives in their share." Iniq made her way over to Cruor and draped her arms around her shoulders.*

*"Demon magic," Iniq mused. "It could sustain us awhile. Maybe a few hundred years."*

*Cruor shook her head. "If every demon in the kingdom was willing, it could be thousands."*

*"I could donate m—" Iniq started but Cruor cut her off.*

*"Don't you even think about it. You know that you need it for the door." Iniq huffed and walked back to the bed.*

*"Opening the door is too unlikely."*

In an instant, I was back on the bed and watching Baecos.

"Why did Cruor try to steal my magic?" I asked Baecos. From the memory that just resurfaced, it looked like she had refused.

"There is only one reason—to save her kingdom. Like mine, it was suffering, and she decided to use you as a means to an end," he explained while slowly turning towards me. "Did you remember something?"

"No," I answered too quickly, his eyes narrowed. "I was just thinking of the ritual you do, why could she not just do that?" I sat up slowly and fidgeted in my lap. Did he feel my lies?

"Truthfully, I don't know. I assume she just found a more coinvent way," he said after a moment of silence. The memories and his words didn't match up.

"What does the ritual you do entail? Is it really that complicated?" Up until now, he has refused to talk about it no matter how many times I asked.

"Not complicated just… *tedious.*" His eyes shone with an emotion I didn't understand. I felt my hair stand on end and I shuddered. From the look in his eyes, tedious may not be the right word.

***

I woke up the morning of the gala with my stomach in knots. This was the first time I would officially meet people from other kingdoms. I tried to force memories of the other people that filled this kingdom to find their way to the front of my mind, but there was always some invisible wall that blocked them.

I heard Baecos groan next to me and turn over. He was still asleep but now facing me. I smiled slightly. He looked so harmless. His face was relaxed and the wrinkles in his forehead that showed up when he concentrated were gone. One of his hands was resting underneath his cheek and the other was stuffed under the pillow. His soft hair was loose and fell over parts of his face.

"Do you like what you see?" he asked without opening his eyes. I smirked at him and fully faced him, moving the hair out of his face while twirling it around my finger.

"Of course, I do," I replied, looking him up and down. Next to me, he was in nothing but thin sleep pants leaving his tattooed chest out in the open.

His eyes lit up and he quickly positioned himself so he was on top of me. I let out a small giggle unable to help myself.

"Let see what we can do about that huh?" he chuckled and attacked my neck.

After a heavy make-out session, we were interrupted by a knock at the door. I could feel that the magic signature was Flayke's.

"We need to get you ready for the gala, miss!" she yelled through the door. How early was this stupid gala? I groaned, and with much effort, pulled myself away from Baecos.

"When does the gala start?" I asked him.

"Not for a few hours, almost half a day really. I think Flayke just wants your attention." He gave me a winked and pushed me towards the door. When it was opened, I saw Flayke standing there with her arms crossed and her foot was tapping impatiently against the floor.

"Finally!" she stated exasperatedly. "We have to get you ready! And I don't just mean makeup and hair!" She grabbed me and pushed me into my room without even a backward glance at Baecos.

It turns out it really was so much more than makeup and hair. Within five minutes of stepping into my room, I was effectively pushed into the bathroom and forced into the tub. Waiting for me were the other maids that promptly started to clean, exfoliate, shave, wax, and moisturize my entire body. Apparently, today was actually kind of a big deal.

I didn't like being waited on hand and foot and I could most certainly shave myself. Every time I tried to push one of the maids away, I would promptly get my hand slapped and receive a verbal beating from Flayke.

As she was doing my hair, I enquired her about a favor that I had asked about a week prior.

"The present?" she whispered, making sure no one heard. I nodded at her and my eyes swept the room to make sure none of the other maids were listening.

Flayke pulled out a small box and handed it to me. I opened it quickly and beamed when I saw what was inside. It was a simple thread necklace with an Amethyst hanging from it. I saw this when Baecos had taken me out to another small town near the mansion. We were passing an antique-looking shop and I spotted it immediately through the window. I begged him to go look inside but left with nothing. I had asked Flayke if she could leave the mansion to buy it for me and she agreed.

I hadn't really thought that I would get him anything nor did I really care, but after being here for so long, it seemed too rude to not even try to get him something. Baecos had once given me some money after one of our trips out. I promptly tried to remind him that our relationship was nothing like that, but he insisted.

I held it close to me and gave her a smile which she returned.

"I hope he will like it," I whispered.

"He will, miss."

Before I left, she made me stand still as she fixed any fly always. "You were always so beautiful, miss." Her eyes met mine and she smiled slightly, patting my cheek. I smiled back at her.

***

After hours of being fussed over, I was ready to make my entrance. The party surprisingly had already gotten started by the time I was finished; the music and the loud voices started seeping through the walls. I was so worried about being late but Flayke assured me that no one would even notice.

I made my way down the hallway and to the main entrance. I could hear people's voices drifting up the stairway and my hands clammed up. The dress that Baecos had picked for me was to die for, it was a scoop neck, heavy, white satin dress with a leg slit and golden embroidery. This was by far the most expensive thing I have ever worn. The fabric was so buttery against my fingers and the beadwork was so intricate, I guessed this was worked on nonstop since our order. The dress of course would not be complete without my dagger tied securely to my thigh.

My hair was pinned up in a complex updo that required way too many bobby pins, but it elongated my neck and elegantly framed my face. I looked the part, but I knew inside I was an imposter. My tattoos told it all. From my back to my shoulder, you could tell that I was the one person that didn't belong here.

I froze in the hallway right before the stairs. My only wish was to be able to go back into my room and hide until this was all over.

"Let me help you out," a deep voice said from behind me. I turned around and realized it was a stranger in this lifetime but I got the inkling that Iniq knew this person. My instincts told me to trust him. No, actually, it was more like they told me to run to him.

He had long hair like Baecos but instead of a low ponytail, it was in dreadlocks that were now up in a bun with only a few pieces left to frame his face. His hair was a deep red, and he had dark black tattoos that covered the entirety of the left side of his face, making his blood-red eyes shine out against them. His amber skin was complemented by what I assumed to be the water kingdom's traditional blue garbs. My heart skipped a beat and my breath caught in my throat. If the red eyes were not obvious enough, his pointed ears and fangs sealed the deal. I tried to steel my face and reply to him.

"Are you from the Water Kingdom?" I asked, noting his tattoos. He gave me a small smile.

"I am their king." I nodded. Regardless of what Iniq may have felt towards him, this was the second demon that I had met, and I would have to stay on my guard. The last one apparently tried to steal my powers. I held out my hand and he looped it in his arm as he pulled me towards the stairs.

"Thank you for your help." My voice almost caught in my throat, but he said nothing.

Just before he reached the step, he stopped and held me there, looking into my eyes deeply... searching.

"I am not sure what the others have taught you about... my kind," he paused, "but I can assure you that I mean you no harm, instead I would like to extend my services to you." I lifted an eyebrow at this.

"Services?" I asked, and he replied back with a soft smile.

"If you ever need anything—or any help—myself and my kingdom will assist." I swallowed and nodded silently.

*It has always lied with you.*

Who was Iniq really?

Below us, I saw the entrance filled with people, but

there was no sign of Baecos. My cheeks flushed as I saw a few people turn to look at us as we descended. I even caught a few whisperings. Whether that was at me or at the king attached to my arm, I could only guess.

Once we reached the bottom, Baecos appeared in front of me with a grin. He eyed the king attached to my arm with suspicion but brushed it away quickly and put on a charismatic smile.

"I am glad that Vien is with someone I can trust." He grabbed my arm and pulled me to him. "Vien, this is Fluvis, I am sure he introduced his position earlier." I met Fluvis's eyes again and gave him a small smile. Even though he was a demon, my mind was screaming at me to trust him. For once, I decided to throw away my dislike of Iniq and trust her on this.

"It was nice to meet you, Vien. I hope we can meet again soon." Fluvis smiled once more and then left.

Baecos dragged me through the party and said short hellos to the people we passed, and they bowed in return. He stopped by a refreshment table and handed me something that smelled fruity. I took a sip and flavor exploded in my mouth, it was a mix between a ripe mango and a lychee fruit. I looked at Baecos and he smiled down at me.

"It's alcohol, don't get too carried away." He gave me a wink and pulled me a bit closer to him. Instead of whispering flirtatious nothings into my ear, his next question surprised me.

"Did you bow to him?" I looked up at him with a confused face.

"Was I supposed to?" I asked incredulously.

"Yes, for other kings you should do the same. I would never ask you to bow to me, but it is custom for you to do it to the other kings." I ignored my discomfort and nodded at him. It was his birthday; I would not make a scene.

After a short break, Baecos saw the Air and Earth kings

mingling together, and he brought me over to meet them. I pushed down whatever insecurities I felt and held my head up high. As we got closer, they both stopped talking and their eyes focused on me. They were both beautiful of course.

The Earth King's long white hair laid down flat on his head and extended far past his waist. His dark brown eyes were framed by his white eyelashes and seemed to jump out against his skin, which was also as white as snow. He had tribal tattoos all the way down his arms and up his neck. He gave me a smirk and I shivered.

The Air King was not much different, handsome as well, but he had an olive skin tone that was painted with swirls. Spiris tried to explain Sylph tattoos, but he always had trouble describing it. It looked like if you could see wind, this is the type of pattern it would make. Its complex swirls covered his forehead and temple area. His white hair was cropped and was slicked back, unlike his companion showing more of his face.

"Good evening," Baecos smiled at them. "This is Vien." He gestured toward me and met my eyes. He narrowed his eyes at me when I did not move right away. My heart skipped a beat and I tried to copy the bow that I had seen others do. Hands folded at my stomach and bent at the waist.

"It is an honor to meet you both," I said as I lifted my face to theirs. I was met with some interesting facial expressions. The Earth King had a mischievous glint to his eyes and a small smirk danced on his lips. The Air King had both of his eyes open wide and his mouth was slightly ajar. I looked away quickly, feeling uncomfortable under their stares.

"I am Terros," the Earth King spoke. "And this is Sono," he said, pointing to the still unmoving Air King.

"You're going to catch flies if you stare like that,"

Baecos half-teased half-growled. Sono shook his head and gave me a hesitant smile.

"You have her well trained it seems," Terros spoke. My face flooded and I felt a prick of anger stir inside me. Trained? I scowled and looked towards Baecos, instead of fighting him, he just shrugged an apology and changed the topic.

Baecos talked to them about some sort of trade agreement and I found very quickly that I did not care or understand the terms they used. I tuned out their conversation and looked at the guests, they seemed to be happily chatting amongst themselves and paying no attention to the kings that were crowded together. If you would have shown me this scene, I never would have guessed that this world was falling apart. I guess money really did exempt you from misery.

I first spotted Spiris chatting unhappily with a few women, and I felt a smile grace my lips. Of course he would hate this as much as I did. Next, I spotted Fluvis in one of the corners drinking alone, I wonder why he was not with the other kings? Red eyes met my own and he gave me a gentle smile. I looked at Baecos and noticed that he was so involved in the conversation that he wouldn't even notice if I left.

I decided that as much as I wanted to save Spiris, the prospects of chatting with a mysterious king was too good to pass up. I walked over to Fluvis and stood next to him with my own drink. He did not say anything and just let me sit in silence with him. I felt his own magic brush up against me—he had an aura as big as Baecos, if not bigger.

"I can trust you," I said, still watching the crowd. I could feel him turn to me, but I kept my face forward watching Baecos; he didn't spot me. I had a feeling that when he did, he may not like what he sees.

"You can, Vien," he replied softly.

"You know about my past?" I asked him, and he did

not respond. I took that as a yes. I looked over to Spiris and our eyes met for a split second, then they quickly looked over to Baecos. I stiffened but Spiris quickly looked back at me and gave me a small nod.

"Are you being treated well here?" he asked me after a moment of silence. I stirred at his question.
"Yes, is there a reason you think I might not be?" I asked, but he did not answer.

"Let's go get some fresh air," he responded and left his spot to head to the main door. My eyes were still on Baecos, who had not once looked over at me, and with Spiris's encouragement, I had no choice but to see this through.

# Chapter Twenty-One

Spiris

Things changed; the plan was progressing much faster than anticipated. I watched Baecos as he spoke with the other kings. He had yet to notice that Iniq took her leave with Fluvis, too excited to brag to the other kings about what he had accomplished.

I tore my gaze from him to the person in front of me. She was from the Earth Kingdom, she seemed sweet, but she was talking far too much about how much her dress had cost. I smiled at her and politely excused myself to get some drinks I said, but instead, I stood by the wall right where Iniq had been. This was a good vantage point, I could watch Baecos and the door. I felt a burst of familiar magic tingle my senses. Quickly looking around, I watched to see if anyone felt it, none save Baecos did. I cursed internally as he made his way over to me.

"Where is *she*?" His frame was shorter than mine, but I made no mistake, I could feel his magic was angry.

"She wasn't feeling good." The lies rolled off my tongue easily. "She went upstairs."

He searched my face, but I made sure to remain calm. He sighed and looked away; I could tell he was weighing his options. The other kings called for him but instead, he walked through the rest of the house… and right out the front door.

My heart pounded and I followed him out quickly. The plan was to fight Baecos if he caught wind of what was happening. I readied my magic as soon as I stepped outside but Baecos had disappeared.

"Don't be stupid," a voice said from behind me, and a burst of magic hit my back so hard it flung me into the rose bushes that surrounded the front of the house. Only one or two people were outside, and when they caught what was happening, they hurried inside.

I painfully picked myself up from the bushes. I felt cuts across my hands and face from the thorns. I turned to look at the culprit only to find Vitos standing there in a suit and tie with his hands in his pockets as though nothing happened.

"What are you doing?" I hissed at him and tried to see where Baecos went but he was already gone. Vitos ruined the plan, where was Fluvis?

Vitos walked up to me lazily with a smile on his face. "Saving you from dying, of course." I threw a spear of magic at him, but he dodged it. "I told you that we are not on the same side. If I saw you attack him, I would have had no choice but to kill you."

"Don't act like you are doing this for me." I saw his magic glow in his hands, but before he could send it flying, I saw Fluvis appear out of the corner of my eye and hurl his own magic at Vitos. Vitos cursed as it hit part of his arm, tearing off the fabric there.

"He is coming back, the window was missed," Fluvis's panicked voice broke through our stare down and I looked at him. I had hoped that this plan would work but we all had our hearts set on the next time, this was only just phase one.

"Go," I spoke to him and watched as he ran back into

the party. As he passed Vitos, I saw Vitos's arm sneak out to grab him, but I growled. "It's two against one Vitos, this is not how we wanted it to play out, but we can do it if you so choose." Once Fluvis was back in, I also felt Cruor's magic disappear.

"That was the plan you've been spending all this time on?" Vitos laughed loudly and walked closer. "You're dumber than I thought you were."

I bristled at his comment. "This is only the beginning." After I met his eyes, I knew that I had royally fucked up. There was a mischievous glint in his eyes and his mouth turned up at the sides.

"Good to know we should expect more." Vitos patted my shoulder and went back to the party. I worried but would have to wait until I saw her next.

# Chapter Twenty-Two

### Vien

I followed Fluvis out the door and into the front garden, but he didn't stop there. He turned right at the fountains and led me into the maze of greenery that was out there. I knew I would not get lost, but I wondered about him.

As I watched his back, I saw that he had no trouble navigating this place. He weaved through the shrubbery so fast that it was me who lost sight of him. I turned right expecting him to be there when I did, but I was met with empty air. I could have sworn that he had just turned, so where was he? I looked over my shoulder and saw a movement in the corner of my eye. I smiled with excitement; it was like a chase. I turned back around and followed the movement quickly trying to catch up.

I turned yet another corner and finally I was met head-on with burning red eyes, but they didn't belong to Fluvis. I quickly took a step back and grabbed the dagger that was attached to my thigh. It was Cruor standing in front of me.

My heart felt like it stopped for a full second and I felt the energy in the air shift. There were no clouds in sight, but it was like there was a storm coming. The air became heavy and I felt it crackle with magic. It was her magic, I realized.

Her dark hair was gelled back showing her face tattoos and pointed ears. She looked battle-ready, wearing leather pants, a white loose tunic, and a leather vest over it. Her posture though was relaxed, and she was reaching out towards me with her hand. Her fingers looked so long and delicate. I saw now that in addition to her eyes' tattoos, she had black flames running up her arms.

"Are you okay, Iniq?" Her voice broke through my thoughts and rang out in the space between us. I braced myself and without warning, I threw my dagger at her, she easily dodged it and got closer to me as she did. "I am not here to fight you."

"What do you want?" I growled. She looked hurt but continued walking slowly towards me.

I decided to speed things up a bit. I started to run towards her and let my magic flare up in my hands. I imagined creating more daggers and as soon as I got close, I tried to swipe her with them. She let out a growl and tried to dodge my attacks as fast as she could.

"I am not—" She ducked under my knife and hit my wrist; the dagger dropped with a clank to the floor. "—trying to hurt you."

She smacked the other dagger out of my hand and brought me close to her. Her face was close to mine and I felt her magic reach out to me.

"I know you came back just so you could steal my magic again," I hissed and tried to push her away, but even as I got my arm free, she quickly and easily brought it back to her.

"What are you going on about?" Her eyes flared and she pushed us to the maze wall. "Stop with the noise, they will find us before we can escape."

"Escape?" She nodded and cupped my face. Against my better judgement, I did not turn or try to run away.

"I have come to save you from them." Cruor looked behind her shoulder and I saw my chance. I pushed her back hard making her lose her balance and tried to run back towards the entrance of the maze. She cursed and ran after me, tackling me to the ground.

"They saved me from you!" I tried hitting her but she held my wrists up over my head, stopping me.

"They lie and you know it, even if you can't remember our past! Think, Iniq! Just think! Why would I do anything to harm you?" Her eyes filled with tears and I stopped my struggling. She let go of my hands and cupped my face again. "Maybe this will help." She started feeding magic into my face. It was hot and made my body jerk as it filled my senses. This was different than when Baecos did it, it was not filled with pleasure, but longing.

As my eyes met hers, I started to get dizzy. It was a memory coming, but this time it was different. Instead of a single memory, my head started to fill—it was a lot of them. Cruor sensed something happened to me and sat me up, pulling me to her chest while still filling me with magic. She was warm and she smelled like campfire mixed with fresh morning air.

It started with meeting her for the first time when we were kids.

Cruor was so standoffish, and she had a scowl on her face as I introduced myself to her. She acted like she didn't want anything to do with me but inside I knew that she was a lonely kid.

The next one showed us running around and playing with our magic, shooting it at each other, and throwing ourselves down in fits of giggles once we were too tired to carry on.

Another was when we were older, teenagers, she was showing me the new tattoos that had just shown up on her body. She was non-stop talking about the honor that was bestowed upon her. Her face was so excited when she showed them to me, it warmed my heart.

There was a time where we were sitting on a grassy hill and just enjoying the breeze. Her head was resting on my lap and she was curled up sleeping soundly. She was so serene in this moment and so unguarded. I was tracing her face; she smiled and woke up giggling when it became too ticklish for her.

The memories kept flowing into me. It became too much; my head was pounding. I brought my hands up to my head to hold it together, it felt like it would crack apart any second. She was rubbing small circles on my back and whispering to me.

"It's okay," she murmured against my head. Her actions surprised me, how was this the same woman that led me to my death? Tears started streaming down my face as the pounding in my head became worse. I felt Cruor jostle me slightly, she was standing up and bringing me with her, but I could not focus on that with her magic keeping the floodgates open.

There were just so many memories, we spent so many years together previously and all those small, seemingly insignificant moments spent together were filling me. Coffee on a rainy day. Laughing at jokes until our sides hurt. Late-night secret telling. There were so many, but none of these prepared me for the one that I saw next. I could tell that this one was buried deep in the seal because I felt my head almost split open as it forced its way to the top.

It was us on a late night with barely any light in the room. I was tangled in dark sheets and pressed against her naked body. She was hovering above me and stroking my hair. She had a small smile on her face. I was panting against her and we were both covered in a sheen of sweat. I lifted my hand to her face and pushed her short hair out of the way so I could fully see her eyes.

"I never thought that I could love anyone as much as I have loved you," she said as she kissed my forehead, both eyes, and lastly my lips. I kissed her back after that and wrapped my hands in her hair.

In an instant, I was pulled away from that safe haven. I

felt Cruor's magic leave me and flare outwards. My magic instantly responded and did the same. I felt our magic melt together and I slowly opened my eyes.

"So, you finally found your way in," I heard Baecos growl from behind me. Cruor only held me tighter against her.

"I see you're still a manipulative *piece of shit*." I felt her hand dig into me as she said this, and her magic flared around her. It looked like flames but instead of the normal red flames, they were painted black and the very tips were a bright white. My magic seemed to be merging with it causing the flames to sparkle. "You will pay for the harm you have caused her."

"She is well taken care of, I assure you," I heard Baecos say, and I could tell he was smirking.

I could feel his magic spike, but it was different than any other time I had felt it. It reminded me of Vitos's magic, sticky and filled with hate. Cruor stepped back in an attempt to get away from the magic that was slowly creeping towards us. Was she going to escape now? I looked over my shoulder at Baecos and I saw that he was alone, and his stance was battle-ready.

"Come here," Baecos growled at me and gestured with his hand. I felt a wave and sense of urgency overcome me, my body acted on its own and I easily let myself down out of Cruor's unassuming arms. I tried to push her away and her face snapped down to look at mine.

"What the *fuck* do you think you are doing?" She bared her teeth at me, and I felt myself freeze a bit. What was I doing? I looked down at our intertwined hands in confusion. She was going to take me out of there so why did I just try to go back to him?

"Are you upset that she left you again?" Baecos yelled.

"What did you do to her this time?!" she screamed back at Baecos, and her magic seemed to roar with her. I shuddered at the pain I had felt in my previous memories. I know Vitos had a part, but I still did not know how Baecos played into it.

Baecos let out a loud laugh. "What did I do? A lot actually, but she enjoyed every single minute of it. She was wet and waiting for me each and every time. Don't forget that you were the one that led her to her death." Baecos took this moment to step closer to us, and I took this moment to step back and out of her arms.

Her face flashed with pain and she tried to reach back out to touch me, but her arms stopped short as Baecos came up from behind and pulled me to his chest so my back was flush with his front. He bent down so his head was at my ear and he took that second to bite it, hard. Hard enough that I felt blood trickle down my ear. I cried out and Cruor's eyes flashed again.

"I didn't—" she choked out. "You know I didn't betray you, can't you see he is lying?!" she screamed at me and clutched her chest. "Why don't you remember the times we had together?! Why don't you remember what he did to us?!" My heart ached for her. I did remember the good times; my mind was still swimming with them... especially. I had the audacity to blush.

"I do," I tried to force out. Baecos tightened his hold against me and growled in my ear. "I remember some, but not everything. I don't want any of this. I just want to go home—he will get me there."

"You are delusional! Remember what he is capable of!" I flinched at her tone.

"We made a deal. After that deal, I want nothing else of this world. You included," I replied softly. Cruor stepped back and she looked like she had been punched in the stomach. Baecos chuckled.

"I am feeling quite merciful today, given that it is my birthday." His arms loosened and he took his time feeling the side of my body and even up to my breasts. I flushed and tried to look down, but he grabbed my chin roughly and forced me to look at her while the other hand trailed down my dress and into the slit dangerously close to my sensitive area.

Cruor's eyes widened and her face twisted in disgust.

"If you can walk away right now, I will let *everyone* live." His magic changed from the sticky disgusting magic to the tingling and hot sensation I was used to. He started pushing it out of his hand brushing across my underwear. I whimpered, unable to stop myself.

Cruor's fist tightened against her side and her body shook with rage. She let out another growl and bared her teeth at us. My eyes started to water.

"You are a disgusting pig," Cruor spit out. "I will come back." Before she could even leave, Baecos skipped us back into the house and into his bedroom.

Before I could even come to terms with how fast we had moved, I was already thrown against the wall. My head bounced painfully against the wall, which made my vision fill with stars.

"What were you thinking?!" he growled at me. "She could have taken you!"

I had no words for him. I only stared at him, hard.

"Answer me!" he growled and hit the wall near my head. I flinched.

"What gives you the right to treat me like that?" I demanded. " You shame me in front of a person you should have saved me from! Not to mention you have been lying to me about my relationship with her!" I felt my magic rise again, this time instead of the cooling feeling that it had left, it felt like I was being set on fire and it only fueled my anger. "I saw myself with her! And it sure as hell didn't look like she was trying to kill me." I felt the air around me crackle as the magic in me started to rise. I felt like I would literally explode. "You have been keeping those memories from me and you have refused to tell me anything of value. Whenever I ask a question, you don't want to answer!"

His eyes widened and he watched me intently.

"Don't think I didn't notice!" I growled at him. I balled my fist and pounded at his chest. As soon as my fist hit his chest, he was thrown back and had to quickly try to regain his balance.

I heard Baecos move and I looked up at him and glared. His hands raised up, palms facing me.

"Let's talk about what you saw," he said softly, his hands were still up as he spoke, and his form was crouched. It was like he was a lion tamer that had come face to face with a lion who hadn't eaten in days.

"Why did you lie to me?"

"What did she tell you?" he growled, and I felt my anger flare.

"I asked you a question. It is obvious that Cruor loved me, why would you say she tried to steal my magic?"

"Love makes you do crazy things," he started walking towards me again, but I backed away from him. "Her love for *Iniq* was strong, but the love for her kingdom was stronger."

"Why didn't you tell me I had been with her… in *that* way?" I looked down to avoid his gaze, but the torn and dirtied dress only soured my mood.

"Would it have changed you wanting to leave here?" I didn't know how he did it without skipping, but he was in front of me again and his hands slid down my arms slowly. "This is why I was not trying to force you to remember, Vien." My name felt foreign on his tongue and left me feeling uncomfortable. "Look at what that memory did to your body? When I saw you in her arms, it looked like you were dead. Not to mention that Iniq lived a long and painful life, remembering your happy times with her will not hurt as much as when you remember the painful parts of your life."

"How would you even know that?" I muttered bitterly.

"It's not like you've been sealed before."

There was some merit to his words. From the start, getting memories back was not pleasant, and if these were this painful, I was scared to imagine what it would feel like to remember death.

Baecos cupped my face softly and I tried not to flinch at his touch. "I am sorry for how I acted out there." He apologized softly and I met his purple eyes. They were also soft, and I saw no more anger in them.

"What was she to me?"

"Before the betrayal, she was Iniq's everything." He watched my reactions intently. "Everyone knew that you two were so madly in love and you would never see one without the other."

"And after?"

"More painful memories."

***

No one from the gala had even noticed what had happened outside. Baecos insisted on rejoining them but I was no longer feeling up to it. I told Baecos that my head still hurt and that I wanted to lay down for a while.

After regaining some of my memories back, I finally threw away the notion that Iniq and I were separate people. It was the easiest and most natural decision that I had come to terms with since coming to this world... since coming back here.

I was once scared of losing myself to this world. Losing what my mortal self had been like, but even as I began to remember, I still relatively was the same person.

Another side effect of the memories was that now my tattoos had shown up again. This time it was in the form of a crescent moon in the middle of my forehead. I never imagined myself with this many markings, but looking at how it fit on my face, I knew that it was only natural.

As tired as I was, it was easy to spot Baecos's gift still on the vanity. I sighed as I looked at it. My body felt heavy and my bed was so damn comfortable, but I knew I should probably give it to him before his birthday came to an end. My bare feet padded their way over to my door, hitting the ground with soft slaps. I shivered against the cold ground. I had changed into my night clothes and I didn't realize it could get this chilly in the Light Kingdom. I pushed the door open and was met with his closed one.

I wondered what he was doing in his room, maybe he wasn't even there right now. I walked near his door and waited. Usually, he felt me outside and told me to come in, but this time I waited and there was nothing. I reached out my own magic and tried to sense if he was in there. He was. I knocked quietly but there was still no answer. Maybe he was sleeping.

I quietly opened the door and peeked my head in. His room was dark, but I saw him asleep in his bed. I smiled and walked in, closing the door softly behind me. I tiptoed over to his bed and peered over at his face. Sure enough, his eyes were closed and his mouth was slightly open showing a serene expression. I gently put the box on his nightstand and turned around heading back to my own room.

I was almost at the door when I felt his magic flare and I was pinned to the door.

"This is a familiar position," Baecos's deep voice chuckled behind me. His voice was thick with sleep and it made it even sexier.

"I thought you were sleeping." He turned me around to face him. His hair was a mess around his head and his eyes were hooded.

"I was," he replied and brought his hand up to cup my face. "I was really worried about you today," he said honestly, searching for something in my face.

"I lost you in your last life and I didn't want to lose you

in this one. I tried to give you your space. I know you do not want this kind of relationship but," he paused and looked away from me, "I was really afraid when I saw you today. I hope you can forgive me."

"You already apologized, Baecos, that was enough. Thank you." I reached my hand up to cup his face as well. He grabbed my hand and placed a kiss on my palm.

"You are too understanding, Vien." I traced the tattoos on his chin and took my time with my next words.

"Iniq," I said simply, and he cocked his head to the side. "You can call me by my real name."

I saw Baecos's eyes widen.

"I realized a couple of things today," I explained. "And one of them was, yes, Vien was my actual name... but Iniq has been my name for much longer, and I should accept that now."

"If this is because of me—" I cut him off with my hand.

"It is not. I think the seal opened more today and I am rediscovering myself," I said, pointing to the moon on my head.

"I think I can help with that," Baecos said with a mischievous grin. In an instant, he pulled me off the wall and threw me onto the bed. I giggled at his desperation.

Baecos pulled off his shirt and threw it across the room. He slowly stalked towards where I was on the bed and positioned himself on top of me. I watched him intently and lifted my hands up to his hair. I started by pushing back his hair so I could see his eyes, and when I did that, I tried to block out the comparison of the blood-red eyes that flashed through my mind. I panicked from what I saw and tightly wound my hand in his hair, roughly pulling him to me. He was surprised by that act, but he met my lips with no complaints.

Using the strength that I had, I pushed him over so he

was on his back and I slowly threw my leg over him, straddling him. His hand grabbed my hips tightly and ground himself against me. I let out a small moan and saw his eyes flash with need. I put my hand on his chest, tracing the tattoos. I started to call on my own magic and let it come through my hand and into his chest. He froze underneath me, and his hand gripped me even tighter. I smiled and commanded more magic into him. He threw his head back and let out a very soft groan.

I needed more than that. I smirked and ground my hips against him, enjoying the friction it caused. His thin pajama pants barely hid his arousal. He sat up and pulled my face to his.

He bit my lip so hard I gasped; he used that to deepen the kiss. I wound my hands around his hair again, forgetting the magic I was doing and letting my tongue explore his mouth. Instead of my magic, I felt his fill the space between us. I moaned at the sensation. My toes curled and I felt my middle become soft. His mouth traveled from my own mouth to my neck. He sucked softly eliciting another moan out of me. More memories of those blood-red eyes, those fangs, and her long fingers entered my mind.

I removed my hands from his hair and took off my shirt. I heard him growl and his eyes met mine. It was his turn to flip us over now, he was back on top of me and he kissed from my neck leaving patches of fire all the way down to my hard nipple. Once he reached his destination, his tongue flicked out lightly. I moaned and arched my back trying to get closer to that mouth of his. He chuckled but obediently gave in and placed his wet hot mouth all over my nipple. I moaned again and wrapped my legs around his waist. The other hand was rubbing my thigh, hiking it up so he had better access to me.

His attack on my nipples stopped and he started to leave wet kisses all over my stomach moving downward. I moaned as he stopped at my silk shorts. His eyes looked up to mine and he smiled against me. I felt myself flush and I knew it went straight to my sensitive core. Suddenly, he pulled off my shorts and I gasped as the cold air hit me. Baecos gripped my thighs and pulled me closer to the edge of the bed. I saw him staring at my throbbing wetness. I tried to protest the nagging feeling of self-consciousness, but he just smiled at me from in between my legs. I felt his long fingers stroke me slightly and I groaned at the feeling.

"You're pretty wet already, Iniq." His voice was heavy with lust and it only made the situation worse. His fingers lightly rubbed against the sensitive nerve bud and I opened my legs even further. He never stayed in one place for too long or put too much pressure. I shifted slightly and he chuckled at me.

"Tell me where you want me." He stopped touching me and his face went between my legs. He gave a small teasing lick. I groaned loudly.

"There," I choked out, he only licked me slightly in response.

"Where?" he growled. I felt the vibrations against me.

"Inside me," I growled back. I heard him chuckle.

"Don't be so impatient." And with that his mouth started to devour me, silencing my complaints. I grabbed at his hair again and he gripped my hips harder in response. My eyes drifted towards him as his mouth was busy on my core. Seeing him like this only intensified my pleasure. Slowly, his eyes met mine and I felt his smile.

I felt him pull away from me and whined. I saw him stand up and start to untie his pants. I sat up slightly and he motioned for me to sit up further. I obeyed and waited for him to fully take off his pants, but instead, he came closer to me with his pants still on. I looked at him in confusion.

"Take them off for me. I did for you, it's only polite," he teased. I smirked up at him and obeyed. I slowly pulled his pajama pants and boxers down. I could already tell he was hard, but nothing prepared me for coming face to face with his fully erected member. He kicked his pants to the side and allowed me to look. I reached out a little to touch his tip, seeing the precum there. I scooped it up with my finger and looked him in the eyes. I smiled and started to suck on my finger, moaning. It was more for show than anything else. It seemed to work, his member twitched near my face and his eyes narrowed.

His hand reached out to tangle itself in my hair and he pulled my face closer to him.

"Suck," he commanded. I gave him a smile and began my work.

My eyes did not leave his as I took his whole length in my mouth. I watched as he threw his head back and moaned. I smiled against him and continued to suck. His hands gripped my hair and he started to forcefully push my head back and forth against his entire length. I heard his breath come out in short pants and I knew that he was close. Instead of letting himself cum though, he grabbed my hair back painfully and forced me to look up at him. He brought his hand up and rubbed the spit off the side of my mouth.

"I need you," he said and lifted me up so I was flush against his erect member, poking me in the stomach. "It is going to be hard and rough—it's too late to go back." I nodded meekly; I need to find release however possible and get those damn red eyes out of my mind. His eyes flashed dangerously, and he pushed me over to the desk. There were still papers on them, but he pushed most of them off and bent me over in one quick motion. He pushed my face down on the desk to hold me in place, fixed my arch, and then positioned himself at my entrance.

Without so much as a warning, he thrust himself in me. I stretched around him and groaned at the sensation of being filled by him. There was no pause. As soon as he entered, he began pumping in and out of me quickly. I was pounded painfully against the desk, but I really couldn't bring myself to care. The magic and feeling of his thrusts made the pain blur into pleasure, and I found myself screaming for more.

He quickened his pace and grabbed my hips to meet his thrusts, driving himself further inside me. My legs started to shake, and I felt my stomach clench.

"Come for me," he growled. I quickly fell over the edge with a scream and he tightened his hand in my hair as I did.

I was a panting mess, but it seemed that he was not done with me yet. He pulled himself out of me and flipped me over. He quickly gave me a deep kiss and went to go sit back down on the bed. Once there, he patted his lap. I quickly followed him and climbed on his lap once more. His slender hands gripped my waist and pulled me onto him. I threw my head back as he entered me again.

"Move," he growled. I obeyed and started moving up and down his length, reigniting the fire inside me once more. His hungry eyes watched me as I bounced on him. He gave a deep groan and threw his head back. I started to move faster, feeling him nearing his end.

He started to meet me mid-thrust causing me to moan even louder. His pace got faster and harder, and with a groan, I felt him tip over the edge inside me. I slowly got off him and laid next to him, panting heavily. I was too weak to talk; I just stayed there lying next to him in silence.

I do not know how much longer I laid there but the exhaustion from the day was catching up to me and I was slowly falling asleep. I was barely aware of when Baecos tucked me in his bed for the night.

Those red eyes did not disappear. Instead, they haunted me in my dreams as if they were mocking me.

# Chapter Twenty-Three

Iniq

I woke slowly the next morning all too aware of the ache between my legs. I looked over and Baecos was nowhere to be seen. I sat up slowly and stretched. I felt a twinge of disappointment but brushed it off. I was sure Baecos was around here somewhere, maybe eating breakfast.

*I know you don't want this kind of relationship.*

He was right, I don't.

I looked around for my clothes and found them still on the floor. I picked them up and got dressed. I knew last night was a long time coming, and it was great, but something in me felt amiss. It was like I felt emptier somehow.

I left his room and went to my own to get ready.

After I was showered and put together by Flayke, I walked down to the dining room. I listened carefully to see if I could hear anyone in the room, but I could not. I felt out with my magic but Baecos nor Vitos were in their usual spot.

To my surprise, I felt Spiris sitting at the table. I walked in and saw him eating alone. I did not speak but joined him at the table. The maids brought over my food and I began eating slowly.

"Are you okay after yesterday, Vien?" Spiris asked me softly, breaking my concentration. I knew he was referencing Cruor's visit.

"Iniq is fine now," I said, "and yes I am fine. I was not hurt." He nodded at that and continued to eat his food.

"Are your memories coming back?" he asked slowly. I nodded meekly.

"It was very painful," I admitted, "but I feel more like myself now."

He just nodded and looked away. Was there something wrong with him? Looking closer now at his face, I could see small scratches on it, they were already scabbing over. Before I could speak, he had already started to get up from his seat.

"Where are the others?" I asked.

"Out," he said in a clipped tone. I didn't ask anymore at that time, but I chose to follow him out of the room. Instead of going to our usual meadow today, he brought me to our home dojo. Something changed in the way in the way he walked, while he was normally really moody looking usually, it seemed to be extra prominent today.

*When I see you freely giving yourself to that bastard it makes my blood boil.*

I sighed and shook my head but said nothing.

The dojo was huge, the floor was covered in padding and one of the walls was filled with mirrors. It was definitely made for fighting. In the few of the corners there were piles of weapons, some I had never seen before.

He stopped in the middle of the room and sat down with his legs crossed, he patted the spot next to him and I joined him on the floor.

He let out a sigh and ran his hand through his hair. I looked at him a little closer when I realized that he had bags under his eyes. His skin seemed paler and his eyes were not as vibrant or playful as they once were.

"Did you remember any more about the dungeon?" he

asked softly. This took a different turn than I expected.

"No," I whispered. I saw him visibly relax and let out a long sigh.

"When you do remember, I ask that for our safety you keep it to yourself." I stiffened a bit.

"Anything more you can tell me?" He shook his head. "Should I start with the door then?"

"We are going to try something different today." I smiled and my stomach flipped. I was always down to try something new.

"We are going to work on your magic control, it could use some work. Up until now, you have been funneling it into the door, but that does not help to build your magic back up."

I nodded and called out to my magic trying to pool it within my hand.

"No," he said. "Your whole body, make it cover your whole body."

I commanded it to cover my entire body, but when I looked towards the mirror, it looked like my magic was spotty. It was very transparent and had obvious holes in it. Spiris was watching too and after a few minutes of me trying unsuccessfully, he sighed and shook his head.

"Stand up and close your eyes." I listened to him and jumped when I felt his hands massaging my shoulders. "Relax, leave your arms at your side and try to release all your tension from your muscles. Your magic will come to you easier." I felt him walk away from me and stand in another corner, most likely leaning against the wall.

I tried to focus myself and call to my magic. I took a deep breath and tried to gather what I felt underneath my skin.

"Visualize it, just like the door," he said, probably seeing how horrible it looks. "Like a thin mucus covering your skin."

I didn't like the visual but tried my best to replace the

"mucus" with what my own magic looked like. I imagined it starting from my head and unfurling slowly covering the rest of my body. I felt a comfortable cooling feeling run down my back. I took it that that meant it was working.

"Try to make it thicker." I nodded and tried to visualize the smoke becoming dark. Instead of the thin fog-like appearance, it had before I tried to imagine it black as night. "Now hold it like that."

I already felt a bead of sweat run down my face, how much longer did he want? I pulled my eyebrows together and grunted as I felt myself strain against my own magic. I widened my stance just slightly and gritted my teeth. This was nothing like the door. Pushing my magic externally was less taxing.

After ten minutes of holding, I felt it flicker, but before I could quit, Spiris spoke up.

"Make it bigger." Bigger? I was almost at my limit. My knees were shaking, but with a groan, I visualized what he said, trying to push out my magic as far as I could.

I heard him let in a sharp breath as my magic expanded so fast that it got to him in a second and covered him completely. It was a weird feeling, feeling him inside my magic. When I poured a little bit of my magic into others, I never stayed connected to it. And that was when I heard it.

*She needs to be stronger before we move.*

It was Spiris's voice. I heard him clear as day and it swirled around my magic like a leaf in the wind. I was hit with an immense amount of pleasure; this was not my own pleasure I realized immediately. I gasped and opened my eyes and saw nothing but black shadow covering the entire room. I lost my concentration and all the shadows snapped right back into me leaving me gasping for air.

I shot my eyes over to Spiris, he was on his knees and his hand was spread out on the ground trying to steady himself.

"Spiris!" I yelled and ran over to his side. His hand lifted and stopped me from coming closer.

"Tell me what you felt," he forced out. I saw him try to slowly stand up, pushing himself off his knees, then he went back over to the wall slowly and leaned against it for support.

"I felt your emotions," I said, omitting that I was pretty sure I read his thoughts. "Sorry." His eyebrow raised like he knew I was lying but nodded anyway.

"That's all?" he asked, and I nodded at him but didn't meet his eyes. "Good."

My head snapped up so I could meet his eyes, does he know what I just heard? His facial expression showed nothing, but his eyes seemed to hold a secret.

"Try again." His eyes met mine again and he smirked. He was testing me. I felt myself get excited.

I widened my stance and tried to find my magic again. I shut my eyes hard. I was already so spent but I knew it was important to try. I forced my magic towards only him this time and tried to visualize it engulfing only him.

When it hit him, I knew immediately because I felt his satisfaction.

*You once told me to keep this secret when we met before. I have not told anyone since, and I would assume that you would want to keep it that way.*

I felt myself smile and felt my excitement rise, I tried to keep our connection strong.

*I can teach you how to do this without people knowing.*

I was about to ask a question out loud, but his voice rang out stopping me.

*We must be very careful about what we say, there are always prying ears. Try to visualize the opposite of what we just did, make your magic clear. And please focus on your intent.*

I felt panic spike in him. Maybe someone was already watching us.

I tried my best to visualize my magic slowly dissolve in

the air. As I did, I had to brace myself on my knees as I found it hard to concentrate.

*Better.* I felt the smile in his words. *I suggest you practice this every day, multiple times a day, but only when you are with me or alone.*

I understood his warning very clearly.

*Open your eyes, Iniq.*

I did as he said and was amazed at what I saw in front of me. My magic was still around us but instead of the shadow earlier it was a very light grey fog with millions of sparkles. It looked like the milky way. My concentration broke a little and I saw it flicker.

*Slowly, bring it back to you.*

I listened and tried to imagine it retreat like a wave. Once I felt all of it come back into my body, I met Spiris's eyes. He gave me a real smile and nodded, pleased. I didn't hesitate to smile back.

"I can't thank you enough," I said and saw him freeze for a second and I was hit with a memory. My head hurt again, and my eyes glazed over.

*The whole room seemed to be splattered with blood. From the ceiling to the floor no matter where you looked, you saw splashes of blood. I had counted how many splatters made it to the ceiling, it was the only way to keep me sane. 482,483,484.*

*I tried to keep my eyes focused on the ceiling as I felt the knife tear through my arm. Screams have long since died in my throat and it only seemed to excite them when I did. I pleaded and begged but they would only tease me. Now the only way to spite them is to stay silent.*

*I couldn't bear to look at them now. I couldn't bear to watch them smile as they tore through my skin. I would never look the same. I was filled with scars because they didn't believe in healing me fully, they liked to see their mark on me. Even my once beautiful tattoos were now scarred over and had ugly lines running through them making them unreadable. I knew my back was worse, I saw them once in a mirror and could hardly believe that the jumbled mess of black was once a pair of wings.*

*After the deed was done, I felt them uncuff me and start to heal me. Just enough so that I wouldn't die.*

*They left and I felt myself being gently lifted into a warm pair of arms. I knew these arms.*

*"I got you now," Spiris spoke from above me. I tore my eyes from the ceiling and locked with his own.*

*"I can't thank you enough."*

My eyes focused back on him as I came back to reality. He seemed to be seeing the same memory that I was. I wanted answers more than anything now, Spiris knew them too but he was unwilling to tell me. His hand came up and ruffled my hair, and then down to my cheek. I leaned against it and gave his palm a small kiss. His eyes widened and I saw a small blush come up his face. I didn't think he could be that innocent, but it was fun to see how I could push him.

"Practice," he said while clearing his throat. "Practice and I am sure the answers will come to you."

What a cryptic little shit. I nodded and sat down with a plop.

"I am done for the day!" I sighed happily and patted for him to join me on the ground. He smiled and joined me. Whatever he was keeping from me I vowed that I would find out sooner rather than later.

# Chapter Twenty-Four

Cruor

Damn all these useless people.

"This plan went as well as it could have," Ash spoke from behind me, reaching out to run his hand across my shoulder. I growled at him and felt him retreat.

"We went there to make her doubt them," Fluvis said, not bothering to get up from his seat. "We knew that she would not remember you right away given the information Spiris gave us. Next time she will come willingly."

"You didn't see the way he touched her," I growled at him and threw the teacup next to me across the room, watching it shatter as it hit the wall.

"This is the best inn in the city, please do not ruin it with your temper tantrums." Fluvis took a sip of his own tea and watched as the now shattered glass was picked up by Ash.

Fluvis was generous to let us stay here while we were hiding from that mad man. It would be safer than my kingdom for now. Baecos would look there first if he ever wanted to come find us. Now that he saw Iniq speaking to Fluvis though, I was sure that he knew the man had switched sides. It is not like he was ever on his to begin with.

"At least we could tell that she was not being… physically harmed," Ash's voice was but a whisper. I knew that he had missed her throughout the years. He had begged me to go see her now that she was back, but I refused to put him through that kind of danger. Baecos had been dabbling in forbidden magic; it made him unstable and there was no telling how much his power had grown.

"I have a plan," I spoke and watched as Fluvis's eyebrows raised. "It would get them away from Iniq and also allow Spiris to steal her from them while right under their noses."

I heard Ash chuckle in the background, and I let myself smile.

# Chapter Twenty-Five

### Iniq

It wasn't until much later that Baecos finally made an appearance. I was in my room trying to make my magic clear when I heard a knock at my door. I quickly withdrew my shimmering magic and went to the door. I felt that it was Baecos before I reached the door, his magic was trying to reach out to me.

I opened the door to a sweaty and panting Baecos. I raised an eyebrow at him.

"What happened to you?" I asked, and he smirked at me, his eyes lighting up briefly at my tone.

He just pushed his way through and laid himself on top of my bed. I slowly went over to the bed and stood in front of it. I watched as he spread out across it trying to regain his breathing, his hair surrounded him like a halo.

"It's okay to join me here," Baecos patted the empty space beside him. I went and sat down. "Some sex is not going to change us," he huffed out when he noticed me being stand-offish. That was not why I was being that way. My mind flashed to the blood-soaked dungeon.

"You left me this morning," I grumbled.

"I had something to do," he explained, and I frowned at that. "Something got on the grounds today, I had to go check it out."

"Something?" I asked, my interest piqued.

"Yes, a lesser creature seemed to find a hole in our barrier and wormed his way in. It was a Wrebil." An image of the creature flashed through my mind from memory. "He won't cause much harm but if he gets you, he will take a good chomp out of you, and he has poison-coated teeth so it's better that we took him out." His eyebrows wiggled at me, and I smiled at his actions. I liked his playful side.

"And the guards?" I asked, and Baecos shook his head.

"He was too fast for them, one of the fastest I've seen."

"I thought you left me without a second thought," I said meekly. "I thought once I gave into you that it would change how you treated me."

I heard Baecos give a small chuckle beside me. Then he was full-blown laughing. I narrowed my eyes at him and scowled.

"You were the one that wanted this type of relationship, Iniq." He sat up and cupped my face with his hand. "Are you going back on that word? I didn't lie when I said you may want to stay by the end of this."

"Never," I murmured to him, and the serious air around us lifted. He laughed at that, but his eyes stayed connected to mine.

"Why don't you show me what you learned today?" His eyes twinkled with excitement and I knew what he was asking for. Instead of putting my hand against him like I did, I concentrated on making the darkest and thickest shadow of magic I could. I watched as it slowly engulfed me and him. He stiffened at the intensity. I tried to see if I could train my eyes to see in the darkness, but I needed more help from Spiris for that.

I felt his emotions and mind immediately. I knew I had to keep this to myself, as well as the ability to change my magic form, so I had to be careful about my own emotions and reactions to what I could hear.

*She is almost ready.*

I almost asked what he meant but I caught myself. His surprise switched to arousal almost instantly.

"I wonder," I spoke, tearing his mind away from his arousal. "Does my magic affect you as much as yours affects me?" I ran my fingers against his arm.

*Vixen.* "Yes," he moaned out. "The stronger the magic, the bigger the reaction."

"I wonder," I whispered, "if I keep this up long enough, can you come?" I felt his arousal spike and he groaned.

I saw an image flash through his mind, it was us from last night, I was bent over his desk and he was pounding into me. I felt my own arousal rise.

I snapped my magic back to me.

"Sorry," I muttered, looking at him finally, his eyes were in slits and he was panting hard. "I can't keep it up that long." He snapped out of whatever thought he was having and quickly threw me to the bed. In an instant, he was leaving hot kisses against my skin.

"That was amazing," he groaned against the skin of my neck. I shuddered as I felt his magic waft across me.

I knew where this was going.

I flopped back onto the bed exhausted after another round with Baecos. He was unstoppable tonight. This was the third time that he had woke me up in the middle of the night. The first time was the roughest. I was awoken by two of his long fingers already pumping in and out of me. The second time he woke me up with his face in between my legs. And this last time he had a mouth on my nipple and was sucking lightly. It seemed as though he was trying to make up for lost time.

"You haven't had enough?" I panted and watched as he left to clean himself in the bathroom.

"Never!" he yelled from the bathroom. I groaned and turned over in the bed. I was bound to fall back asleep in the next few minutes, but I felt the bed dip next to me. I let him climb in and hold me to his chest.

The after was when he showed the most tenderness for me. Baecos was always coarse and rough, I couldn't help but compare him and Cruor to each other. Cruor always took her time; she could be rough but never unintendedly, I remember a time—

I froze at my own thoughts and tried to force them out of my head. It seems every time I am like this with Baecos, Cruor's eyes plague me.

The next time I awoke was interesting.

It was morning for sure, but still quite early. Baecos was kissing my face and neck. His body was flushed against mine and I could tell he was already hard. I groaned as he positioned himself between my legs and thrust gently.

"Which way did you like best?" he asked in a husky voice full of sleep.

"What do you mean?" I muttered against his lips as he met mine again.

"Which." Kiss. "Way did you like best? Last night when I woke you up. Which was your favorite?" I blushed at his question.

"Fingers," I said, surprising myself.

"I knew it." He wasted no time at all. I felt two fingers feel for my clit. I groaned again and I felt my magic show itself. It was wafting across my skin and his. He growled when he felt it.

I bucked when I felt his fingers move towards my entrance.

"I can't believe you are already so wet." *She's never leaving.*

I froze once I heard his voice, but he plunged his finger in me immediately after and I moaned again. He pumped in and out of me fast and hard. Paired with his magic spilling over me and my exhaustion, I was almost ready to come.

While his fingers were pumping in and out of me, he paused for just a second and started to beat into me harder than before. My body writhed against him and I shuddered feeling my orgasm coming along quickly.

I arched against him and screamed out his name as I did. My magic was still attached to his mind, so I heard the last of his thoughts as my magic pulled away from him.

*This will keep her here. She will never think of another as long as I have her like this.*

I was so exhausted that I couldn't keep a hold of anything he said. I immediately relaxed against the bed and stared up at him. His eyes were still hungry.

What was this man made of? I couldn't take anymore. I used to dream about this type of relationship, fuck until you can't anymore. Pure need for each other. But this was something different. While I was always filled with pleasure with what Baecos did, I could not keep up.

I saw him still hard and waiting for me. I groaned against the soreness in between my legs and turned around with my ass up in the air waiting for him to enter me.

"I taught you well," he chuckled darkly. "Wet and begging for your master." I shuddered at the eroticism that hung in the air when he said *master.*

I felt him enter me in one long thrust. I moaned against the covers and gripped the sheets beneath me.

All at once, he started to pound into me from behind. His hands gripped my hips and painfully brought them back to meet him mid thrust. My moans got louder and louder. I felt him hit the end of my cervix and I wriggled against the feeling.

It was beginning to be too much.

"Fuck, Baecos," I moaned. "I can't handle much—" He stopped my words by thrusting even harder against me, each time hitting that sensitive spot. I felt myself clench around him and I threw my head back as my orgasm came over me.

He was not yet done though, even after my orgasm he was thrusting in me with such verbosity that I felt myself wind up again. I grabbed the sheets even tighter.

"Baecos, again, faster," I choked out as I felt myself getting close. Baecos groaned and increased his thrusts into me. His arm snaked around me and rubbed my clit, helping me along.

I threw my head back again and felt myself once again tighten around him. This time I felt him come too. With one last thrust, he spilled everything inside me.

His grip lessened and he fell next to me in bed. I could not turn around, but I laid back down on my stomach and tried to catch my breath. I looked over at Baecos and saw him give me a tired smirk.

"Okay, I swear this time I will let you sleep," he panted out. I left out a breath and let myself fall asleep again. He did not hold me to sleep.

# Chapter Twenty-Six

### Iniq

It seems that every day there was another creature that got onto the property. I didn't fully remember or understand how it worked, but I did know that there was some type of magic barrier that stopped unwanted people and things from getting on the property.

My own thoughts recently drifted more towards Cruor in the past few days. It always came at random times and I could do nothing to swipe them away, and I was not sure I wanted to. I had a feeling that the thoughts I had of Cruor were not actually thoughts, but memories.

These memories never hurt me the way the others did, it was like they were slowly creeping up on me. It was like an ache in my body, a small part of me felt that I was missing something, and when I felt my mind drift to her, that was when I began to remember those small moments. At some point I started willing them to come, actively searching for them to fill the hole that it left me with.

Today I was back with Spiris just like I had been the other days. The first time Spiris didn't ask me to reach out to his mind, but instead, he focused on me shaping and expanding my magic. I found out that if I wanted to, I could make it as hard as steel. Spiris told me that if I practiced even more, I could make it almost impenetrable.

I noticed that as I got used to my magic more and more, I felt my reserves of it grow and my control over it become almost perfect. It only took me a few days to almost perfectly control it, but I knew that my magic was still largely untapped. If the door were able to be summoned by a magic reserve this small, how easy would it be for me to open it once it grew?

It only took me three days to fully make my magic transparent. I didn't tell Spiris but while we were resting one day, I decided to test it. I concentrated on making my magic transparent and pushed it towards Spiris. He was laying down on the ground lazily like he always did, and he thought I was in deep thought.

As my magic coils reached out to him slowly, I tried to focus on making it as undetectable as possible. I felt myself touch his mind, and it took all my might to not smile. I steeled my face and let the thoughts fill me.

*I am so tired. I wonder how much longer it will take to get her ready. She is moving very fast, too fast. I am sure Baecos has caught on and—*

*Oh.*

*Would you look at that.* I froze. How did he know? He let out a chuckle.

*It's all about intention, darling.* My eyebrow raised at the pet name.

*You did very well actually, I barely even noticed, but you wavered when you heard my thoughts. It let me sense that something was there. Usually, a normal person would not notice, even then, but the more skilled people would. I would be careful using this on anyone else until you get it down.*

I nodded and closed my eyes, trying to stretch my invisible magic and cover the room. I was trying to see how far I could get it, but I wanted to be careful in case anyone was nearby.

A memory flashed through Spiris, but I am not sure he

was totally aware of it. It was me, back then, we were in the meadow again and we were laughing together.

*Don't look.* I heard his panic in his thoughts, but they came out anyway.

My head was thrown back and my hair waved around me, not a particularly pretty picture of myself but I could tell he was holding on to this memory. There was a feeling attached to it, a longing of some sort. He longed to fix the scars that marred my face and arms, longed to run away with me, longed to find the courage to speak out. I watched as I climbed over to him—much like I did in the meadow that day—but instead I straddled him and brought his hand up to my face and bit his finger softly. I felt the arousal waving off him.

I pulled back hard. So hard that when my magic slammed back into me, I had to gasp for air. I had a feeling that they were too close to be just friends, but I didn't know I had been so open about it.

I shot a look at him and his cheeks burned red.

"Did we…?" I asked hesitantly.

"Never." He didn't look at me when I said this, but he didn't tell me anything else. "I would never take advantage of you."

A thought hit me, could I project? He said he could feel my intent. Does that also mean I could push something towards him? I closed my eyes and tried to push a reassuring feeling towards him. When my magic hit him again, he stiffened.

*I said st—*

His inner voice cut off when he felt the emotion, I was pushing out towards him.

*You shouldn't be able to do that yet.* Panic again. *Too strong too fast. Baecos will notice.*

I tried not to recoil at his thoughts. So what if Baecos knew? I tried to push curiosity to him, and he swallowed hard and panic shot through him.

*You are so powerful, Iniq. This is just the beginning. Who wouldn't want someone as powerful as you near them? People who don't know your power just assume that you have always had a certain way with people and that is what made you powerful, but in reality, once you are strong enough, you could bend people's will if you really wanted. You should focus on just opening the door and leaving here.*

I froze. Would I really do something like that?

*I can't speak much for before I knew you, but when I did, you never used it on me.*

I nodded. I wondered how long we knew each other for. Spiris seemed to hear my question before I even said anything.

*You were actually only here for less than two years. We built our... friendship during that time.* He couldn't stop the next sentence and it made my blood run cold. *Then not long after that time, you killed yourself here, and they made me clean it as punishment.*

Wait... I killed myself here?

# Chapter Twenty-Seven

Spiris

I saw her mind whirling inside her head. Her eyebrows were pushed together and I saw a bead of sweat fall down her forehead. My mind went to the night that Baecos had brought her here, she looked like she was in a trance and she followed his every move. I knew that Baecos had used his power on her. She was vulnerable and weak when she came here, nothing like the girl she is now, but he used that to his advantage and made her come here willingly.

It only took one time. One time strapped to the table. One time being thoroughly destroyed by Vitos and Baecos. One time helplessly screaming while I stood out in the hallway unsure what to do. I didn't know her well, I had only seen her a few times before this, but after this one time, she did not fight anymore. It took just one time to break her completely, I don't know what she went through before she came to Baecos, but after he was done with her, she had lost all her will to live.

I watched as Iniq's eyes widened, and I felt panic rise in me. I hadn't known she was still connected to my mind.

*I can explain,* I rushed out, but her magic had already

retreated, and she began clutching her head again. It wasn't long before she started screaming. I tried to rush to her, but I was stopped when her magic covered her in a ball of shadows.

Baecos and Vitos came not long after they heard the screaming. Baecos shot daggers at me and tried to rush towards me but Vitos put a hand on Baecos's shoulder.

"I don't think he caused this." Vitos's eyes met mine and for the first time, I saw panic there. I gulped and looked back down at the shadows covering Iniq. I may not make it out of here.

# Chapter Twenty-Eight

## Iniq

It was the kingdom of light that took my magic from me. They were the ones that led me to my death. I saw the memories of me arriving here and the subsequent tortures. They were harvesting my blood—my magic—for themselves. Baecos lied to me, they all did, it was never Cruor that was trying to take my magic from me, it was him. I didn't know what happened after I felt my head split in two, all I knew was that I was surround by blackness and there was a strong memory that was trying to force its way up. I felt tears streaming down my face, but I knew it was time for some answers.

*I was in a dark room and was shackled against the wall. My magic was depleted, and I knew that I was close to death. I was afraid that I would starve to death. I felt a hole where my stomach should have been, they must have forgotten to feed me.*

*The scenes changed and I was in a new room, the ones where they held sacrifices and rituals. I knew this room, but it was the one that I had seen so many times before. The blood speckles were well over a thousand by now. Suddenly, two people appeared in front of me and they seemed to be struggling against each other. It was Cruor and Baecos. I cried and screamed at them to stop. Saying I would do anything to stop them.*

*Baecos, of course, had the upper hand, and he easily withdrew the dagger that he and Vitos had stabbed into me so many times before and held it up to Cruor's neck. Cruor headbutted him and his grip on the dagger loosened, it fell to the ground and clanked its way towards my weak form.*

*This dagger was a special one. Instead of the normal magic daggers that they would use when they wanted it to really hurt, they would use this one. The hilt was intricately carved and had three blood-red rubies adorning it. The blade was as grotesque; instead of the normal straight edge, this one had a wave. There was blood still coated on it dripping to the floor leaving a small pool there. I reached for it; it was heavy in my hand. I held not only my own life in my hands but everyone that came before me. Every magical person who had had their life ripped away from them with the blade. It was the weight of death.*

*I held the blood-coated dagger to my own throat; I would end this suffering now. If not for me then to at least guarantee Cruor's safety. I focused on the pain, anger, and sadness that I had felt throughout my entire life and used it to craft a seal that would hide my powers. This would make sure that they could not trace me, they would not feel my magic, no matter where I was… I hoped.*

*Baecos pushed away Cruor and tried to reach me before I acted.*

*"Let me die!" I screamed at Cruor and watched her try to drag Baecos away from me. She had found me too late; this was the only way out of this. I was too weak to fight and Cruor would never win with me here. I could only hope that after I died, Baecos would lose interest in her, or at least this would allow her to escape.*

*And I sliced my own neck.*

I was thrown violently back into my own body. My throat was burning uncontrollably and I felt as though my head had been run over by a truck.

I was still screaming. I abruptly stopped and tried to digest what I had just witnessed. I ignored everything around me and retreated into myself. I had fanned my magic around me like a shield and I heard people outside it yelling for me.

I killed myself. I could see with sudden clarity now,

there was no real use for the door. It was a meaningless journey and everything I had done up to this point was solely to prepare me to be sacrificed for his own personal gain—*again*. I felt like I was a pig going to slaughter, they came and fattened me up—dressed me up, fed me, had me train my magic—all so they could just strip it away from me again.

I was so desperate and in pain when I took the knife to my throat, I thought the pain alone would kill me. That is what I used to seal myself. It was the emotions that gave life to the little bit of magic I had left. But the biggest emotion that I used for the seal was regret, I regretted every choice I had made up until that point. I shuddered.

I took some calming breathes and tried to think about what I would explain to the others. I would tell the truth, but I needed to reach out to Spiris's mind so I could collaborate his story. I tried to separate an arm of magic and make it as transparent as possible. I waved it around and sensed where Spiris was. He was to my left I quickly entered his mind.

He was quite literally freaking out. I heard my own screams in his mind and shuddered. I tried to ask what he said and convey that to him in one emotion. I hope he understood.

*I told him you were just practicing extending your magic like we have been, and you started complaining of a headache. Then you started screaming.*

I sighed and pulled back from him; from now on I would have to act as though I was not literally sleeping with my murderer. I felt bile rise but I pushed the feeling down. I would escape when he is least expecting it and I would be taking Spiris with me.

I pulled back all magic, including my shield. I was met with bright lights and Baecos's form. Spiris was to my left and Vitos was behind Baecos. He was smiling darkly while

Baecos had a concerned look on his face.

There was a loud gasp from Baecos. "Your throat." My hand shot up to it, did my wound follow me? It was smooth and Baecos started demanding answers.

"What happened?"

"I was practicing my magic when at one point it extended all around me and it was so dark that it brought me back to a memory. I was locked up and had nowhere to go, I was in a room where two people were fighting and one of them tried to kill the other. In order to stop them, I took a dagger... and killed myself." Baecos's expression was hard, and I felt Spiris stiffen as the lies came smoothly off my tongue.

"Did you see their faces? We have been searching for this person for years and have yet to find them. Your memory could be the key to getting rid of him." The most dangerous type of liar is one that has nothing to lose.

"The seal would not allow me to see their faces, but this person was very powerful." I swallowed loudly. Baecos's eyes narrowed slightly and even with my magic pulled back in, I could feel the anger coming off him.

"You need some rest, let me take you upstairs." I let Baecos help me get up, trying not to flinch as I felt his hands on me. I thought they were so beautiful once, now they just felt slimy.

I caught my reflection, and it only fueled the anger inside of me. There was a long, black, intricate dagger tattooed right on my throat—the top of the dagger was pointed directly at my head. It was the same one I killed myself with.

This was my hideous punishment for killing myself. I would be stuck with this constant reminder of my choice for as long as this body lived.

# Chapter Twenty-Nine

Iniq

Baecos insisted on staying with me that night. He assured me that he, Vitos, and Spiris would be here to stop whatever threat came to me.

I was disgusted by the reminder of my own weakness, but I was disgusted by the monster in front of me even more. When he was sleeping, I watched and imagined all the ways that I could kill him. He didn't expect me to strike, I could do it right now. My hand itched as magic pooled in it.

Baecos eyes opened suddenly and I dispersed my magic quickly.

"Trouble sleeping?" His voice didn't sound like he'd just been sleeping.

"A bit." I smiled and turned around giving my back to him. I tried to calm my heartbeat, but I could not. I felt his eyes on my back, I could hear him thinking. He had to be catching on by now. He sighed and wrapped a heavy arm around my form.

"Just relax."

I had a part to play and I wanted to make sure it was as believable as possible. I needed to be the weak person that Baecos believes I am. The next few days I stayed in my room and schemed. I acted as though I was scared and depressed that I had killed myself, but in actuality, it only fueled my anger.

I wanted to run but I didn't know a way out.

I wanted to skip away but I didn't know how.

I wanted to bring Spiris with me, but I had no plan.

I waited until Spiris came to my room. I knew he would come at some point, but I had to wait. Both Vitos and Baecos stopped by my door and I refused to see them, luckily, they listened.

I waited and waited and waited, but Spiris never came. I was worried that they had hurt him. My mind raced and instead of me being tortured, I imagined him in my place. His neck was bent over a stone slab and I watched as they slit his throat. I shuddered. I had never seen them hurt him before, but I knew that they had to. Being Vitos's brother was not enough now.

Looking back, I should have known that they would never allow me to leave. I was stupid to believe they only wanted to open the door. It was so obvious now.

*He's lying!*

*Remember what he is capable of!*

Cruor's message rang through my head. My heart hurt when I remembered my own words to her.

*We made a deal. After that deal, I want nothing else in this world. You included.*

I wondered briefly if Cruor would ever come back for me. I sure had a way of burning every bridge I made.

Each night I spent in this room I was plagued with the same dream. I was in total darkness and a fully completed door stood in front of me. It was teasing me; it was showing me what I could have done. Every time it showed up though, it was filled with its own magical signature, and I swore that I could feel the emotions radiating off it. It made it hard to sleep, I woke up many times throughout the night.

On day four, I left my room for breakfast. I had

stopped eating and Spiris had not come to my bedroom even once. I was feeling really weak by that time and a weak me would not allow me to run. I made my way through the hallways and felt my stomach grumble. I couldn't really complain, this was again another one of my choices that I made.

That day I decided that the bastards needed to face what they did to me. I would not hide it, hiding it makes it only seem like they have won. I am playing a part, but I will refuse to bow. I put my hair up high showing the tattoo that was so kindly given to me by the High Kings.

God-chosen my ass.

When I finally reached the dining room, I tried to sense who was there, and to my surprise, they all were. I took a deep breath and entered the room. When I did, I saw all three of their heads snap up. I chose to sit next to Spiris as Vitos was in the one besides Baecos, and I would be dammed if I openly sought out Vitos's company.

Baecos had his normal smirk on his face when he saw I joined, but I also sensed a hint of relief. Spiris stiffened.

"Wow, look who is still alive," Vitos sneered. Ah, there he was.

"Was everything okay on the grounds this morning?" I asked Baecos, ignoring Vitos. I had to openly stop myself from sneering at the pair of them.

From the look in Baecos's eyes, I could see that he thought his mind games were working. He thought that I had come out still believing. I saw no hint of aggression or suspicion cross his face. I hated that face.

"Surprisingly today, yes," Baecos replied and continued eating. There was a plate put in front of me and I also dug in.

"How are you feeling?" Spiris spoke up beside me. Baecos shot him a look but I ignored it.

"I feel much better. I am sorry about the way I've acted

the last few days. I appreciate all you guys have been trying to do for me." I'd never once uttered words of appreciation while I was here. Just a sprinkle of deceit, reel them in, make them underestimate you.

"So, now that you remember... how did it feel to kill yourself?" It was Vitos, of course. "It's a coward's way out if you ask me." Baecos let out a loud growl towards him.

"Don't you dar—" it was Spiris who spoke this time, but I cut everyone off by waving my hands at them.

I tried to keep my face as calm as possible when I spoke, but it took everything I had to not jump over this table and ram my fork through his eye. "It was the scariest thing I have ever gone through. The pain, sorrow, and regret were raging through me, and if didn't kill myself, surely those emotions, at that strength, would have." I took a sip and finished. "I was so scared of what I had to face. If I didn't know that I would be reincarnated, I would have probably been too fearful to go through with it."

There was an eerie silence that spread across the table at my words. Even the maids had stopped.

"You're a lucky one," Vitos replied. "If Spiris or I killed ourselves, there is no way we would be able to come back. Let's hope neither of us makes such a stupid move." His eyes narrowed at Spiris.

Baecos sighed. "Who knows?" he chuckled lightly. "Maybe the gods will favor both of you one day and they will make an exception."

"Like they would ever favor a sadistic litt—" Spiris kicked my leg to silence me.

"I supposed nothing is impossible," Baecos said, amused.

"Just highly unlikely." It was Spiris that said that.

They waited for me to make the decision on what to do after breakfast. They didn't speak, only stared and waited for me to decide. Training with Spiris was the obvious choice, Baecos reluctantly agreed. I mumbled something about wanting to be stronger to protect myself.

Instead of the home dojo, because there was nothing roaming around the grounds today, we went back to our meadow. I tried not to jump into the conversation right away, I was afraid people were watching us.

I stole a look at him and when he noticed, he rubbed his forehead like he had a headache; he left his hand there for a bit too long. For anyone else, I am not sure this would have looked out of the ordinary, but for me, I knew what he was asking.

I closed my eyes pretending to be dosing off, but I made my transparent magic reach out and caress his mind.

*You are getting much better at that. I didn't feel it this time.*

I smiled at the compliment.

*I would still refrain from using this on Baecos just yet. Which I know is your plan—don't lie.*

He must have felt my intent turn to denial.

*With this power, you should be able to talk back to me at some point. You didn't do it often last time, but I knew you could when the time was needed.*

I knew what my next task was.

*If you can do that, I will answer whatever question you may have.*

My heart skipped a beat. I focused on trying to push words out, but they were slowly, and barely, strung together.

*...hh-urtt?*

*Holy shit,* his voice replied, and I let out a chuckle.

*Y-ouu hu-rtt?* Pushing this message made me break out in a sweat.

*You need to work on this more, I can feel your magic when you try to push a message. It spikes externally and I can feel your intent. You need to learn how to do this without risking your life.*

*Answer.* This message stuff was hard, but I actively tried to respond to everything he said. I felt him swell with pride. I also beamed at his emotions; he was so supportive.

*No, they did not hurt me. I am sorry I could not visit. It would have been too suspicious.* I was sent a picture of him pacing in his room late at night debating whether or not to come see me.

*'S oo-kay. Need to leave. Soon.* This sentence came easier than the rest, but I still had a sheen of sweat covering me.

*How much do you know?* I focused on pushing my memories to him, and I felt his disgust rise and he was filled with regret.

*Enough. How?*

I don't know how much longer I could stay connected to him. We were losing precious time.

*Trust me. We wait. I have got this. I have planned from the start.*

My heart swelled and I felt my tears behind my closed eyes.

*Together?*

*Never imagined it different.*

I sighed loudly to signal that I pulled out of his mind. My magic felt like it was at its edge and I wanted to preserve it until we could run. I would trust Spiris on this. I went through every interaction I had with Spiris up until this point; he was always looking out for me even if I didn't realize it. He deserved nothing less than my faith.

# Chapter Thirty

## Iniq

I had tried to go back into Spiris's mind but he insisted that I rest and just try to enjoy the fresh air. He said that this meadow was the only fresh air I was allowed back then, and I rarely even got out there. I shuddered at the thought.

Spiris had a… unique way to keep me out of his mind. Each time I did, I was met with either screaming or something widely inappropriate. When he could not keep up the constant screaming, he started to remember the times he had spent with various women. The first time I saw him taking a woman from behind in his mind, I pulled back so fast the magic felt like it hit me head-on and I fell on the ground. That made Spiris laugh pretty hard. At least it answered my question about how innocent Spiris was. I craved a comforting physical touch but every time I thought about it, I remembered the memory I saw of me straddling him and backed away.

Nonetheless, I loved seeing Spiris enjoy himself. When I first met him, he looked so sad and gloomy, but now watching him throw his head back in laugher made me also feel very happy inside. His happiness gave me hope that I could achieve some too.

"Do you have a mate?" I asked him after seeing yet

another girl in his mind.

"Not that I know of," he huffed out. "This body was not born with an indication that I had one. I am surprised you know about this."

"I have a few tricks up my sleeve," I said and winked at him. "That is what my feather means doesn't it? My mate has the same?" He nodded at this but did not comment any further.

I knew who my mate was, but I refused to even think of them. My hand twitched to touch the hidden tattoo on my shoulder, but I kept it in my lap.

"I hope I can find mine one day," I made my voice wishful and girly. Spiris raised his eyebrow, but he felt it.

The air intensified around us and suddenly, with a flash of light, Baecos stood next to us. I felt proud that I had finally bested Spiris, but it was short-lived; I was filled with anger as soon as I saw Baecos's face.

"Something is on the ground—we have to go." Baecos's eyes looked wild. My heart stopped, is this what we were waiting for? I felt a strong magic force start running towards us. In an instant, Spiris and I were on our feet looking around us.

It was too late. It was here already. I saw Baecos and Spiris form weapons of light out of their powers. I followed Spiris's lead and called forth a bow and arrow.

I saw the creature but just for an instant. It was huge. It was humanoid that had grey skin and long fingers that looked like claws. Its eyes were solid white, and its teeth were jagged. This creature had its own magic signature, and I could tell that it used a dark type of magic; it was sticky and felt vile as it caressed our skin. I hesitated for a second, Baecos's eyes were trained on it. We could take him out right now and he would be none the wiser.

I looked at Baecos from the corner of my eye and wet my dry lips. Now, I would do it. He started to stalk towards the edge of the forest, and I pointed the arrow straight to his back. I took in a steady breath and started to pour my magic into the arrow. If it does not kill him, it would at least injure him greatly. I imagined it lodging itself so deep in his head that it came out the other side. I felt the sides of my lips curl and my heart race, just the image sent a thrill through me. I remembered the way he smiled at me and touched me... was he remembering how I screamed when the knife cut my skin? Did he find some sick pleasure in controlling me the way he did?

Who was I kidding? Of course he did.

Spiris's hand clamped down on my shoulder and I stifled my scream.

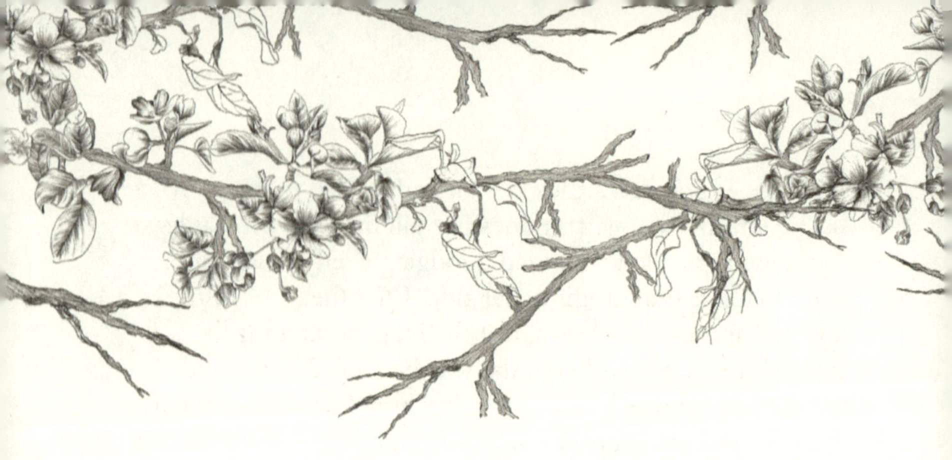

# Chapter Thirty-One

Spiris

That damn smile was back. It was plastered on her face as she watched Baecos stalk towards the edge of the forest. I clamped my hand down on her shoulder.

"Not yet," I whispered. "Trust me." She shivered then nodded, the feeling of her body reacting to me should have made me happy, but this was not the time for such pleasures.

"It felt the magic, it's running," Baecos spoke up and turned back to us. His eyes focused on my hand. His eyes met mine briefly—he was testing me.

"What the hell was that?" Iniq asked as if she was startled, forever playing a part. She must not have realized that her smile was still proudly worn on her face.

"A Giant Wendigo, they are some of the most dangerous creatures out there. They roam dead forests and eat whoever goes in them. I heard that some have gotten to the mortal realm," I explained to her, removing my hand slowly, but only to rub it down her bare shoulder and arm. When we were together last time, I would steal every chance I could to feel her skin, but I never wanted to force her into more when she was so unstable. I watched as the muscles in

Baecos jaw clenched. Iniq tried to look up at me but I kept my eyes square on Baecos and smirked. I knew what he saw. My lips were close to Iniq's ear still and he saw how she reacted to my hand that trailed down her arm. He hated it back then and he hated it now.

"Bring her back home," Baecos ordered. I nodded and held her arm. "I'll finish it off." And Baecos ran off after it.

We did not linger, as soon as Baecos took off, I skipped us to the mansion.

We went straight into my room without talking.

"You shouldn't have goaded him like that," her voice rang out as we entered her room. I squeezed her hand slightly refusing to let go.

"It was for you, not him," I whispered. She did not need to know what he planned for me. "I don't care much for what he chooses to do with me."

"I care," she hissed and grabbed my hand, bringing it close to her heart. My own heart thudded painfully in my chest. I could steal my chance now if I really wanted to. I felt her magic enter my mind.

*Were you lonely when I was gone?* Her question caused me to smile sadly.

*You may have been the best friend that I ever had. I was a coward before. I promise to not let you down this time, or ever again. There is not a day that goes by without you crossing my mind.*

I spoke only the truth. Since she had died, I could not stop thinking about how I had failed her.

*Thank you for everything you have done. I am so glad I met you.*

"Thank you, I look forward to our practice tomorrow." I gave her a smile and she returned it.

"I will see you tomorrow, Iniq." The magic was gone now; my thoughts could roam wherever they wanted. I let my eyes look over her small heart-shaped face and pouty lips. I knew that if I were any less of a coward, I would kiss her right now. Instead, I leaned down and gave her forehead a small kiss. I felt her hand clench at my shirt, pulling me closer to her. I sighed and stepped away, and without giving her another glance, I skipped to my room.

I did not have to wait as long as I thought. Baecos was already there waiting for me.

# Chapter Thirty-Two

### Iniq

I let out a sigh I was holding as he left. I had lied to Spiris. Because of his goading, I know that Baecos would come to me tonight, to prove himself. He wants me to think that he is the only one that I should feel for. I will let him believe it and when he is least expecting it, I will enter his mind.

I was waiting in my bed until later that night. I never heard him enter his room, but I was sure that he was there due to his magic bleeding through the door.

Once I felt him enter his room, I made sure to give him a good twenty minutes just in case he decided to come into mine. He did not. I sighed and turned around in my bed. It was a sigh of relief. I debated going to go see him to keep up the image, but I decided against it and I felt myself slowly fall asleep.

Sometime late in the middle of the night, I felt my bed dip. My eyes shot open and I froze.

"It's me," Baecos's gruff voice came from behind me. I swallowed loudly. I knew he would come.

"I knew you'd come." I heard him chuckle behind me and he slowly wrapped his arms around my waist.

"I am glad you know me so well." His lips brushed my

ear and I had to swallow the bile that rose. "I wanted to give you your space." His hand moved slowly across my stomach. "It must have been hard for you."

"Maybe harder for you. I can't imagine what it's like to lose someone so close to you." I knew I was playing a dangerous game.

"Did you remember how close we were?" His hand drifted down to my thighs. I wanted nothing more than to stab that hand.

"Unfortunately, I do not." I could not keep the venom from my voice as I spoke.

He has yet to use his magic and it made me very uncomfortable. The magic was an aid to his manipulation. Without it, I was too aware of how awful he was. He started kissing my neck and spreading my legs slowly.

Bear it. I told myself. I chanted it—no—I screamed it repeatedly.

I used this chance to try my best to discreetly enter his mind.

I felt a spike of apprehension from him. I tried not to panic; focused on my intent. Discrete and undetectable.

"I could show you of course," he whispered, and his hands glided over my underwear. "It has been a while. You must be aching."

*You can lie but your body cannot.*

I felt his magic spike in his hand, and I had to whimper at it. Shame and disgust filled me; my eyes pricked with tears. His mind was filled with thoughts of me. How my hair felt, how I smelt, how I was acting. He was testing me.

"Tell me how much you ached." His voice was sharp again. Panic rang through me. He must know that I know.

*I wonder if Spiris has made his move on you yet?* His mind replayed the image of Spiris's hand trailing down my arm. In his mind, Spiris was smirking at him. In an instant, an image of Spiris being tied to a pole and whipped by Vitos flashed through his mind. I clamped down on whatever I was feeling. Oh my god. That was not just a thought, that was a real memory. He had hurt Spiris before. My heart started pounding.

"I managed," I answered. "Been preoccupied with training." I felt him nod against me.

*Good, but maybe it's too fast. We do not want a repeat.*

I turned around so that I faced him instead and brought my hand up to his face, slowly trailing my fingers across his skin.

"What are you thinking?" I made my voice barely above a whisper. He smirked and brought me closer to him, his lips brushing mine.

I tried not to shudder as an image of a body bloodied and mutilated entered my mind. This body was not my own. He had killed others, and by the spike in arousal and excitement, I could tell that he enjoyed it.

"You must have an idea."

I leaned in and brushed my lips against his. He pulled me closer and deepened the kiss.

*She is a really bad actor.*

I couldn't help myself, I stiffened against him. He chuckled against my lips and slipped his hand under my shirt to cup my breast. I had no bra on.

*Do you like that?*

I moaned against him and he pinched my nipple. I forced myself to act normal and to try and not let his comment scare me.

I pulled away slightly and he met me with a smirk.

"Second thoughts?" *Maybe I didn't give her enough magic.* I shivered at his voice in my head.

"What will you do after the door opens? Do you even know how to reach them when you are in their realm?" I felt his grip tighten on my waist. I felt his annoyance grow sharply.

*Definitely needs more magic.* I felt his magic hit me at

lightning speed and my head became dizzy.

"It should not matter to you. Will you not just leave as soon as you complete it?" he growled as he kissed down my neck and bit it hard. I felt my concentration waver and I had to really focus on keeping the connection strong. I was already sweating profusely but he hadn't seemed to have noticed.

I saw images of myself fill my head, but they were not ordinary images, they were during the ritual. I was tied and bloody, sometimes even begging for him to stop. I felt the bile rise in my throat.

*Ohhh…*

His thoughts were cut off with his own laugh. I knew better, his emotions turned from arousal to blinding fury.

*Spiris is going to pay for that mind trick he taught her.*

I felt a cold chill run up my spine. He knows. He has known. I blew our cover. My magic snapped back to me.

I met his eyes slowly and saw that a sinister smirk was plastered on his face.

# Chapter Thirty-Three

Iniq

I stiffened and refused to speak. He watched me carefully and lifted his hand to my face. I flinched.

"You are a very bad liar," he growled and stroked my hair. I knew at any moment those soft strokes could turn with the snap of a finger. "How long did you think you could keep your power from me?"

I struggled to find an excuse.

"It happened when I remembered that I killed myself. I am sorry for invading your privacy but Spiris had nothing to do with this." I saw his eyes tighten.

"I know that is an obvious lie, I would be a fool to believe it." He spit his words out at me. I had never seen him so angry before. It scared me and I didn't know how to react. "I have known since you first started training with him in the dojo. You don't think I had ears everywhere? It has just taken you this long to use it against me."

"This has nothing to do with him, leave him out of it." My voice cracked. So Baecos had known the entire time.

"Are you fighting for another man while in bed with me? Did he show you a better time than I have?" Did he really not care that his secret is out? I reached out again.

It was jealously, he felt extremely jealous.

*She was MINE. And he had the nerve to teach her this without my permission?! Spiris will be the ruin of me.*

Thoughts filled his head of images; me and Spiris laughing together, laying in the meadow, and sitting next to each other at breakfast. Every single glance Spiris made towards me he caught, every time his hand lingered on my back, and even the time in the meadow where he saw me tease Spiris with my hand cupping his face. I felt relief fill me as I realized he had not known how much I had seen.

"I am sorry," I blurted. "There is nothing going on with me and Spiris. I just really didn't fully understand what was happening and was scared to tell you. I promise it won't happen again."

*You are looking inside again.* He chuckled outwardly once he realized I was in his mind again.

*Are you trying to make me jealous on purpose?*

"No," I gasped at him. "Why would I want to do that?"

Before I could hear his thoughts again, his mind displayed pictures of us in very intimate positions. The first one to pop up was from the first night. I flushed at the picture and he rolled over to my side with a huff.

"It's not nice to pry," he said and gave me a pointed look. I reluctantly pulled back my magic.

The rest of the night I refused to look back in his mind. I got lucky to only get caught with having this power and not knowing what he did to my past self.

I did not see Spiris the next day.

When I woke up, I knew what I had to do. I dressed and acted as I normally did. I tried to portray as much normalcy as I could. I did not want Baecos catching on any more than he had already.

When I reached the dining room, my heart dropped. I walked in as I normally would but Spiris was not at the table. Baecos and Vitos were sitting there waiting for me as usual. I froze in my tracks and my heart began beating in my chest. He must have gotten to him.

Both Baecos and Vitos looked up at me. For the first time, Baecos did not smirk when I entered the hall. His face remained void of any emotion. If anything, it looked as though he was bored. Vitos on the other hand, his expression chilled me to my core. It was the most sinister smile I had ever seen on a human being.

"Why are you waiting there?" Vitos's snide voice cut through the room. His hand slowly reached out and pointed at Spiris's empty seat. "Sit down and eat."

My instincts were telling me to run. Runaway as fast as I could. Find Spiris in whatever way I could and run away forever. My hair stood up on the back of my neck. I understood immediately that if I tried to run, they would catch me. I had to buckle down and deal with this as best I could.

I jerkily walked over to the empty chair and sat. I tried not to pay attention to the bile rising in me when I saw the food in front of me.

"Eat," Baecos ordered. I froze at his voice and my eyes snapped over to him.

"We are going to be spending the day together," Baecos announced as he finished his meal. I nodded and refused to look at him. I knew it was stupid, but I tried to reach out with my magic. I am not sure if it was on purpose but there were images of Spiris that were showing there.

I dropped my utensil as soon as I saw what was going on. It was hard to make out but from Baecos's position, I saw Vitos's back; he was holding what looked to be a whip and something was laying on the ground. No, it wasn't something, it was someone… Spiris. His back was open and bleeding. The cuts seemed to be covering his entire back. There was not a spot that did not have blood on it.

Spiris tried to get up but Vitos stomped on his back. When he put more pressure on his back, I heard Spiris's earth-shattering scream. I left his mind as quickly as I could.

No. No. No. No. How could he do this to him? This was all my fault. Spiris told me to be careful, I was such an idiot.

Tears freely fell from my face and hit the plate in front of me, the guilt was overwhelming.

"Iniq, what's wrong? Did you see yourself committing suicide again?" My blood started to boil I shot a look at Vitos. I decided to enter his mind as well, maybe he could tell me where Spiris was.

Instead, I saw myself, but it was a different version of me. Not Iniq and not Vien, it looked like another mortal, but it was eerily similar to what I looked like when I was a mortal. The only difference was that I had brown eyes.

What am I seeing?

*The other me was crying and Vitos stood in front of her in clothes from the mortal world, the ones Baecos wore at night sometimes.*

*"How did you find me?!" she screamed. She knew him. She recognized him.*

*Vitos gave a loud laugh.*

*"You are so unbelievably stupid, Iniq. Your seal was weakened too much, one step in the human world and I found you almost immediately." The other me had another dagger in her hand, different from last time, but I had a feeling I knew what was going to happen. In an instant, the other me brought up her shield as black as night. Vitos tried to attack it but he failed. There seemed to be an explosion from the shield.*

*Vitos was thrown back about a hundred yards and when he looked back, the other me was bleeding out on the ground. As he looked over the body, he could tell that I'd cut so deep that I bled out in mere seconds—he couldn't heal me. Vitos let out a laugh and kicked my dead body.*

Before I pulled out of his mind, I heard Vitos's voice. It was as cold as ice and I felt it stab me when he spoke his next words.

*Did you really think that this was the first time that you were reincarnated?*

I snapped my magic back and I heard him chuckle.

"No matter the life, you were always the coward," Vitos spat.

My gaze snapped towards Baecos and he glared daggers at Vitos.

"Do you want to end up like your brother?" he snapped at him. Vitos looked hurt but shrugged it off.

"You manipulative monsters!" I yelled at him and stood from my seat. The chair fell backward, and I threw everything in front of me off the table. I felt my magic rise in me. I was so angry and hurt that I could not stop it from whipping out around me. Everything breakable in range shattered. I heard some of the maids scream in terror. "I told you he had nothing to do with this," I glared at Vitos. "And you hurt your *own* brother for something I did!" Vitos also stood up letting his own magic out.

"If you both do not stop it this instant, I will not go easy on either of you."

"I don't give a fuck what you do!" I yelled at them and whipped my magic out at them both. I made sure it was as hard as diamonds and as sharp as a sword. Before they could hit their targets, Baecos's magic exploded from him with a blinding light and stopped my attack dead in its tracks.

Baecos got up slowly with a chuckle and started pushing his magic out further, making mine shrink. With each step, his magic overcame mine and came closer and closer to my body. It felt like I was hit with a thousand tiny blades. I let out a scream and fell to my knees. The pain did not stop right away; I gritted my teeth and tried to hold in my screams—he was keeping the pain there to punish me. Baecos's shoes came into view and his hand gripped my chin, forcing me to look at him. My narrowed eyes met his. I could tell he was enjoying every second of this.

"You will behave if you do not want anything else to happen to Spiris. He is in recovery for what he has done, we did not kill him." His face got so close to mine that I felt his breath fan across my face. "I can easily change that."

I nodded but he only gripped my chin harder.

"Tell me you understand."

"I understand," I spat. As soon as I did, his magic disappeared and I was left panting.

"I do not enjoy hurting you, Iniq," he said while helping me to my feet. "But you have to understand that disobeying me has its consequences. Lying like last night included."

"What do you even want from me?" I snapped. He laughed and pulled my hair painfully. I was forced to look at him.

"I have always just wanted to own every single part of you." His lips brushed mine softly and I felt disgust rise in me. "Ever since I first laid eyes on you, I needed you. And who better to power my kingdom than someone favored by the gods themselves? We only deserve such special treatment."

In an instant, he had skipped us back to my room. I felt panic rise in me. Fear must have been evident on my face because he chuckled.

"Don't worry Iniq, I like my partners consensual... for the most part." I felt bile rise in my throat. "Then again, everyone says yes once they have a bit of magic pumping through their veins."

He started to walk away from me. "I was going to spend the day with you if you behaved, but it looks like you will have to stay here until you know how to." And with that, he threw me away roughly and he was gone.

I let a breath out and fell to the ground.

# Chapter Thirty-Four

### Cruor

When Spiris had yet to contact me, I knew something was wrong. He'd missed our meeting time. This was supposed to be the last meeting before the next phase. I had Ash keep a lookout for me as I ran through Baecos's compound trying to follow Spiris's weakening magical signature while concealing my own. It was easy to find the others. Iniq, Baecos, and Vitos were all on one side of the mansion while Spiris was on the far end, no doubt so that Iniq cannot reach him.

It was easier than I thought to sneak into the room he was in. His head snapped up from his laying position as soon as he felt me enter, but he cursed slightly and laid back down. He was forced to lay on his stomach and his back was wrapped with bloody bindings.

"What the fuck happened to you?"

"We fucked up," he groaned. "I got a little handsy with his goods and Iniq used his powers to read his mind."

I groaned and rolled my eyes. "Can't you two just lay low for a little while?" I really thought he was dead but looking at him now… this seemed worse.

"You have to take her, now," Spiris's voice wavered as

he spoke. "She remembers how she died. She will go to you willingly now, but I am afraid for what Baecos has planned for her."

I took in a sharp breath. If she remembered how she died, does that mean she remembered us? I tried not to get my hopes up but the thought of welcoming her back into the castle was more than I ever thought would be possible. I felt magic spike from the other side of the house, it was Baecos. My stomach dropped when I felt the intent, I prayed to the High Kings that they would take pity on Iniq.

"I did not bring reinforcements," I whispered and tried to clamp down on my magic; it was trying to rage to the surface. "I have to go back. Prepare her and yourself, two weeks from tomorrow we will leave. If there is an immediate danger, Ash will be waiting near the opening. He can get a message to me and we can be here within twenty-four hours if needed."

"She could die in that time—you need to leave with her now," Spiris hissed.

"That's why we have you. You pray to the High Kings that he lets you out soon," I hissed at him. I went to leave but I felt a small amount of guilt rise in me. "I am sorry, get well. I was just… jealous when you mentioned getting close to Iniq."

Spiris chuckled but stopped with a hiss when he felt his back strain against the act.

"I doubt it's me she sees in her dreams at night, but I would be damned if I didn't at least try." His playful attitude brought a smile to my face.

"See you on the outside, Spiris. Stay safe." I left without another word. I had stayed too long already.

Two more weeks.

# Chapter Thirty-Five

### Iniq

He really locked me in here. Picking up my chair, I threw it as hard as I could against the locked window. It just bounced off, not without even leaving a small scratch on it. I screamed in frustration and began throwing stuff off my vanity and around the room.

I commanded my magic into a bow and arrow and aimed at the window. Still nothing. The door sadly had the same result. I kicked it and punched it as much as possible, but I only ended up hurting myself.

Images of Spiris's bleeding body and painful screams filled my mind. I was so stupid. He clearly warned me to just keep to myself and trust him, but I had to let my impulses win. Did I really think I could come to no harm here? I growled in frustration.

I felt a nudge on my cheek, and I looked up to see the faerie that I saved not so long ago looking at me with concerned eyes. I almost forgot about her. I gave her a small smile through my tears and brushed my finger across her forehead. She smiled back at me with her sharp teeth and promptly bit the tip of my finger.

I cursed and pushed her away. There were small

punctures made in my skin and they started to well up with blood. I put my finger in my mouth to suck the blood away and tried to shoot her a dirty look, but she was gone in an instant.

"Useless faerie…"

***

It was dark before I woke up again. I did not know when I had fallen asleep, but it had to have been after I tried to light my room on fire. My magic must have run out. It was not long before I realized that I was not in my room.

"Look who finally woke up, it seemed you used a good portion of your magic," Baecos's voice said from behind me. I was in his bed and lying on his chest as I normally would have. His hand stroked my hair. "I wonder what you were doing to have spent all that magic?" I froze against him and he clicked his tongue disapprovingly. I tried to push him away, but he held onto me tightly.

"Did you forget that I had asked you to behave?" His grip on me became tight and painful, tears pricked my eyes and threatened to spill over. "If you are good, I will not hurt you or Spiris. We can live as we once were, together and happy."

His hands rubbed circles in my back.

"I am sure you want to know about your past selves. Think of it as my gift to you," he started, I refused to move. "You see, you have been reincarnated over six times since you first died." It was like a bucket of ice-cold water was thrown at me. "I found you *every. single. time.*" His voice was razor-sharp and filled with an unspoken threat. He would find me again if he had to. "For some reason this time, you came right to us."

I would not let him win this time, nor would I leave Spiris alone.

Tears were flowing down my face freely. He patted my

back in fake concern.

"Your life was a wreck there—it was easy for you to get swept away in the wonder of this world." His hands squeezed my sides again.

Silence.

"Still nothing? I hope you are not thinking of killing yourself?" His hand was in my hair now. "While you may think at times you are alone, I can promise you that you are not."
"If you are good," he continued and brought my face up to his, his eyes had a glint in them, "I will give you another gift. I swear I am not as bad as you make me out to be, Iniq." He brought his lips to mine and gave me a small peck. "I can be nice, but it's a two-way street, remember that." His tongue brushed across my lips, but I stayed still. He sighed and let go of my face.

"From now on, you will live in my room." I felt panic run through me. "If you are good, like I said, you can get your *privileges* back."

I did not respond; I used my anger to fuel my scheming.

***

Sleep did not come easily for me that night.

It was almost dawn when I finally was able to get a few hours of sleep. As soon as I felt the bed next to me move, my eyes shot open. Baecos was getting up out of bed. I watched him stand up and stretch as he shot me a sleepy smile. He acted as if he had the most restful sleep of his life.

"You never wake up at the same time as me." His hair was down but he was in the middle of tying it up as he spoke. "Join me in the shower."

I stiffened, there was no question in his voice. I slowly got up out of bed and followed him into the bathroom. He started the shower for us and looked me in the eyes as he took his pants off. I did not hesitate. I took off my clothes and entered the shower, I felt his eyes following me as I did. I held my arms against me and waited for him to enter the shower, but he just continued to stare at me.

There was no glint in his eyes or smirk on his face. Instead, he looked a bit annoyed. He walked over to me and put my arms down.

"It's not anything I haven't seen before—you don't need to hide." He huffed and joined me.

The hot water washed down my form and I felt my muscles relax. I was so exhausted that I felt, even given the current circumstance, that I may just fall asleep in here. Baecos poured shampoo into his hands and started to wash my hair. His hands were gentle and when his fingernails scraped against my scalp, I shivered.

"I can be gentle and caring, Iniq," he whispered and started washing the shampoo out. "If that is what you require of me, I can do it." He applied conditioner to my hair as well, he did not wash it out right away, instead, he moved me out of the way and washed his own hair. I turned my head away from him.

Baecos sighed and pulled me flush against his body. He used this as a chance to wash the conditioner out of my hair. He then washed my body; I tried not to show any reaction when he brushed across the sensitive areas.

"I don't want to hurt you," he reminded me and started kneading my back. I couldn't control myself, I leaned into it. "I just want us to live happily together until your powers are fully back."

I decided now was time to show him I could act as well.

"I know I may not agree with your methods… but I can tell that much." I did not wait for him to wash me, instead, I washed myself and tried to step out of the shower but he pulled me against him. I took everything in me not to freeze at him hardening against me.

"Do not take my actions as forgiveness. You must still *earn* your rights back." He placed his hands under my face and brought them up so I could look him in the eyes. He leaned down to kiss me, and I reluctantly kissed him back. I felt his magic seep into me, and I began to hate myself.

I would obey for now.

***

I looked myself in the mirror and hollow eyes with dark circles under them looked back at me. The dagger on my throat seemed to haunt me. I shuddered and tried not to cry. I took a deep breath and tried to pull all my emotions inside me, leaving nothing left to be felt. My empty stare told it all, but I would be dammed if I let him ruin the rest of our lives.

I joined him in the room and got dressed. I decided to put my hair up again. When I did, Baecos found the extra feather tattoos on my neck and his fingers traced it softly. I said nothing and let him lead me to the dining room.

Spiris was absent again. I didn't comment on this.

Vitos, of course, was sitting there and smiling at us. It was a shit-eating grin if I ever did see one.

"You get to train with me again today." His eyes glinted mischievously.

"Looking forward to it," I replied dryly. My eyes stung from the lack of sleep. Or maybe it was the crying.

I looked down at my plate. I still had a lot of food on it, but I could not bring myself to eat it. I just pushed my plate forward and waited for the others to finish.

"You ate very little," Baecos said, staring at me intently. I nodded at him.

"I am feeling a bit nauseous, I am sure it will pass," I

217

reassured him. He seemed to accept my excuse.

They both finished and we were off to the training fields.

This time I was determined to fight Vitos back. Before this, you couldn't even call this a fight, it was a beat down even when I was at my best.

Vitos stood about twenty feet away from me. His dark eyes were filled with malice and he rested in an attacking pose. He always attacked first. It only took two seconds before he attacked, I threw my arms up to block his incoming attack and made sure to turn my magic into a protective shield. His glowing fist hit my shield right on. I was pushed back a few feet before he came at me with his second punch. Instead of blocking this one, I ducked, allowing my body to follow its instincts, and tried to let go of my mind.

I pushed my magic to my feet and shins making them as hard as rock and sent out my leg to kick his. The impact on his leg was hard, I could have sworn I heard a small crack. Vitos screamed and was thrown off balance, he fell flat on his ass. I tried to move back as far as I could. It took a second for him to get back up, but I could feel his anger building, his magic flared wildly around him.

"What happened, Vitos?" I chuckled at him and stood in a wide stance. I made a bow and arrow out of my magic like I did the other day and pointed it straight at him.

He deserved this. I aimed at his form and let the arrow fly through the air. Vitos gave me the most sadistic smirk I have seen to date; it made my insides freeze and my hair stand on end. In a flash of light, he was gone. The arrow hit the ground he was previously sitting on. I looked around wildly.

Where did he go? Before I could turn around, I felt his magic flare behind me. I was too slow to throw up my open magic and I felt it hit me full force on my back. It sent me flying across the yard and I hit the ground hard. I whipped my face back to see him stalking towards me. There was a sword in his hand. I gasped and tried to look at my back; while I could not see the wound, I could see the blood that was falling from it. I grit my teeth and tried to get back up, tried to ignore the pain that was coursing through me, but I let out a scream nonetheless as I stood.

"That was cute, you need to find new tricks." Vitos laughed across the field, and in an instant, he was in front of me again. I rolled out of the way of his strike. His sword hit the tree where my head had just been. I turned my body towards him and sent an arrow flying for his face. He only smiled again and skipped away.

He would not fool me this time. I felt for his magic. Behind me again, I didn't hesitate. I dove away from him, turned, and sent an arrow flying to him.

It landed in his chest and he howled in pain. He dropped to one knee and gripped the arrow with his free hand, but before he could pull it out, I shot another one—it was close to the heart. His body flung backward and he hit the ground hard.

I followed my instincts and changed from a bow to a long sword. Memories started to come back to me leaving me dizzy. I stood over many bodies, just like Vitos, and swung my sword down at them, killing them without a second thought. There were so many people I have killed throughout my years, I noticed most were during wars, but I never hesitated, I always swung my sword down without a second thought. I felt a smile grace my face just as before; I ran to his body and raised the sword above my head ready to deliver the killing blow. Vitos's eyes widened and he brought up his hand to stop the blow, my guess is he was too weak to skip away.

"STOP!" It was not Baecos that said this. It was Spiris. My eyes shot over to the voice and I saw Spiris walking towards us with Baecos. Spiris looked like he was struggling to walk, his skin was pale, and he had a sheen of sweat on his face.

I was relieved to see him; I shot my invisible magic to him.

*I am okay, please do not do anything that stupid.*

I got rid of my sword and started to walk towards him.

*You did good, I am sorry that I left you alone.*

Tears filled my eyes. *It's all my fault,* I shot back.

I took one more step and my world fell around me, I vaguely felt myself crash to the ground.

***

I woke up sometime later in my own bed. Baecos was absent but my heart stopped when I saw Spiris beside me. My back was aching, but I could tell that Baecos had healed most of the damage. I reached out to Spiris with my mind.

*He didn't heal you.*

I could only guess as much when he sat next to me looking as pale as he did.

*No, he did not, part of my punishment. Did he hurt you at all?*

*No, he didn't.*

*Looks like maybe you can hold your own against Vitos.* He teased me; he may have sounded like himself, but I saw the pain in his eyes.

*I just let my body do what it does naturally, apparently killing is one of those things.*

*No shit,* he snorted.

*I can heal too, right? Let me help you.*

I saw Spiris shake his head, but his voice rang out. *You should not heal me though, you were on his good side today apparently, I would keep it that way if I were you.*

I swallowed my self-hatred and disgust—I knew why.

"Where is Baecos?" I asked aloud. Spiris shot me a look but responded aloud as well.

"There is another Giant Wendigo on the grounds, he is

hunting it. Vitos is resting in his room." I nodded but did not withdraw my connection.

*We will leave here together.* Spiris's head shot up and he stared at me with emotions unknown to me. His fists tightened and his breath came out unsteadily.

*We cannot risk much, please do not do anything rash.*

*Do you not want to leave?* I started to panic.

*I do, believe me, but we have to wait a little while longer. I have to heal.*

I nodded at this, it made sense. We could not have an injured person on the run, it would only slow us down.

*Give me two weeks. Everything should be prepared by then.* I felt myself freeze.

*Have you been planning this?*

*I have waited a hundred years to redeem myself. Give me a little credit.* My eyes stung and pricked with tears. *I have put so much into this. I ask that you trust me on this, it will become clear once it is time.*

Reluctantly agreed to this, I would trust him.

*I trust you,* I said, and his mind flashed to a time many years ago where I said the same thing. It was only a second, but it warmed my heart. I knew in no matter what life I was in, Spiris would be there to protect and guide me.

I reached out and held his shaking hand. He squeezed mine in response and gave me a warm smile.

*Thank you, I promise you that this one will work.*

I nodded and pulled my magic from his mind.

# Chapter Thirty-Six

## Iniq

Spiris left not too long after our conversation. We both knew that he shouldn't be caught dwelling too long. It was a good thing he did, Baecos showed up in my room not twenty minutes after. Baecos's hair was messy and he was out of breath, his clothes were dirty and ripped in some places. I did not speak but only watched as he crossed the room.

Baecos walked towards me and sat down on my bed next to me. He gave me a small kiss on the head and rested his forehead against mine.

"You behaved well." I almost scoffed at him. "Seeing you bring down Vitos like that reminds me of how powerful you once were."

"I just let my body do what it wanted to," I admitted.

He leaned back and looked me in the eyes, no doubt to search for any lies that I may be hiding. He didn't seem to find anything alarming and he let out a sigh.

"It seems there are more and more of these creatures getting onto our lands." He stood up and ran a frustrated hand through his hair.

"Is there anything stronger than a Wendigo?"

"Yes, but I have not seen any Hell Hounds or

Banshees… yet." He shuddered. "If you ever see either of those, you are better off dead. They are intelligent. Not easy to fight." He grabbed my hands.

The rest of the night was simple, I had to go back to Baecos's room, but nothing happened between us. Even next to the monster that Baecos was, I had no problem falling asleep knowing that Spiris was now safe.

***

Baecos was not kidding when he said there were more and more creatures getting on the grounds.

Over the next five days, we had found that three more Wendigos had gotten close to the mansion. I was not worried about the Wendigos, Vitos and Baecos could handle them. And if anything, we could use this as an opportunity to escape.

I was nervous about the plan Spiris had come up with and I was constantly walking on eggshells around Baecos; it was beginning to get exhausting. He would not allow Spiris and I to train together again, though with both Vitos and Baecos defending the grounds, it is not like they would know. But to keep Spiris safe, I listened anyway.

Baecos had once said that he had ears everywhere, so whenever I had to talk to Spiris I would make sure to do it in his mind. We were lounging in one of the many resting areas in the house when I reached out to him.

He was sitting against the window staring out of it, possibly looking for the Wendigo.

*How is your back?*

I saw Spiris smile a bit from where he was sitting. His mind brought up an image of his back. It was painfully scabbing. I shuddered at the sight.

*Sorry, the healing process is nasty looking*, he said sheepishly.

I smiled at him and shook my head.

*I have a question and I am not sure you can answer.*

*I will try, go ahead.*

*How did you come into your position?*

I felt the shock that ran through him when he asked this question. He chuckled softly.

*That's all? I was prepared for something much worse.* I saw his shoulders visibly relax. *Vitos and I lost our parents during a war a long time ago, Baecos's dad took us in. After he died and Baecos took over, we made an oath to stay by his side and help protect him.*

An image of Baecos's dad ran through Spiris's head and I felt a weird sense of anger well up in me, and I did not know why. His hair was short, unlike Baecos's, but besides that, they looked like carbon copies of each other.

*How did his dad die?* I asked this question, but I had a feeling that it may not be a good answer.

*He killed himself,* he said simply and remembered his funeral, but there was more. I could almost taste it, the secret he was unwilling to share. I wanted to know more.

*Why?* I pushed.

And then Spiris started screaming in his mind. I recoiled my magic and held my head in my hands.

Okay, so that was something I guess I could not know yet. I sighed. I knew Spiris—unlike Baecos—had no ill will, so I let it go.

I looked back up at Spiris and he had a smirk and tapped his mind again. I raised an eyebrow but he gave a pleading look. I shrugged and entered his mind again, prepared to pull back just in case.

*I have a question of my own.* My interest was piqued, it was usually the other way around.

*Go on.*

*Has Baecos,* even his mind paused at this, *forced himself on you?*

I stiffened and gave him a small smile.

*He likes them consensual.* I left it at that, but I

remembered the times he had pushed previously.

225

# Chapter Thirty-Seven

## Spiris

*Did you plan this?* I shot back at her through my mind. I felt anger and disgust towards Baecos fill me. I studied her; she had been losing weight at an alarming rate since Baecos had found out.

*Do not worry about what I am doing with him, it is essential that he trusts me again.*

I felt her withdraw from my mind. It was for the best. I was fuming as I imagined his hands on her in this state. I wouldn't put it past him though, he was a monster in more ways than one, but that did not excuse anything.

I let my mind wander slightly. I should have taken my chance in that room. Now I was sure the guards were watching us as we spoke. Maybe the meeting would be worth it. I winced thinking about how bad another lashing could be. I needed to be healthy for the escape. That still didn't stop me from flirting with the thought of going over there and kissing her until she was breathless. I couldn't wait until the day that without warning I would be able to go up to her and feel her lips against mine.

I swallowed loudly and her eyes shifted back to mine. I waited for her to reach out to me again and instead of letting the feeling raging inside me leap out, I settled for a question.

*You are also not taking care of yourself lately. You have been losing weight. Are you even sleeping?*

*I am eating as much as I can, and yes, I have been sleeping better now that I know that you are safe.*

*You need your strength, please try to eat more.* I hinted as much as I could at our plans.

*I understand.* Her voice was clipped, and she returned to her own mind again. It's not that I couldn't tell her. Cruor even asked me to. But seeing how Baecos's power worked, I didn't want her to implicate anyone in the plan in case he did use it on her. It's a horrible thought but a necessary precaution.

I sighed and looked out the window again, hoping to not find a Wendigo but instead, a Hell Hound and Cruor coming early.

# Chapter Thirty-Eight

## Iniq

I knew it was stupid, but I felt it call to me. For days, the door had shown up in my dreams. It was different from before; the presence was bigger and more demanding. It called to me stronger now, just like when I first entered this world, I felt a pull to it. I had gotten close to opening it in my dreams, but I was always awoken just before I succeeded. I felt it grow impatient, angry at the lack of attention it was getting.

Today was different, this was the first time I felt it even when awake. I was lounging with Spiris, but my mind was preoccupied. The door never spoke in words but in feeling. I imagined it was the same feeling that I gave off when I entered people's minds. The sensation got so bad that I had to excuse myself with an excuse of my stomach hurting.

As soon as I got to my room, I dropped to the floor and poured my magic into creating the door. This time I barely had to exert much magic because as soon as I gave it the confirmation that I wanted it, it seemed to appear in front of me. This was not the door that I had seen previously. There was no transparency to it, it was real and as solid as the dagger attached to my thigh. This door was so black that it seemed to absorb the light around it. I slowly stood up and started walking towards it. It seemed to purr at my actions, enticing me to come closer.

I ran my hand over the front of it, I felt the vibrations of magic rumble through it. I heard its voice.

*We have been waiting for you…*

*Come… just a little further…*

My breath hitched. The voice was velvet smooth. It felt thick like honey and surrounded my senses. I pushed lightly on the door and saw that it cracked open, the inside was just as dark as the outside. I felt the dark tendrils from inside reach out to me and caress my body. I imagined myself being wrapped in it and never leaving. I took one step forward—

"She's going to skip!" Baecos's voice broke me out of the trance I was in and I felt a hard body collide with mine, sending me crashing to the ground. I struggled to get back up, the person that crashed into me had their hand on my face and forced it to the ground, their body on top of me stopping movement.

"This is gonna be fun." It was Vitos, of course. From my position, I saw the door slowly disappear and its magical presence as well.

But not without one last parting gift.

*Do not die for this is your last life.*

"I was not. The door called to me," I tried to force out under Vitos's weight. "You're fucking heavy, get off." I heard his laughter above me.

"You must take me as stupid, there is no door, and we felt your magic spike," Baecos called from above. "You know what to do with her."

Vitos gave another laugh and pulled me up with him harshly.

His laughter never stopped. It was getting on my nerves, but I had bigger things to worry about. Like how I was going to get out of this goddamn torture chamber.

They had done a little redecorating since the last time that I was here—there was more blood on the ceiling.

I was struggling against the magic holds that they used to fasten me to the table. I used my own magic to try and break them, but they stayed firm. Vitos was in the corner laughing as he watched me struggle, he was probably waiting for Baecos to come and enjoy this torture. I felt the door's magic creep up on me again and it materialized right next to Vitos. I watched his expression, but he seemed to not notice the huge door in front of him.

Why was it choosing this time to not let the others see it?

*Reach the door…* the voice wafted through the air again. I sighed and laid back down. Surprisingly, the door came with me, it was now stuck to the ceiling.

*Just a hand…*

The door opened and the tendrils made their way towards me again. I shifted my gaze to Vitos and his eyes were trained on me, an evil smirk gracing his lips. At least he'd stopped laughing.

*Just a touch…*

The space around me turned dark from the blackness that was spilling out from the door. When I breathed in, I felt the magic partials follow. It left a sweet taste in my mouth and made my blood feel as though there was electricity in it. I tried to move my arm again, but it was still tied down.

"You will not break these," Baecos's voice came from beyond the darkness, but I could not see him. "We have had years to perfect them and *multiple* subjects to try them on."

"The rituals…" I spoke, but my voice felt foreign to me. Still staring into the darkness, I started to see shapes form.

"Yes," he purred. "You were always too smart." I knew Baecos was touching my arm, and maybe even my face, but I could not feel it. "Right until the end, then you became weak."

The shapes in the darkness started to move and I swore it smiled at me. There was something like a hand reaching out for me. My arm would not move to touch it though. The smile widened and flashed its sharp teeth at me.

*We have been waiting… do not disappoint us Iniq…*

The feeling of a knife burying itself into my thigh was the thing to scare off the door this time. I let out a scream and reality came crashing back down on me. Vitos was the one with the knife in his hand and it was fully buried in my thigh; his face was already sprayed with blood. He laughed as his hands left the hilt, it was my own dagger that he used to stab me.

Looking around I saw that this was not my only wound. All up and down my arms I was bleeding. It was dripping off the stone table and to the hard floor, by now it sounded like there was a pool of blood.

"So, you are finally back huh?" Vitos grabbed my hair and forced me to look into his eyes. "You always had a knack for tuning it out, but I guess the wounds were just too light."

The door saved me from pain. The door took me elsewhere. The door was nowhere to be seen but Baecos was in the corner watching as Vitos continued to carve my skin with the knife.

I could focus on nothing but the searing pain. I had to bite my lips to keep from screaming causing a sweet iron taste to fill my mouth.

"You are worse than demons." I spit the blood in my mouth towards Vitos but it only got on his sleeve.

"If we are demons." His knife delicately traced from my stomach to my neck and sat there poised, ready to be joined with my tattoo. "Then you are nothing but an imposter. They gave you all this power, and here you are hardly able to harness it enough to put up a fight." I felt the tip of his blade break the skin on my neck.

"That should be enough blood," Baecos spoke, stopping Vitos from carving something permanent into my neck. Vitos growled and threw my dagger on the ground, shattering it into pieces. Baecos came over to me, carefully walking around the blood puddles, and started to heal my wounds. Vitos was about to protest but Baecos spoke first. "You are lucky this time, next time I will not heal you and your body will be marred as punishment." I refrained from spitting in his face.

"He always had a soft spot for your looks," Vitos muttered. "Don't feel special."

Ah yes, I felt so special right about now. As he healed the wounds, I realized that the wound was far from gone. Even though my leg was fully healed, I felt ghost pains all over it and my muscles kept spasming. Not to mention I felt my magic was practically drained, so much so that his healing made me swoon.

Baecos tried to speak to me as we made our way back to the rooms, but I was too far gone to even try to understand what he was saying. I was beyond relieved to see that he placed me in my own bed. Not like I could escape now. He left a wet kiss on my throat and left; it wasn't long until I slept. This time the door did not visit me, someone else did.

# Chapter Thirty-Nine



True to Cruor's word, Ash was waiting for me in his hound form outside the hole in the barrier. He stood up as soon as he saw me run to him.

"We need her now. It needs to be faster than twenty-four hours, they are draining her as we speak." My voice was just short of a yell. Ash's eyes widened, and in an instant, he was gone.

Wasting no time, I ran back to the house and skipped into Flayke's room. She was in the middle of undressing and yelped when she saw me. I grabbed her shoulders harshly.

"It's time. As soon as Iniq has had a few hours of rest, we need to take her."

"What happened? Is she okay?" Her eyes were wide and they started to fill with tears.

"We don't have time for that," I growled at her. "I do not know the state that she will be in when they are done with her, but we can only afford a few hours in between. Baecos should be high off the energy he received from her. Stay away from him."

She nodded and went to her closet to prepare the clothes for her and Iniq's departure. I was worried about trusting her at first, but I could not have done this preparation without her. This whole time she had been feeding us Baecos habits, wherever he was she knew about it. If I had not seen her mourn over Iniq with my own two eyes, I would have had to do this alone.

Going back to my room, I found a small pack to use for the road. It was not long until I felt Baecos's magic enter the mansion again, it was stronger this time and I could feel Iniq's magic intertwined with his. I felt my hands start to shake as I changed my clothing. My back was far from healed and Baecos was not someone who could be fought right now. I had to warn Ash before we moved, they needed to know that if worse came to worst...

Two hours had passed since they came back, I felt Baecos's magic flare again and move in the mansion. This was the time that he would be most distracted. I felt Vitos's magic flare as well. I swallowed my disgust.

My brother was at least useful for something.

I looked outside at the forest, it was hard not to miss the two large dogs that hid out there, Ash being one of them. I nodded to him and set off to Flayke's room.

It was time.

# Chapter Forty

## Iniq

It was Flayke who came knocking. She was speaking in hushed tones and trying to get my attention. With a start, I realized she was in my room. I woke up with a jolt and saw her worried expression.

"Flayke, are you okay? What's wrong?"

"Get ready miss and hurry. It's time," she whispered and helped me to my closet. The pain was still there and my movement sluggish, but my mind came to me quickly. It was happening now, and Flayke was helping us.

I accepted the clothes she handed me: leather pants and a long-sleeve tunic. I met her by my door, and she handed me a cloak. I put it on and before we left, I grabbed her hand and cupped her face.

"I cannot thank you enough for taking this risk." She smiled and a memory of her flashed through my head. I realized that she was always on our side, even last time. She was always there when I was allowed out of the dungeon, dressing me and braiding my hair.

She said nothing and led me out of the room. My heart was pounding so hard I only hoped that no one could hear it.

We silently made our way down the hallway and to the

side door. I had never used this door before but Flayke knew the way and she expertly took me through the winding hallways and through a few doors. Before I knew it, the cool air hit my cloaked face.

As we stepped outside, I became aware that Spiris was around here somewhere. I felt his magic. Flayke took me to the maze that was on the grounds and used Spiris's magical signature as a guiding light. I tried to hurry but I was still feeling sluggish. I had no idea how long I was asleep, but it felt like my body could not keep up.

As Spiris came into sight, a grin broke across my face and I felt hope fill me. He was dressed similarly to me and had a small pack thrown across his shoulder. He looked ready to run for his life. We were doing this; we were getting away from this together. It took all that I had to not rush at him right away, but when he held his hand out to me and gave me the biggest smile I had ever seen him muster, I couldn't contain myself. All the fear and doubt washed away from me and I could only focus on him. He did it, after years of waiting and planning, he was doing as he promised.

I ran to Spiris as fast as my legs would carry me. I felt a magical signature flare from behind me and Spiris's face twisted. I stopped in my tracks and dread started to fill me. We were careless. This was a trap.

"Run! Iniq! Run!" It was Flayke. I whipped my head around and saw Vitos towering behind the small woman. Her eyes were wide with fear and Vitos arms were raised. He had a sword in his hand. I reached out my arm, but my legs could not get me there fast enough.

Vitos brought down the sword and sliced her head clean off her shoulders. I felt the warm blood splash across my face.

"No! Flayke!" I screamed as I watched her body and head fall to the floor. Vitos's eyes were glowing, and he smiled at the dead body under him. I felt Spiris grab my hand; I tore my eyes away from the body and ran with him.

I reached out to touch his mind.

*We are so close just a few more feet.* Even in his mind, his voice was panicked.

In a flash of light, Baecos appeared in front of us. His eyes were glowing orbs of purple and he had the ugliest sneer across his face. His magic was overpowering again, just like all the other times he performed the ritual. His magic was distinctly mixed with my own. It was a more volatile combination than the others, the magic seemed to crackle in the air. He used my blood for the ritual.

"You think I was stupid? You think I didn't know your plan Spiris?!"

Before either of them could respond, Baecos had grabbed Spiris and put him in a chokehold. Spiris struggled against him but with Baecos's enhanced magic, there was no way he would win.

*I know you are listening, Iniq. Hurry, pay attention.*

I didn't know what to do. I felt Vitos appear behind me again, but he made no move to come towards me.

*Behind me is the tunnel, follow it and Cruor will be waiting for you on the other side.* He sent me an image of the tunnel; it was hidden by his magic made to look like the maze.

*NO, I can't le—*

*YOU HAVE NO CHOICE! Let her take you to safety. For me, please…*

Everything seemed to happen in slow motion. My breathing was coming out in shallow breaths and I watched in horror as Baecos summoned his sword and brought it to Spiris's throat. There was no hesitation in Baecos's face, only blood lust. Spiris had tears running down his face as he looked at me.

"NO!" I screamed.

*Iniq, you were the only thing in my life that gave me purpose, you gave me a will to live. You showed me a way out. You trusted me. It was always you who kept me going.*

Memories of us across all my lives flashed through his mind. We were smiling, laughing, and hugging. I could feel his love coming through these memories. I could feel his loneliness disappear when he was with me. Our own memories mixed together, I remembered the first time I cried in front of him, our first hug, the first time he showed me a real smile. I remembered when I couldn't sleep, he met me downstairs and we shared a warm tea together. His only regret was that he did not show his feelings for me when he had a chance. An image of us almost kissing filled my mind.

*Live, Iniq. Run and be free. Do not fall into the darkness. I love—*

Baecos's sword silenced the last of his thoughts. I watched as he decapitated Spiris's head and threw his body to the side like it was a piece of trash. I could not take my eyes off of Spiris's frozen face. His eyes were wide, and I watched as the light slowly drained out of them.

"I thought you were smart. We *let* you escape—we knew he would not stand by while the woman he loved was tortured." He took his sword that was still coated with Spiris's blood jabbed at his body.

I heard Vitos's cruel laugh behind me. He was a different kind of monster. I felt my own magic boil inside me but before I could act, I saw Baecos fall to the ground grabbing his head and trying to claw his ears off. I turned to look at Vitos, but he was the same, and behind him was a black shadowy figure screaming.

It had to be the Banshee. There was no other explanation for what I was seeing. It was a figure that had a cloak made of black shadows, I could only barely make out what was beneath it. The skin hiding there seemed to be leathery and dark grey, if not black; its boney fingers were peeking out of the coat as its outstretched hands reached for Vitos's hair. The only part of its face that I could see was its mouth wide open showing rotten teeth. I realized that it was not that the other features were in the shadows, it's that the creature didn't have any eyes or a nose. Its mouth took up almost its entire face.

Even though I knew its screams should have had me writhing on the floor, it felt like my head was dunked in water and everything around me was muted. I could hear the screams faintly, but they did not hurt me. I took my chance to run.

I tried to run past Baecos's crouched form, but his hand reached out and grabbed my ankle. I tripped and fell flat on my face. He was climbing up my form trying to reach for me with his bloodied hands. His hands were about to wrap around my neck when we heard a deep growl. I saw a large form run at him in a blur. He was torn off me and I pushed myself off the ground, pushing myself towards the tunnel that Spiris had shown me in his mind.

I froze in my tracks as I came face to face with what could only be described as a Hell Hound. The fur was as dark as night, eyes blood-red, and he was as big as a horse. He had an odd white spot in the middle of his head. His mouth was softly growling but instead of lunging at me like his partner had done to Baecos, his muzzle softly butted my head. I heard a low whine come out of its throat like it was worried.

My eyes widened in surprise, but I didn't have time to think. He turned and was running towards the tunnel. I followed him and tried to run as fast as my weak legs could carry me. My eyes burned with tears at the thought of Flayke and Spiris giving their lives to save me. They were innocent and deserved so much more than their life to end in such a horrible way. I pushed away the thoughts as the Hell Hound turned his face towards me. I could feel another one a few yards behind me, but I had yet to see it. After a few more minutes of running, we burst out into a forest, much like the one I was in when I first came to this world.

There was a clearing in front of us and—just like Spiris had said—Cruor was there, but she was not alone. She sat on top of a hell hound that seemed to be fastened with a saddle, its eyes were also blood-red but instead of black fur, it was a dark grey. Next to her on top of his own dark-grey, slightly smaller Hell Hound was Fluvis the Water King. Cruor's eyebrows were pushed together and her eyes glowed red. I was not scared. Spiris told me what I needed to do, and I knew I could trust her.

"Where is Spiris?!" Cruor yelled and held out her hand for me to climb on the Hell Hound. I let the tears flow freely and mounted the Hell Hound behind her.

"They got him and Flayke. They are gone." Cruor cursed and yelled for the Water King that we needed to leave. He nodded and all the Hell Hounds raced through the forest. The Hell Hound that led me through the maze was close to our side. I recognized him because of the white spot on his head. His eyes would look at me every few moments; he knew me. The other one that followed me through the tunnel was on the other side. His eyes were focused ahead and this one was a russet color. Three distinct claw marks that ran down his face. I was confronted by the fact that I was not the cause of these beautiful creature's pain. As if it knew I was thinking about him, his eyes met mine then turned back forward.

"Hold on!" she yelled.

They moved so fast that I felt like I was going to lose whatever was left in my stomach. I circled my arms around Cruor and hid my face in her back. This time my head did not split open with memories, it seemed to sense that right now, all I needed was the comfort her scent brought me. I let the tears flow freely onto Cruor's shirt. If she minded, she did not tell me.

As we were riding away from the Kingdom of Light, I could only think of the memories that I had shared with Spiris and the ones that he had thrown in at the last second.

His dying words and love hit me like a train.
     *I love you too, Spiris.*

241

# Chapter Forty-One

### Cruor

It took everything I had in me to not turn around and tear Baecos limb from limb. Ash nearly depleted his magic in order to get to us, it was only thanks to a soldier that selflessly offered up his magic that he was able to keep going. Iniq's face was buried in my back and her hands were held tightly around my waist. I would be filled with joy under any other circumstance, but I could feel her tears soaking through my shirt.

Damn it, Spiris. I felt guilty when I look back at our last conversation. I should have ignored my jealousy and helped him more. I could have healed him or sent more hounds, or hell even went in myself to drag him and the maid out of there. I regret not taking her back with me that day of the gala, I wanted to bring them both back, but I should have forced her out of there while I had the chance.

I looked towards Ash. He was keeping up with us, but his eyes never left Iniq though. He was beside himself when she died last time. He did not make it in time to help me fight Baecos and save her—none of them did. I barely made it myself and when I did, I was losing quickly. He looks to be keeping up okay, but I knew that he must be tired.

We had almost reached the point where we would

travel, close to my kingdom, but we wouldn't stop here. He would go straight there and demand to be heard, so instead, we would go to Fluvis's kingdom and stay there until she was healed enough to continue on. After that, I would kill Baecos with my own hands.

"The Hounds will travel soon, be prepared," I spoke to Iniq, hoping my voice carried through the wind to her.

"Travel?" her muffled voice asked. Of course, she wouldn't remember.

"Like skipping, but for demons." She nodded against me and said nothing. I felt her arms tighten around my waist and I stilled against it. It was not the act that made me still but instead the spike of power that came from behind us.

"He followed us!" Fluvis yelled.

Not a moment later, a flash of light appeared in front of us causing the hounds to stop in their tracks. In front of us stood Baecos, his chest was rising and falling violently, and his face was painted with blood.

"Give her back to me." His magic spiked and began to cover him and the area around him.

"Back up!" I yelled to the hounds. My eyes shot to Ash. If it was anyone else, we may have been able to have a better chance, but he was so exhausted, we would have to rely on the others for this. I felt Iniq shake violently behind me. I wondered briefly what was going through her head, but I wasn't sure that I really wanted to know.

Fluvis's magic spiked as well, and I watched as his magic slowly came together. Starting from the ground, the water he had conjured slowly rose and started braiding together intricately to form a small barrier between us and Baecos.

I knew it wouldn't hold.

Fluvis met my eyes, he knew it as well it seemed. I cursed and felt my heart rate pick up. Baecos just used this time to catch his breath and his eyes were on me the entire time. Everyone was waiting for me to decide.

My blood turned ice cold. Not one idea on how to escape filled my mind. There was nothing I could do.

I looked to Ash again, his eyes were focused on Iniq. He would be devastated if we lost her again.

"What are you doing?" Iniq hissed at me. "We have to fucking go."

There was no use. He found us and by the look of his lips twisting up into a smile, he had the same thought. Dread filled me and I felt the hounds shift anxiously still waiting for me to decide.

Baecos's magic spiked suddenly. The barrier between us exploded into thousands of tiny sparkling pieces.

"Go back! Run!" Iniq's voice was filled with a powerful magic and shot out across the space between all of us. All the thoughts and doubts were pushed out of my head and all I could think about was the will to flee. Without hesitation, we all followed her orders as if we were attached to one mind. The hounds were now running back the way we came. I shot a look at Fluvis but he refused to meet my eyes. I wondered if Iniq realized the extent of the power she just used.

Iniq twisted her body so that she was now facing where we had just come from.

"You will fall!" I yelled at her, but in response, she just leaned back to steady herself against my back.

She conjured a bow and arrow and tried to fire at Baecos. He was now running after us again. Did she not realize that keeping up with the hounds by just running was a crazy feat as is? Her arrow would not do anything to him.

Instead of firing at Baecos, she fired straight up.

"Fluvis, above!" she yelled, and Fluvis threw his magic above them. As her arrow hit the cloud of magic, we were suddenly shrouded in a mist-like substance that made it hard to see. The hounds did not stop though, they all continued forward and easily went through the trees and mist. Without her memories and with her magic as weak as it was, an action like that was surprising. The last time we saw her, she didn't know Fluvis, and now suddenly she knew how his power worked?

Before I had time to comment, Iniq was pulled from the back of the hound and I watched as her body disappeared in the fog that covered the area around us. As Iniq was pulled, so was her magic that kept us going. I made Callum stop and tried to scan the area with my eyes and magic to find her. Nothing came up in the near vicinity. Panic wafted through me as I found Claire without a rider. I cursed and sent my magic out even further to find them. Sending it over trees and through the fog searching for anything recognizable, anything to grasp onto.

*There.*

Baecos was fighting with Fluvis, and Iniq was not too far away from them. I jumped off Calum and ran towards the magic. Fluvis would die if left alone.

The fog had begun to dissipate, and I was able to make out the form of Baecos and Fluvis now. I threw my magic out and commanded it to reach his form. I focused on all the anger and panic that filled me and tried to fuel it into the fire that now covered his entire body. He stepped back and tried to pat the fire away. He was distracted enough that Fluvis was able to slice his abdomen open with an ice sword.

I grabbed Iniq and pulled her back towards Callum, but she attempted once more to shoot an arrow. I knew it was aimed at his head, but it landed in his bicep. Her body was shaking so hard it was almost like she was convulsing. She was in no shape to expend any more magic. Felix's hound sped over to Baecos's form and gripped his body in his giant jaws. Felix tried to violently throw him away from our group leaving him to fall in a hump against a nearby tree. I felt a sick satisfaction as I watched him struggle to regain his footing. His body was broken and bleeding as he tried to desperately heal himself.

We'd won this battle.

"We leave now!" I yelled to Fluvis. This was as lucky as we would get—to even get this far was just pure luck.

I pushed Iniq back up onto Callum. Fluvis once again sat on top of Claire. Ash was in a defensive position watching Baecos as we readied once more.

"Travel!" I yelled at them and watched as the scene shift in front of us.

# Chapter Forty-Two



The door woke me up sooner than I wanted it to. It filled my sleep again, begging me to come in and enticing me with promises for a better life and a safe passage, but I ignored it. It seemed to hate that because the next moment I was up gasping for air. Cruor's hands were on me instantly, covering my mouth so I could not make noise. The Hell Hound next to me did not stir but I heard the other ones jump to their feet.

"It's okay, it's a dream." Her face was close to mine and I saw her red eyes were wide and panicked. I nodded and felt her take her hand off my mouth slowly

"I'm sorry." My voice was barely above a whisper. I heard the hounds relax and Cruor waved her hand. I assumed to dismiss any guards that were around. I saw them earlier but chose not to comment; they were doing their job and staying well-hidden and I wasn't in a mood to talk. I was far from Baecos, but I could not bring myself to get over the fear of him breaking through the trees and finding us.

After Baecos had been defeated, we had traveled for another full day before resting. We were constantly looking over our shoulders and feeling for any type of magic spike. After we reached a certain point, we had met up with Fluvis's soldiers and were finally able to sleep for a few hours. I was still amazed that we were even able to stop him. I had never seen him that injured before and with my magic flowing through him, I was sure he would have destroyed us. Cruor swore that it was because of the distraction that I caused that caught him so off guard, but looking at my hands now, I am not sure that that was the case. I felt the power the surged through me during that time, it didn't feel like my own yet felt so familiar.

"It's okay, really. Just want to make sure no creatures find us," Cruor said. I could barely make out her form in the dark, only her eyes and a small idea of the motions she made. I swallowed loudly and reached out to grab her hand, and before I could change my mind, I tugged it close to me. She got the hint and laid down next to me, I reached out to cover her with the blanket and she accepted, making sure it covered us both. She was further away than I wanted but it was enough to feel the heat from her skin.

"Thank you," I whispered. "For coming for me."

"When we heard the Banshee back there… we thought we were too late." She was changing the subject. "I thought we failed you, again."

"I couldn't hear it," I admitted and brought her warm hand closer to me.

Cruor stiffened and then laughed weakly. "Only you."

I don't understand why but her laugh struck something in me and tears started to flow. Her eyes widened and she came closer to me, her hand pushing my face into her chest.

"I'm sorry," I spoke between sobs and grabbed at her shirt.

"For what?"

"For saying I wanted nothing to do with you. You risked everything to save me and yet I told you I never wanted to see you again."

She sighed and continued to pat my back until my tears ran out.

"You didn't know. There is nothing to apologize for." Her lips were in my hair and she gave me a small kiss. "Rest please."

I nodded and tried to relax against her. Sleep came almost immediately.

The door visited again… but this time it was far away. Watching almost. It made no move to stir me this time.

I woke up still in her arms.

I had the audacity to blush when I realized my curled hand flattened slightly and was now cupping her breast.

"We need to get up soon. You slept a little too long," Cruor's voice sounded above me. I nodded and got up slowly trying to stretch out. I winched when I tried to stretch my legs. I still felt where the knife had stabbed my thigh.

Fluvis came into sight and nodded to us. Cruor nodded back and started to get the hounds ready for riding. It was not long before we started riding again.

"Are you sure you would not rather sleep?" Cruor asked Fluvis as he boarded his hound.

"Don't insult me," he scoffed. "You have yet to give me a full night of sleep since you were born."

Cruor flashed him a smile and we were off again. It was not much easier to tell where we were going even in daylight. The dead forest was still so dense that I was surprised the hounds could push their way through it.

At night, the dead forest had seemed like the black tendrils that floated out of the door, reaching to grab anything—anyone—and trap them. I knew realistically that the trees could not move, but every time I saw something shift, I would look towards it and find nothing but more dead trees. They had an aura around them, one that was dark and seemed to reach with death.

"Is it magic that keeps them dead?" I asked after looking at the trees in daylight once more. They looked much tamer when you looked at them head-on. There were no hands reaching to grab you off your hound, just thin twig-like branches that could easily be broken if hit too hard.

"I would say it's the opposite," Cruor spoke from in front of me. "It's magic that keeps them alive."

I looked at them again. They were definitely dead.

"There is a tale," she started again, "that when the High Kings still roamed this land, they put a spell on this forest. It was once filled with trees of all different kinds of fruits, apples mostly. One of the kings had caught their lover here dining on fruit with another and was so angry that they cursed the forest. You will only be able to see the beauty of this forest if you can come here with the one you truly love. Like a gift for those who can love."

I tried to make out if there was any dead fruit on the ground, but the hounds were moving too fast to see.

"It must be a lie then. It looks pretty dead to me."

"I wouldn't say that." Cruor stiffened slightly. "I have seen leaves and fruit on the ground that looked just barely rotten before. But I have not, nor has anyone I know, seen it in full bloom."

The ride was deathly silent after that. I wanted nothing more than to demand that she tell me every single thing about Spiris and their plan, but I could not bring myself to breach the subject. I pushed down the pain that I felt when I thought about him. My hurt was still there but a new emotion started to pop up: guilt. I shouldn't have let the door overrun my thoughts like that. If I had an ounce of self-control, I know that it would be different. I could have fought Baecos, stopped him before he found out we were leaving. I was too groggy to think of how stupid it was to leave so early, that we should have waited until they were further away to make our escape.

"Don't think too hard," Cruor's voice cut through my jumbled mind. "You could have done nothing to stop it."

"How—"

"It's how you have always been."

I sighed and held her closer. After another half day of riding, we traveled again. I was beginning to get wary, how much longer did these trees go on for? No one had spoken a word all morning, even the hounds were as silent as ever.

"How much longer until we get there?"

"We have to be careful with how we get there. We will ride until late tonight and then we will arrive." Cruor's voice was low making sure not to make unnecessary noise.

"I didn't know it was that far."

There was no response.

We did indeed ride into the night, we only took a short break before sundown for the hounds to catch their breath and hydrate. I knew Fluvis was the Water King but watching him pull it out of nowhere seemed too good to be true.

"It's not out of nowhere," he said. "Just like the darkness and light, water is in everything living."

I could not tell what time it was but I assumed past midnight. I could slowly see the forest thinning; there were lights up ahead. I felt the tension in the air rise. I felt Cruor stiffen and heard the leather reins strain in her hands. She kicked the side of the hound lightly and he sprinted faster than ever before—I had to hold on to Cruor tighter to not fall off. My heart pounded in my chest.

The hounds broke through the barrier.

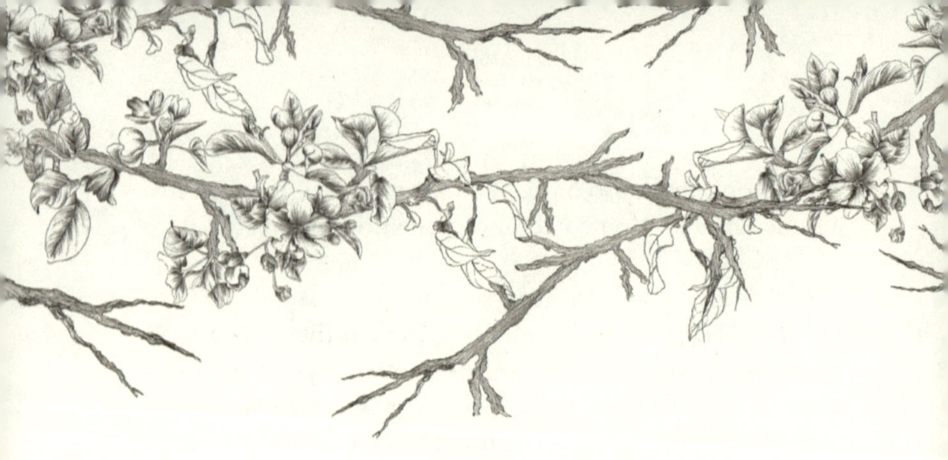

# Chapter Forty-Three
## Iniq

It was unnerving to see a city so still. There was not a single
light on in the many houses. The paths were lined in
cobblestone and there was a river that seemed to run on all
sides. The hounds slowed down to a small jog and led us
through the area. No one spoke until we stopped in front of
what seemed to be an inn.

"Welcome, Iniq," Fluvis said as he led us into the inn.
"The Water Kingdom is yours as long as you need it for."

I smiled at him slightly and relinquished in the warmth
of the inn. It seemed cozy, all the way from its laced-lined
curtains to its roaring fireplace. The lady at the front desk
waved to us and I followed Fluvis up to the rooms. Cruor
stated she needed to take care of the hounds and said she
would catch up. I plopped down on a chair in the sitting
room that Fluvis had shown us; tea was ready for us.
Through shaking hands, I was able to start drinking the
bitter liquid. I sighed as the warm liquid chased away the
coldness in my toes. I would lie if I said that I was at ease
though, I did not know the likelihood of Baecos barging in
here any moment now.

"This is where we are now," Fluvis said as he rolled out

a map and pointed to the edge of the Water Kingdom. "We traveled through the dead forest and to my kingdom. When we are ready, we will take a similar way to Cruor's Kingdom."

"Why did we not go straight there?" I asked, noting that the Light Kingdom and the Fire Kingdom seemed closer.

"Because he would expect that." Cruor made her way into the room with what looked like a guard. The guard had ivory skin and hair black as night; he had tattoos that I had never seen before, but I thought better of mentioning it.

"We match," I said to him, noting the small bit of white hair that was hidden behind his shaggy black hair. His eyes were as red as Cruor's. He smiled and gave a small wave.

"The names Ash if you don't remember." I nodded in appreciation.

"Thank you," I started and cleared my throat. "I am sorry that I could do nothing to save… Spiris, and I really appreciate your help in getting me out of there." It was hard not to choke on his name.

Fluvis laid his hand palm side up on the table. I slowly gave him mine and he squeezed it.

"It is our duty. There is no need to thank us." I blushed and the image of the door floated through my mind. Yes, I am a savior to them. I understand now why they needed to save me.

"It's nice to hear some life in your voice. We will leave once you are ready," Cruor said as she sat next to me. It was nice to hear my lie was working. I was not sure how long I could keep it up with Spiris face in my head. "You need to heal."

"I am healed," I pushed, ignoring the phantom pain of the knife and my shaking hands.

"We aren't talking about physically," Ash spoke up

from his standing position in the corner. I frowned. He reminded me of something, but I couldn't put my finger on it.

I sighed and continued to drink my tea. I was too high strung to begin to contemplate sleep, so instead, I stayed and listened to Fluvis update Cruor on the happenings in his kingdom. This town it would seem was the oldest of this kingdom Fluvis explained to me, the rumor was that the High Kings used to gather here and host a feast that lasted nearly six months. Before the division and the war, this place was a safe spot for all. No matter what powers you possessed, demon or not, you would be welcomed here. Fluvis took pride in the history of this land—his eyes were gleaming, and his fangs showed through his wide smile. He was bragging, but I did not mind.

"Can you tell me more about them?" I asked. "They are behind the door, are they not?"

"They are, they can control anything and everything here. They are the source of our magic and the destruction of it," Cruor explained.

"I was told they are similar to gods." As I spoke, I saw a few puzzled faces meet mine.

"Gods?" Ash spit out the tea he was drinking making a mess on the table.

"I suppose the Light Kingdom would call them that, but they are nothing like gods." Cruor picked at the bowl of nuts in front of her. "They are closer to demons—devils—than they are to gods, but *some* refuse to believe that."

I swallowed loudly as I remembered the feeling of the black tendrils reaching out to me and the imprint of a sharp tooth smile in the black abyss. The darkness would always leave a lingering feeling and would cloud my mind and judgment. I could believe the devil's story.

"Yet they have the power to take ours away."

"Magicians," Cruor corrected. "Magicians take powers away. Not demons."

"And creatures," Ash piped in. "Some creatures are affected."

"Just some?" Ash shrugged and took a fist full of nuts from Cruor. She gave him a pointed look but didn't say anymore.

"Who knows what they are thinking, they are fickle kings. Senile with age." Fluvis sighed and stood up. "It's half past three in the morning, I don't know about you, but this old man needs to sleep." I nodded and let Cruor guide me to my room. She brushed Fluvis off when he offered and said she was more than capable to find her way.

She stopped at a door and opened it, gesturing for me to go inside. Inside was a small twin bed and a fireplace that was already started for me.

"I will be in the room over. Let me know if you need me." She was leaning on the door frame and it looked as though she had more to say.

"I am sorry again," I said and stepped towards her grabbing her hand. "Thank you for coming to save me." Her body was stiff but she brought my hand up to her mouth and a kiss was softly brushed across my bruised knuckles leaving heat in its wake.

"You never need to apologize to me." Her fangs were visible as she spoke, and I imagined them piercing into my— "Get some rest and do not worry about the dangers outside. You are safe now."

I nodded and watched as she shut my door and left me alone to my thoughts. I used my hand to fan my face.

"Stupid…"

I dreamt about the door again. It was like every other time, appearing in front of me and slowly cracking open. The black tendrils weaved their way out of the door and wrapped around my body. I tried to fight them off, but they didn't budge.

I slowly saw a clawed hand wrap itself around the door

and try to pry it open. I tried to dig my nails into the ground and things around me, but I was still being slowly dragged into the door.

*This is your last.*

I woke up in a cold sweat. The blankets were strewn across the end of the bed leaving me bare and shivering in my thin nightclothes. I could still feel the tendril wrapped around my wrists and ankles. Looking down at my wrist now, I was less than surprised to see a small bruise forming, but it was not solid like in the dreams, it was in the shape of fingers.

I decided not to stay in bed much longer anyway. The sun was up high enough in the sky and I could smell food wafting through the inn. My stomach gave out a rumble and I realized that it has been more than a day since I had eaten. I found some simple clothes in the closet that came with the room, washed, and was walking down the stairs of the inn not ten minutes later.

It seems that everyone else had the same idea as well. Cruor, Fluvis, Ash, and a few others were seated in the dining room around the large middle-table inhaling the food in front of them. Cruor waved me over to the seat next to her and I gave her a small smile. Her hair was standing up in all directions giving her a sleepily and unkempt look… so much for a queen. My mind flashed to the times where we enjoyed coffee together in a previous life, she seemed to have never changed.

"Surprised to see you up." One of the unnamed men spoke up. His hair was a dark grey and was cropped short, the ends just brushing his ears, which had multiple hoops in them. His face seemed ragged like he hadn't slept well, and his nose was a bit crooked, probably from being broken. He had red eyes and matching tattoos with those around him, intricate neck tattoos that almost spilled onto their faces, and their hands were covered in intricate designs that flowed up their sleeve-covered arms.

"Bad dream," I explained and started helping myself to some food.

"That is Callum, his sister, Claire, and Felix. Don't expect any tantalizing conversation from Felix though, he's not the smartest of the group." Claire had the same grey hair as her brother but hers fell in waves down her face. Unlike her brother though, her features were more petite and delicate, but the muscles showing through her clothes would tell anyone not to underestimate her.

My eyes shifted to Felix; he was the most shocking as his face had three old scars on it that went from above his left eye to his right jaw. I am surprised he still had his eyes, but they were very much intact, and they met mine carefully before pulling his attention away. His own russet hair was shoulder length and half-pulled back into a small bun, even with the scars he was ruggedly handsome with a strong jaw and high cheekbones. Ash may have said he was not the smartest but the way his eyes watched the others proved differently. I made the decision to try not to fight him any time in the future, even if the pounding in my chest told me to run at him.

Felix growled at Ash and threw a piece of his bread at him. Ash smacked it away and it landed on Claire's plate with a splat.

"You're the useless one, Ash," Claire huffed and pushed her plate away in disgust.

"A little dirt won't hurt you." Callum grabbed her plate and started eating her leftovers.

"You'll get reaccustomed to their banter. Like children," Cruor said and shot me a smile. She motioned for a server nearby and in an instant, a cup filled with dark liquid entered my eyesight and a small cream jug in front of me. I sniffed it and I felt happiness radiate from inside me when I did. It was coffee. I dumped some cream inside and started gulping it down, suddenly parched.

Baecos's mansion never had coffee, always tea. I assumed it was because this world didn't have any, but maybe he was just pompous. It had been forever since I was able to enjoy some, and I took comfort in the familiar bitter liquid. I shot a smile at Cruor and watched her eyes widen as a soft smile flitted across her own face.

"I hope your preference hasn't changed," she said, watching my reaction.

"This is perfect, thank you." I had the idea to reach down and squeeze her hand, but I refrained.

I drank my coffee, slowly watching those around the table. They seemed so content and happy, even Cruor seemed so at home here. Ash was in the middle of a story that I was barely paying attention to when he turned to me.

"When Claire first shifted, she freaked out. No one was her breed, we thought she was a normal demon," Ash explained to me through laughs.

"Shifted?" I echoed. The table silenced and then burst out into laughter. I felt irritation tickle my senses. "What's so funny?" I elbowed a laughing Cruor, but she couldn't talk between bursts of laughter.

"Ash doesn't look familiar to you?" Callum asked while ruffling his hair to show his white spot that landed directly in the middle of his head.

"Would you look at that." I plopped my head in my hands taking in their appearances thoughtfully. "Why did no one tell me you could change into hounds?"

"We thought you knew!" Ash exclaimed, reaching over to ruffle my own hair. "You didn't see us shift last night because it's not like clothes come with the form."

Cruor patted my back in mock sympathy. I knew she was just trying to joke but the move didn't sit well with me. It was not the human contact, if anything this body needed it and craved it. But the pity was not welcomed.

"Still much to learn," Fluvis commented, shaking his head softly. They were back to joking in an instant. Even the siblings had smiles on their faces. I wondered if there was ever a time here when I was able to display such a smile. I tried to remember if there was ever a time that I felt truly comfortable, but even from the beginning, I knew I did not belong here.

In the corner of my eyes, I saw blond hair shoot through the dining room, and I jumped slightly searching for it. I sighed in relief when I realized it was just a maid and not Baecos. Looking at the others, it seemed no one noticed my actions.

"What will you do today, Iniq?" Fluvis was done eating but he still hung around while the others were finishing. I found myself not being able to finish and pushed my plate away. I had to think about it. I never had much of a choice. It was an allusion of a choice, I assumed this was the same. My mind wandered back to the door.

I looked down at my hands in my lap.

"We could explore the city if it pleases you," Cruor whispered to me.

"And if I say I would rather not?" My voice came out harsher than I intended.

"Then we can stay here and read or sleep, or really anything else. We have time to kill."

"Maybe a small shopping area if they have those here..." I refused to look up at her, afraid of what I would find there.

She and a couple of others let out a laugh. I felt a hand pat the top of my head gently. Smiles and Spiris's scent danced through my mind.

"Oh, you bet we have those here." It was Ash who spoke, and it was his hand that rested upon my head. He ruffled my hair slightly. My eyes pricked with tears.

***

No one paid us any mind as we walked through the crowded street. Shoulders brushed against my own and Cruor's hand found its way to the small of my back guiding me around. It had been so long since I had been around people like this, the noise itself was almost too overbearing for me.

Fluvis did not come with us today but the others did. They were a part of Cruor's personal guard—where she went, they went. I learned that they had been with her for three hundred years. Looking at them I felt another wave of fresh envy come over me. Ash, Callum, and Felix were always chatting and messing around with each other, and Felix made sure to stay close to Claire. His eyes would always catch hers and she also smiled when he cracked jokes. I could guess the relationship they had. And here they all were, living it, enjoying their lives with each other.

Instead of being able to enjoy this moment, I was constantly looking over my shoulder. There were people here that had Light markings on them and every time I saw them, I was filled with a whirlwind of emotions. The most prominent and obvious one was fear, but the other ones were hatred and anger. I hated seeing his people being able to laugh and look happy. I wanted to scream at them and ask them if they knew what their king had done. And every time I saw purple eyes, my knees shook, and I had to grip on to Cruor. It was a bad idea to be around so many people. I chose the wrong type of outing to go on. I thought that I could be normal, or at least try to be normal, but my emotions were betraying me.

We made it to the shopping area where stall upon stall was set up, and people would stop in front of them to check the goods. I saw jewels, knitted goods, food, and even jewelry stands. Cruor let me walk to the stands that interested me, following me silently. I caught sight of a small stand selling baked goods. My eyes went to what looked like a cinnamon roll and my mouth watered. They were fresh and the sugary topping was still warm and dripping down the sides of the pastry.

"That one, please. And two lattes please." Cruor gave the woman at the stall money and she quickly handed us the items.

"You didn't—" I started but she cut me off.

"I wanted to. And how can you shop without the proper snacks." She pushed the roll to my mouth and I hesitantly took a bit. It was cinnamon. She smiled and took a bite for herself; her tongue shot out to clean her lips afterward, a star fang popped out just slightly as she smiled. The roll was gone soon, and I absentmindedly sipped my coffee as I looked at a jewelry stand.

My eyes lingered on a beautiful blood-red stone that was fastened into a necklace. I loved it. Rubies were a favorite of mine. The bloodied dagger that plunged into my throat flashed through my mind. I sipped my coffee and looked away from the beautiful stone. Maybe one day I could love it again.

It was not long until the eyes of everyone started to make me too anxious. On top of that, the hate and anger that filled me only seemed to be getting worse as I passed more of those with Light markings. After a child with Light markings bumped into us, I begged Cruor to take us back to the inn. I was not sure what I would have done if Cruor's hand had not been fastened tightly to my elbow.

Cruor's panic-filled face did not get past me. She must have known what I was thinking. Or if she did not know, she at least had an idea of what I was capable of.

*** 

The day left us quickly and before I knew it, I was back at the inn eating dinner with the group. I listened to Ash explain how ridiculous Callum had once been as a youngling.

"He had no care in the world, just for shits one time he walked in front of the whole dining hall butt naked." I forced a smile and watched as Cruor grimaced at the picture.

"They were incorrigible at a young age, all of them," Cruor said, giving Claire a pointed look when she was about to disagree with her. Claire's eyes shifted to meet mine then she looked back down at her plate.

"They do not compare to the two of you," Fluvis spoke. "You and Iniq would not leave the library for days on end. One time the entire kingdom was in a panic because we couldn't find you two, and it turns out you had just made it to the very top shelf of the highest bookshelf we had, and you couldn't get down." Cruor shook her head and let out a small laugh.

I frowned and tried to will the memory forward, but it refused to come. It was being blocked, like most other memories.

It was not long before I pushed my half-finished food away and excused myself from the table giving an excuse that I was tired.

When I was back in my room, I let out a sigh and allowed myself to fall to the floor, tucking my face into my knees. I stayed this way and let my emotions and thoughts flood me. I know I was just pretending, but even now, I was so lost without Spiris. I felt like I was just following the others without really even being here, every time they spoke about my past, I never felt like it was an extension of me but someone completely different. I wondered if they knew the anxiety that plagued me. I wondered if they knew the types of images the filled my mind. The instincts to spill blood. I wondered if they realized that even though I was filled with envy and wanted to be normal, an even bigger part of me didn't care about them at all.

Cruor and Fluvis, I knew they cared. Even Ash was carefully watching me the whole time. But could they feel that I had no feelings for them? Could they feel that I am not the person they once knew? I felt guilt but even that was muted by an overwhelming numbness.

The air shifted around me and I knew that if raised my head from where it was tucked, I would see the door. You could feel the darkness seeping out of it, covering the room with a heavy feeling, a suffocating feeling. I felt the tendrils reach out to me again, but I ignored their advances.

"Leave me alone," I spoke to it. I felt it hesitate for a second.

*Come to us… We have been waiting…*

"I don't care." The tendrils squeezed my ankles painfully. "Stop bothering me," I hissed and felt the tendrils withdraw. That was it? I looked up and instead of the door in front of me, it was Cruor's face. She was kneeled and reaching for me as if she wanted to move the hair out of my face. Her eyebrows were pushed together and her lips were set to a straight line. She looked to me then down at her hand. She sighed and left without another word. I started to call out to her, but it died in my throat as she slammed my door.

I looked at the floor at my feet and spotted a small bag. I picked it up and felt the weight in my hand; it was small and felt delicate. Opening it, I spied the blood-red stone necklace that I spotted in the stall earlier. I felt the stone and could feel some magic pulsating out of it. It felt like Cruor had put some of her magic in it and it was now shining through the stone. She wouldn't know that when I saw this it only brought up bad memories. She wanted to make me happy. I sighed and carefully wrapped it around my neck. I vowed to give her my thanks in the morning.

For now, I made my way to the bathroom for a much-needed shower. I spotted myself in the mirror and was shocked to see something I didn't notice this previously. The light tattoos were back, taking up space on my chest, now the only missing pieces were the eyes. I prayed they would not come; these were the only things that I had left of my previous life.

# Chapter Forty-Four

## Cruor

I stormed out of her room and into the seating room where Fluvis was waiting for me in. He was waiting there for us to discuss a plan for Baecos, but when he saw me come in, he raised his eyebrow.

"She told me to leave her alone," I muttered and poured another cup of tea for myself.

Watching her today made me feel uneasy. I didn't expect her to jump back into life here as soon as she arrived, but the haunting emptiness that filled her eyes is what scared me the most. Even when Ash teased her, she barely responded to him. If anything, I thought he would be able to get her to speak normally, but the last time I heard her speak more than a few sentences or show any emotion was when we arrived here last night.

"It's her first day back into this world away from Baecos, Cruor." Fluvis's tone was scolding. "We have no idea what he has done to her, you can't expect her to act like the person she was a hundred years ago." I looked down at the tea in my cup, but it gave me no answers. I scowled at it.

"She wanted to go shopping but complained when I bought her stuff. He is gone now and she has full reign to do whatever she wants but she…" I couldn't finish my sentence.

"She is not used to the freedom," Fluvis explained. "Maybe she wanted to go to the shopping area to be around people. Maybe she can't stand to be alone by herself, the person she was closest to just *died*." My thoughts went back to when she had just died, I acted worse than this. I bit everyone's head off and destroyed half the castle. I sighed and plopped down in the seat next to him. I would not be doing anything productive tonight.

"Let's forget about planning for now," I started and summoned a deck of cards, smirking at Fluvis. "You ready to get your ass handed to you, old man?"

He threw his head back and let out a laugh. "You're on."

# Chapter Forty-Five

### Iniq

That night, the door did not visit me in my dreams, but
Baecos did. I thought I had a chance tonight when I realized
I was in a dream; it was beautifully refreshing to be
surrounded by white roses. I could even smell them. I let
my hand glide across the white roses softly, enjoying the
feeling of their velvet petals. I plucked one and brought it
up to my nose to inhale its scent. Before I could even lift it,
the rose's white petals started to wilt. From the stem up to
the petals, I watched as the flower turned grey and the head
of the flower snap off and roll to the ground.

The ground was now painted with blood and the rest
of the white flowers had turned grey. The pleasant clean
smell turned rotten. The blood was something I had gotten
used to, but a voice from behind me made my blood run
cold. I turned around and came face to face with Baecos,
and in his hand was Spiris's head. Spiris's eyes were wide
open and his mouth was moving as if he was trying to speak
but nothing came out. Instead, Spiris's blood dripped all
over newly rotted roses.

Sitting up in my bed, I tried to catch my panting breath
and calm myself. I took in my surroundings looking for

Baecos. I even sent out my magic to feel if he was around. When I had checked the entire room, I finally felt okay to sigh and lay back in bed. My face was wet with tears and my covers were in a disarray. I tried to calm my breathing and clenched the blankets in my fist.

After a few moments, I realized I would not be getting any more sleep. I washed and dressed and headed down to the dining room. The sun was just barely coming out and I prayed that they had some coffee ready, which they did. The workers suggested that I go to the garden out back and enjoy my coffee there. Luckily, there were no white roses here. I tried to focus on the beauty of the garden in front of me and not the death that lingered in my head.

Sitting in the garden at a table sipping my coffee, I was glad that I listened to them. I watched as the sun came over the buildings that surrounded the garden. It was calming and best yet, quiet. I was thankful for the normalcy the other brought me, but that paired with the door's voice popping up in my head made everything too loud. I wondered if this was actually me just going insane, the years of torture catching up to me. I felt a magical signature from behind me—it was Cruor. I held in my sigh and went back to pretending. I gestured to the seat next to me without looking at her, so she sat down but did not speak. I watched as she sat straight and looked at the sun rising. Her eyes did not meet mine but when I looked at hers, I could see the smudge of purple beneath them.

"Thank you for the necklace, it's beautiful." I fingered the delicate stone that now resided on my neck.

"No problem," she muttered and drank her own coffee while watching the garden.

"What is the plan today?" I took a sip of my coffee. The tension was thick.

"Whatever you want."

I didn't know what I wanted. I felt the lack of sleep starting to get to me, and if I stayed here much longer, coffee or not, I would be forced back into bed. And I was afraid of what I would see there.

"I don't know what I want. I don't even know what to do in this world," I answered truthfully.

"What did you do in the last one?"

More of nothing, I guess. I would read at times, shop if I needed to. I rarely went out unless someone pushed me to.

"I liked to read."

"Then let's do that." She got up and started making her way back to the inn, so I had no choice but to follow her.

A short while later after a quick breakfast, she brought me to a small bookstore and pushed me down one of the aisles. I looked through the titles and saw that some were in a different language. I was beginning to get overwhelmed by all the choices.

As I was looking at the spines, a book and Cruor's hand blocked my view. I looked at her and she shoved the book into my hand. I saw that she already had a pile of her own. She pulled me to the front of the shop and paid for the books. The woman here seemed to recognize her and started blushing, talking about the honor of being visited by a king.

"Are you not a queen?" I asked as she brought us back to the inn's garden to read. She decided to sit in the grass against a rock and opened up the first book in her pile.

"We are all kings, regardless of gender," she started. "Some kings don't even have one—a gender." I nodded and opened my own book.

She had good taste I had to admit. My eyes seldom left the book. It was about the High Kings—or a retelling of a story involving the High Kings I should say. During one of the feasts, a girl recounts how she fell in love with one of the most beautiful of the High Kings and tried to extend the feast for as long as possible so she had a chance to see him for longer. I only ripped my eyes away from the book when I heard Cruor laugh. She had done that a few times, and every time I felt drawn to it. It was a pure sound, unbridled by hate or anger. She was now laying on her stomach and the book was on the ground. I think she was already on her second.

The door chose this moment to show up behind me again and tease my ankles and whisper to me.

*I could tell you a secret.*

This was different than the other times it spoke to me, it must have seen that the other ways did nothing to stir me. My heart pounded with excitement at the thought of knowing something others didn't. I cursed internally. The door knew what to do to pique my interest. I ignored it and went back to my book.

*Or should I remind you of something you are forgetting?*

I shot a look towards Cruor again, but she did not look up. I was forgetting a lot of things. I couldn't even remember my parents' faces. Whatever it told me would just lead to more questions. I sighed and continued to ignore the door. I did not want to go on any quest for more answers.

It hadn't stayed for this long before. I frowned and reread the passage I was on, losing my focus as I felt the tendril wrap around my ankle. What was its game? I felt curiosity tickle at my mind.

*Curiosity killed the cat.*

Baecos's voice filled my mind again. I shut my eyes tightly ignoring the stars I saw there. With a deep sigh, I turned back to my book, ignoring the door once more and fully forgetting any curiosity I may have felt.

I finished my book shortly and with a sigh laid it on the ground. Cruor, without tearing her eyes away from the page, felt around blindly for another book and, once she found the one she was looking for, handed it out to me. I grabbed it and lifted an eyebrow at her actions.

"The next book in the series." She still did not lift her

head.

I smiled and dove into the next one, forgetting the world around me and enjoying the thrill of watching someone else for just a moment.

"How was the reading today?" Fluvis asked at dinner later that night.

"Good," I swallowed. "I was a bit overwhelmed by the choices, but Cruor helped me pick out a good series."

"Don't tell me she gave you *The High Kings' Betrayal*," Claire grumbled, and I looked at her in surprise.

"She did." I heard a collective groan and gave a questioning look to Cruor.

"We have very… very *different* opinions on that book. And," she paused and ruffled her hair a bit, "there were many times we kept the whole castle up with our heated arguments about whether or not Yara's love was true."

I let out a small laugh. "Of course it's not, she was only interested in High King Nitri because of his power. She said as much that that was her motive. She would have left if he could not have supplied her with his power. Looks aside, it was always about power."

Cruor's lips slowly lifted at the corners and ended up giving me a toothy grin. "See, now we are getting somewhere. Your argument previous was always that she could see past it once they were together and that became her motive instead."

"She gave him up when she realized what he could not supply her with! What kind of partner would do that?" I was startled to realize I was not pretending at this moment; I really did enjoy the story she had given me. I ignored the door's presence when it appeared again. It must have heard about the High Kings and came to see what the commotion was about.

The dinner easily became more comfortable and Cruor and I drifted into talks about the book. Even when everyone was done, we tried to talk more, but Fluvis reminded us that there was always tomorrow.

I went to sleep that night feeling excited for the next day.

***

I was back in the dungeon, but there was no door here this time, just me and Baecos. I felt his hand slowly trail up my bare leg.

"You know why you thought that Yara could truly love Nitri?" He brought a bloody hand up to his mouth and his tongue reached out for a small taste.

I felt disgust fill me. "I don't give a shit," I spat. His eyes flashed and his hands found my throat, squeezing the breath that was caught there. I tried to kick and scream but I was bound, and my screams never left my throat.

"It's because you saw Yara in Cruor and you wanted to believe that your love was true." He laughed as I struggled. "Let's be real, Iniq. She only wants you because of your power. At least I was always honest."

I felt my consciousness slip from me. Is it possible to die in a dream? I felt dangerously close.

"Iniq! Wake up!"

I was brought back to the real world by Cruor shaking and yelling for me. It was still dark inside the room, but I saw Cruor's face above my own, her hands holding mine down against the bed. She was dressed in similar night clothes as I was.

I swallowed and felt tears prick my eyes. Cruor's mouth drooped slightly, and she moved over to lay besides me.

"You were screaming." Her hand came up to wipe my tears away. I did not push her away this time.

"I'm sorry." My throat was sore and dry as I spoke.

"Do you want to talk about it?" she whispered. Her eyes were intense as she spoke.

"I was just back there again. I will be okay." She nodded and started to get out of the bed, but my hand caught her wrist. "Would it be okay… if you stayed with me tonight?"

She seemed to contemplate the idea.

"I am just scared. I won't even touch you. I just need someone here," I explained quickly, not wanting her to get the wrong idea, not that I would complain, but I was in no mood to seduce the demon across from me.

"Someone…" she muttered under her breath and ruffled her hair slightly. She sighed and pulled the covers back so she was lying next to me in the bed. She was watching me carefully as I brought the covers up to my chin and met her eyes.

*She only wants you for your power.*

She reached out to move the hair from my face and I flinched slightly remembering how Baecos had touched my face in my dream with his bloodied hand. Cruor pulled her hand back, brow furrowing. She turned around so her back was now facing me. I felt the need to reach out my own hand and twirl her messy hair around my fingers.

I found sleep not too long after that, and this time I dreamt of how Cruor's hair would feel when my fingers were tangled in it.

# Chapter Forty-Six

## Cruor

I woke up before her the next morning. I watched her as she was sleeping. She did not have any other nightmares after I came in, she curled up on her side and slept deeply. It was hard to tear my eyes from her face, and when I saw her tear-stained face, instead of getting angry, I just wanted to kiss her senseless and wash away her pain.

*I am just scared. I won't even touch you. I just need someone here.*

I knew I shouldn't have let that stupid sentence hurt me so much, but I debated sending in Ash as soon as she said that. I watched her stir softly and her eyes fluttered open. I saw the realization click in her mind and she used the blanket to cover her face slightly.

"I forgot you came in," she muttered, still staring at me. I smiled slightly at this and pushed her hair out of her eyes. Her eyes held some light just now, but this was far from how her usual personality was.

"I will leave you to get changed," I whispered. "And then we can get breakfast and start our day of reading." She nodded and I watched her as she left the bed. She glanced backward at me as if she wanted to ask something, but it seemed as though she decided it was unimportant and left to the bathroom.

I sighed and left for my own room to shower and prepare for the day. Callum was in the hall when I left her room and he only raised an eyebrow at me, I shrugged him off. I remembered how her eyes shined when we started talking about our books, but the disappointment was quick to fill me when I saw how her stance had changed. I wondered what had happened in her previous life to make it change so drastically. I smiled as the memories of her yelling at me filled my mind. She would do everything and anything to convince me that Yara had loved Nitri. She had even begun highlighting the spots in the book where she thought they would prove her point to show to me later.

It was not long until we met downstairs in the dining room. Iniq was already sitting with her coffee. Today she wore a baby blue dress with fabric so soft it almost clung to her body, and her hair was up in a bun leaving some messy strands to fall around her face and neck. I smiled softly when I spotted a feather on the back of her neck… I remember kissing that exact spot hundreds of times in our years together. The dagger on her throat was a topic no one would breach, but it was obvious why it was there.

Ash met my eyes before anyone else and I saw his brows furrow when he did. Were my emotions that obvious to everyone? Iniq followed his gaze and sent me a small smile that did not reach her eyes, maybe not to everyone.

Breakfast was filled with easy banter; I kept my eyes on Iniq, but I stared at her hands more times than anyone's face here. I assumed that maybe she had given up trying to make connections with the people here, but something she said yesterday flashed through my mind.

*I don't know what I want. I don't even know what to do in this world.*

"What was the thing that surprised you the most coming here from the mortal world?" I asked her and watched as her head slowly lifted her eyes. They shone in the light slightly. The others around us stopped talking.

"Carriages," she responded quietly, and I saw her grimace slightly. I was about to ask her if she did not like them, but Callum beat me to it.

"Carriages? Not that people can use magic?" His voice was cautiously playful, but I shot him a look. Iniq chuckled slightly and my gaze snapped back to hers.

"I guess not." Another chuckle. "When I first came here, people were throwing it left and right at me so that one I had to believe—fast. But with magic so ingrained in peoples' lives, I hardly saw the need for that type of… transportation." I nodded at her explanation, but her face seemed to still hold a grimace.

"Mine was faeries. I was born here but those suckers scared the living hell out of me." Felix spoke up and looked at her pointedly, tapping a space on his cheek. "I remember the first time I met one, they almost attacked me right there. I was still a pup, but they had no problem sinking their teeth into me." It was rare when Felix joined the conversation. I looked over at Iniq's face and saw that there was a tiny faerie mark on her cheek, which she rubbed slightly.

"Ya, mine bit me too," she sighed with frustration. "I would have expected more help from the bastard, but she bit me and left right after."

It clicked so fast in my mind that I had to laugh out loud. Fluvis joined me not moments later but everyone else looked at us with confusion.

"Why didn't I think of it before." I pushed her forehead softly with my fingertip. "That is why she was immune to the Banshee's scream. The faerie venom must still be in her system and the Banshee's screams do not work on the little creatures." Her eyes widened and she looked down at her finger, the one—I'm assuming—it bit.

"Maybe not so useless after all," she muttered. I met

Fluvis's eyes and he had a smile on his lips as well; it was a start and that was better than nothing.

Breakfast after that was easy, she spoke up when she could and began to relax slightly in her seat.

Today I had her read the last book in the High Kings' Betrayal series, and just like I thought she would, she began sobbing uncontrollably at the end. I smiled when she did and put down my own book to comfort her, and to my surprise, she let me and even pulled me closer. Her crying lasted way too long to just be about the book, but I did not pry.

I enjoyed watching her read. She got way too close to the book, but it was interesting to see her facial expressions change as the story progressed. She'd started reading much faster now and I knew that I would have to stop by the bookstore again soon to get us some more material.

"Thank you," she spoke as I was reading. "I appreciate you trying to help me get reacclimated to this world."

I nodded at her but said nothing. I would let her continue to talk if she wanted to.

"My mortal life was unhappy, and I came to an even unhappier life here, even if I did not realize it at first." She took a deep breath and continued. "I remember bits of our life together. I think my mind went to those parts when I was lonely over there. So even if things are not the same now… thank you, for before."

I felt my throat tighten. I did not know what to say. I wanted her to tell me every last detail of the things she remembered and demand her to tell me how she felt. But looking at the bags under her eyes and considering that this was the most she'd spoken in a few days, I decided to go against it.

***

The rest of the day was filled with even more reading and a few snacks. I was glad to see her eating some more. She was headfirst in a book sipping on her tea when I heard her speak next. I felt her stiffen and when I looked over to her, her green eyes bore into mine. Her eyebrows were pulled together and her mouth was slightly pouted.

"Two years?" Her voice was unsure when she spoke.

"Two years?" I echoed back at her, and I felt all the hope that I felt earlier shrivel up and die inside me. I tried not to show it on my face and watched as she searched my own. Whatever she was looking for I guessed that she did not find it because she was right back to her book like nothing happened.

I felt panic bubble up in me slowly but forced myself to take a sip of tea... as if that could wash it down. I had hoped that most of that was erased from her memories; my eyes found her form again. If she was not blowing up this whole place, I could only assume not all of it had come back to her… yet.

"Does that ring any bells for you?" she asked, not looking up at me.

More than a few.

I cleared my throat. "Not particularly?"

She hummed slightly and turned the page in her book.

It was getting close to dinner time. I excused myself stating I would like to talk to Fluvis before dinner and she waved me off nonchalantly. I did not run, it would be too slow, I traveled to the sitting room that I hoped he was in. He was and so was Ash. Ash had been separating himself from the group for god knows whatever reason and has now been keeping Fluvis company.

Fluvis eyes sought mine and he stiffened when he saw the panic that laced my face.

"Two years," I said slowly, watching his face. "She

asked me if two years rang any bells."

"Two years?" Ash echoed from his seat. He had been stationed in front of Fluvis, and they were playing a game of cards. I saw Fluvis's face falter and I was brought back to the day she died; I was destroying the castle. Ash was grieving by himself during that time so he did not see the outburst, but I watched as he connected two and two together.

*She was there for two years! And I let her rot in there!*
*You didn't mean—*
*I LET her rot. I didn't look for her!*

"What was her facial expression like when she asked you?" Fluvis asked.

"Confusion."

"I would try to explain to her before her memories get to her first. I am not sure what made her ask that question but once she figures it out…" his voice trailed and he looked back at his deck of cards.

Fluvis was mad at me too once upon a time. He never gave up searching but I did long ago. If not for Spiris, I would have never even known she had been taken. Ash was different, he tried to support me, but I saw that she left, he wanted to find her right away… it was I who convinced him not to.

"Tonight, after dinner I will tell her." My voice was unsure but before I could look back at the two, I left and waited for dinner in the inn dining room.

It was not long before the others came to join me. Callum, Claire, and Felix were the first. Even when they had free range of the city and their services were not needed, they never strayed far and always banded together. Images of their hound forms curled up next to each other flitted through my mind. Ash even then was seen as a leader of them; even if no one had decreed it, they all followed him. Ash and Fluvis joined not too much later. They both looked at the empty seat next to me and back up to me. I shrugged trying not to show them how on edge I was. Felix was watching me. I could feel his gaze and it only made me more on edge, he was always so damn quiet.

"Sorry, I was too into the book," Iniq said while entering the room, showing us the book she held in her hand. She sat down just as the food was placed in front of us and we all began eating slowly. Callum and Claire both settled into easy conversation with Ash piping in every now and then, but everyone else stayed silent and I kept my eyes trained on Iniq.

"Your leg is bouncing," she noted, and I made it stop immediately. "I didn't know you do that."

"Habit," I explained and took a drink of my water. I felt her eyes burn holes into the side of my face as I did.

"Are you anxious about something?" she mused, her voice nowhere near accusatory, but I felt the words stab through me. Yes, I was terrified of something. I met her eyes and all I could think about was throwing myself to my knees in front of her and begging for her forgiveness. Begging her to forgive those two years I neglected her and explaining that I couldn't bear to lose her again. I saw her eyes search my face and slowly I saw her make the connections. "Two years."

I couldn't stop my eyes from widening. That fast? She remembered that fast?

# Chapter Forty-Seven

### Iniq

*She remembered that fast?*

No, Cruor. I didn't remember that fast. I was suspicious ever since she had left me that afternoon after I had asked her what the door had told me.

While I was reading, the door came to me again. It taunted me by asking me if it wanted to help me remember something. I managed to nod when Cruor was reading and not watching me, and it told me to ask her about two years and enjoy the show. Nothing else just… two years. It goaded me to take a look in her mind, but I didn't want to until I saw how on edge she was.

I didn't remember until I saw her in her mind. I saw her begging me to forgive her, trying to explain why she did not search for me those two years. I saw Spiris coming to see me in the middle of the night and almost getting killed for it—even then he was the one that had tried to get her out. He was the one to reach out to Cruor to come get me. When she… didn't even try.

"Oh…" It came out of my mouth before I could stop it. I saw her in her mind with other women, she was drunk and cursing at me for leaving her. "You lied."

*"It wasn't my fault we never finished the ceremony," she slurred*

*towards the half-naked woman.*

*She took another swig of alcohol and the nearest giggling woman towards her. It was not long before the door burst open showing an enraged Fluvis. He stalked over to her, picked her up by her shirt, and slapped her across the face with a resounding CRACK.*

*Drunken Cruor was so unphased by it that she started laughing.*

"You told me you didn't remember."

"I didn't know how to tell you," she tried to explain, but I held up my hand to silence her.

*I am going to lose her again. She was so close to resembling just a small amount of the old Iniq and I ruined it.*

Yes, you did Cruor.

"Do you want to know what I was doing in those two years?" My voice was dark, and I felt the familiar tick of my lips and pounding in my chest, there was no more pretending. I sent a silent apology to Spiris.

I felt guilt crash into her again, and I was so tired of it that I pulled out of her mind and rested my head on my hand. I felt disappointment fill me. The High Kings left me without vital memories only to bring them up when I was just beginning to settle and form relationships here. I was even the tiniest bit excited to see what I had seen before when I was with Cruor in my last life and build on it here, but not after seeing her reaction to me being taken and tortured. Another memory of Spiris filled my mind.

*If you had only been fully mated, she would have been able to find you by now.*

*Please, let's not talk about her.*

*It's been a year, Iniq. How could she let you go through all this pain?*

*She doesn't know.*

Oh, Spiris. I felt my magic spike around me and felt it spill out of my skin, but my eyes were still locked onto Cruor's wide ones.

"Spiris was the only reason you came to save me," I started. "If he never came to you, you would have been content on drinking yourself to a stupor and *fucking* anything with a vagina."

"Don't you talk to her like that." It was Callum that spoke, but he made no move to get up and fight me.

"It's well deserved," Cruor spoke softly her eyes remaining fixed on mine. "I messed up. I thought you left me—"

"After six hundred years," I piped in.

"Yes, I thought you left me after six hundred years because I refused to go through the mating ceremony with you. You have to understand Iniq, we were fighting—"

"No, Cruor, you understand." I stood up and walked as close to Cruor as I could, her face almost touching my breasts. I put my hands on either side of her face, caressing it like a lover would. "I think I should show you. Actually, maybe *everyone* should see." My magic flared out again and I shot Cruor a smile. "Could your demon magic help with that?" I purred at her, running my thumb across her quivering lips.

"Iniq I don't think—" It was Fluvis that spoke up, but I silenced him with a look.

"You can do it without her help," Ash spoke softly. "You've done it before… with your power, you connect our minds and project your thoughts." I did not smile at him, only nodded and did as he said, extending my magic to each one of their minds. I tried to drown out the thoughts of anger and panic and solely pushed select memories to them.

I started with Vitos torturing me. I made sure they felt the pain I went through, and they got a good look at his face when he caused it. There were hundreds of these memories, and I made sure to go through each and every one of them painstakingly slow.

"Stop." Cruor's eyes met mine and I saw tears welling up in them.

"We didn't even get to the best part," I purred at her,

running my hands through her hair. I felt all their emotions and I felt satisfaction bubble up in me. This was power. This is what it meant to be powerful.

I showed them how many times Spiris sat by me, bandaging me up while crying with me. I showed them how I looked when I saw myself in the mirror when Flayke was able to dress me up. I showed them the times in the meadow where Spiris longed to fix the ugly scars on my body, showed them Flayke's sad smile and tearful gaze as she told me I was beautiful.

I had debated leaving the next one out, but I felt my adrenaline sore as I heard their reactions and disgust throughout their minds. I pushed the memory of Baecos and I after I found out who he was. I showed them how I obeyed him. I showed them how I got Spiris free. I showed them how much more violent he got after he knew he didn't have to hide anymore. How he left me bleeding and delirious, how he used his magic as a drug.

"I beg you, please," Cruor was freely crying now.

Last but not least, I showed them what it looked and felt like to see Spiris's head being cut off.

I pulled back from their minds but kept my hold on Cruor's face.

"You let me thank you. You let me feel bad when I told you I never wanted anything to do with you." I let my hand run through her hair, it was just as soft as my dream. "I will never feel bad for it ever again. I thank you for risking your life this time, but I will *never* forgive you for leaving me there to rot."

No-one stopped me as I left the inn and walked down the streets. I didn't know where I was going but I knew if I stopped, I would just do back and destroy every living thing in that house. Gone was the numbness and sadness that filled me, now all that was left was pure rage, but somehow even that felt muted. I imagined the rage I would feel once I finally got my memories back; I could just feel the satisfaction radiating off the door.

It was not long before someone came to find me. Twenty minutes to be exact. I found a quiet rock near the river and so close to the forest that I felt the magic barrier vibrate next to me; it was a reminder to myself. A reminder that I could leave at any time. Maybe Baecos would find me but I could leave anyway, and that was a choice that I made consciously.

"It's not safe to be so close to the barrier." Fluvis's voice broke my musing, his hands were buried in his pockets as he walked over to me giving off a nonchalant attitude. He was the least kingly-looking person I had seen.

"Not like it matters," I muttered and tried to refrain from throwing a rock at his head.

He did nothing, I reminded myself. He tried to find me, he actually cared.

"I'm sorry you went through all that." Fluvis sat on the ground next to me placing his hand on my back.

"Me too," I answered simply and shrugged his hand off.

"I've seen both of you grow up. Losing you was like losing a daughter. Once I found out it was Baecos who took you, I was about to wage war on his entire kingdom." He lifted his head up to look at the star-filled sky. His red eyes filled with emotion.

"But you didn't."

"No, I did not. I tried to get close enough to get him to let me in his court." His eyes drifted to mine again. "It worked too late."

"When did she find out?"

"When I did." I felt a sliver of hurt run through me. "But she took your magic intertwined with his as a ... different meaning."

"I saw her at the end." The only time she was desperately fighting for me. It was stupid of her. If her reasoning were that she was waiting to become more powerful or even that she knew she was unmatched, I would understand. But the problems lie with the fact that she didn't even think before my end that I was worth looking for.

"Yes, Spiris came to us before your death. He said that he was afraid that you weren't going to make it much longer. It was risky for him to come—we did not know who's side he was on. Imagine my surprise when an inner court member of his showed up screaming at the border of the Fire Kingdom. He woke the whole city that night." It was hard to hold in my tears at the thought of Spiris doing that. "True to his word, you were gone the next day. We waited for any sign that you were to return but it was hard to get to you before Baecos did. He always seemed to find you… Cruor really beat herself up those years and her kingdom suffered greatly."

"Don't ask me to forgive her." Fluvis shook his head and gave me a small smile.

"If anything, I thought she deserved a few punches, you let her off easy." I let out a bitter laugh. "I just want you to understand. You deserve some type of explanation. Up until now, your whole life everyone has treated you as someone who is obligated to serve them. It's time that people realize that you are much more than someone to be ordered around. This tore you down in your last life, and I will be damned if it tears you down in this one." He squeezed my hand softly. "You do not owe anyone here anything. You need to live for you and only you. You get to decide what you want to do with your life and how you want to do it, even if that means spending it without Cruor."

His words stirred an emotion I didn't quite understand. I see now just how much of a protector he really was. It was in his voice, his eyes, the way he smiles at you. He's been here the whole time silently watching, observing as I live here. The anger, the worry, the sadness, even the shame, he let me feel it without once stepping in. He's letting me live.

"What about the mate issue?" Thinking of being tied to Cruor my entire existence made my stomach twist.

"What about it? Even in this world mating bonds can be broken if you truly desire." The snort he let out was woefully uncharacteristic and I felt a smile tug at my lips.

"And if I choose to go back to the human world?"

"Will you be happy there?"

The answer was a resounding no. I couldn't imagine going back to my parent's house and living on as if I never learned anything about this place. It wasn't even the place that made me wary of going back, it's the loneliness and darkness that seemed to live there.

"I don't know if I would be happy here either," I admitted.

"The door is always another option." His eyes twinkled in the moonlight.

He didn't bother me with anything else after that, he just accompanied me as I watched the stars. I really didn't need to think that hard, the decision was easy.

"It's getting late," Fluvis commented getting up slowly. I was about to do the same but froze when I heard a voice come from behind us.

"You seem even more miserable here than when you were with me." I didn't have to turn around to know it was Baecos's voice. Fluvis wasted no time, he flared out his magic, and I struggled not to fidget against the strength of it.

We both turned around to face him. Fluvis put an arm out in front of me and slowly backed us up until we were at least twenty feet away from Baecos. His violet eyes shone in the moonlight and his mouth was set in his signature smirk. I narrowed my eyes at him, but it only seemed to amuse him. The only thing that brought me relief is that I no longer felt my magic intertwined with his.

Baecos's eyes never left mine, even as we felt the magical signatures of Cruor and the hounds approach us. As we waited for them, I let every scenario run through my head. I wanted to hurt him and cause him pain, I tried to draw from that. But looking at him now, I still felt my knees shake and my hands become unsteady.

"I just wanted to chat," Baecos drawled while his eyes roamed my body. "You didn't have to call for reinforcements." His eyes shifted to Fluvis for only a split second and then they were back to mine.

"You are not welcome here," Cruor hissed and rested her hand protectively on my shoulder. I shrugged it off and shifted closer to Fluvis. Baecos's eyes caught the motion and a bigger smirk tugged at his lips.

"Yes, the barrier makes that very obvious." Baecos reached his hand out but as soon as he laid it on the barrier, it shimmered and stopped his hand's descent.

Vitos decided to walk out from their cover of the forest and stand by his king. His eyes were hallowed now and there was purple smudged underneath them. There was no malice or excitement in his face, only a stand-alone scowl and emotionless eyes. I felt a pang of hurt fill me; I could have easily mistaken him for Spiris at this point. His eyes shifted to mine and then quickly back to Baecos. Ash in his hound form brushed up close to my side, conveniently putting himself between me and Cruor. I didn't stop myself from running my fingers through his fur, his move was deliberate, and I appreciated him for that.

"What do you want?" I spoke to Baecos.

"I wanted to check on you, of course." He tried to take a step forward closer to the barrier, but the hounds growled. "Easy. It looks like there is trouble in paradise... wanted to see if you have come to your sense and will return to our kingdom."

*Our kingdom.* I scoffed at him. It was a ploy.

"Do you even hear yourself, Baecos?" Fluvis growled at him. Baecos's eyes traveled to him and he gave him a small smile.

"And here I thought I could trust you, Fluvis. Didn't know you were on Cruor's side."

"I've been on Iniq's since day one." Even on the other side of Ash, I could feel Cruor flinch.

"There is no way I would return to your hell hole of a kingdom. You are a sick monster and you killed Spiris, it just shows how insane you are to even think that I would listen to you." His eyes traveled to mine and he gave me a shit eating grin. Vitos stared at the ground and I could have sworn his eyes widened when I mentioned Spiris.

"Why doesn't being next to Cruor bother you so? Or maybe it does seeing how you react to her." He let out a laugh, Vitos did not join him.

"She did not murder Spiris in cold blood," I spat. I felt my magic burn hot under my skin. Baecos's eyes flitted to Cruor and he lifted a brow at her. He was goading her, daring her to say something.

"But she is just as responsible." Baecos's eyes came right back to mine. "Do you really think someone as powerful as her couldn't steal you from my kingdom?"

I froze. I didn't want to think about how Cruor failed me yet again.

"It doesn't matt—" My voice was cut off by Baecos.

"It does matter." Baecos put both of his hands on the barrier causing it to light up the area he touched. I watched as his hands became red and I heard sizzling in the air. "Even before you came, she entered my kingdom hundreds of times. When you were there, she had the chance to take you multiple times. She could have just walked right in, in fact… she did. While you were in your room—none the wiser—she was already inside the mansion. How could you stand next to someone who didn't even take the chance to save you when she could? No, she waited until Spiris dragged you out of the house, and even then when you were so close to escaping, she never re-entered the grounds. She waited outside."

I felt bile rise in my throat and my head spin. I had to lean on Ash in order to stay upright. She could have saved him.

"What is your real reason for coming here?" Cruor's voice came through gritted teeth.

"I come to make a deal. Iniq, come back with me and I will leave the Water and Fire Kingdom alone." I scoffed at his audacity.

"And if I don't?"

"Then we will start with her kingdom." He conjured a sword and pointed it towards Cruor. "Yours is the weakest, is it not? They have been suffering more than anyone because of the number of magic refugees they take."

"Threatening our kingdoms will not do you any good, Iniq will stay with us," Fluvis responded before I could say anything.

"Come, Iniq." Baecos's voice wafted through the air and it seemed to carry some magic with it. "You know that your life is not worth the cost of two kingdoms." I flinched but didn't move.

"Has it maybe occurred to you that I don't give a damn?" My hand clenched on the fur of the hound and I forced myself to look Baecos straight in the eyes.

"I think you do, more than you let on." His voice sounded desperate. I watched as he shifted his stance.

"I don't." Fluvis also shifted besides me. "Whatever you are playing at is not working. I will not come with you nor will I be staying here. My magic will forever be out of your reach and there will be nothing you can do about it."

Baecos let out a growl and hit the barrier with his fist; it did not budge.

"If you go back to the human world, I will find you."

He hit the barrier again and bared his teeth at me.

"No one said anything about the human world." My voice was clipped. I turned my back to him, walking back toward the inn.

"This talk is over. Don't visit again unless it is for your execution," Cruor growled, and her and Fluvis followed me back. The hounds stayed to watch after him as we left.

When we made it back into the sitting room, both Fluvis and Cruor jumped into plans of action. They spread a map on the table and listed out possible areas he could attack.

"Did his voice not affect you at all tonight?" Fluvis asked. I shook my head at him.

"It did before," Cruor paused. "Maybe it's the faerie venom." I highly doubted it. I would have liked to believe it was my own resolve that strengthened it. Or maybe there was just no light in me to be exploited anymore.

"If I leave, won't he lose the will to attack your kingdoms?" There was silence after my question.

"He is a sore loser." Ash and the others came in now in fresh clothes. I imagined the face of the innkeeper when they all walked through the door naked and couldn't help but smile. "He does everything for revenge."

"She can work around his voice now," Cruor mumbled.

"If she were to get her powers back, she could probably kill him," Callum huffed and sat down on the floor.

"How do I get the rest of my powers back?" I asked.

"You can't be actually thinking of fighting him?" Claire's snide voice was the only indicator that anyone even heard me.

"Why not?" I asked raising my eyebrows at her. "He killed my only friend and tortured me—I have reason enough to want him dead."

"The only options are breaking your seal… or begging the High Kings for your powers back," Cruor sighed and fisted a hand through her hair.

"If I beg for magic back, will it make Baecos more powerful?" I asked, walking over to where Fluvis and Cruor stood. My fingers brushed across the map they were looking at pausing when it reached the Light Kingdom.

"It may," Fluvis spoke, and his hand rested on top of mine. "But if you go through that door, there is an even bigger chance that when you come back, it is you who will become more powerful."

"Don't encourage her," Cruor grumbled. I gritted my teeth as she spoke. My hand twitched under Fluvis's and his response was to put more pressure on it. I wanted to let my anger out on her so bad I couldn't think straight.

"Why are you so afraid of me going to the other side?" I hissed at her, pulling my hand away from Fluvis's and crossed my arms.

"We just got you back, Iniq." Her own hands balled into fists and her frenzied eyes met mine. "We can't just let you go off into an unknown world. We have no idea what will happen to you there."

"You can't *let* me?" I took a step closer to her. "You don't *let* me do anything. I am my own person, and you don't get a say in what I choose for myself."

"Let's give them some privacy," Ash grumbled and started to usher everyone out.

"Why are you doing this?" her voice barely above a whisper. She tried to bring a hand up to cup my face but I smacked it away.

"I am choosing a path for myself." I leaned against the table creating a small distance between us.

"You are doing this because you are angry at me." Cruor took another step towards. "I want to be able to spend my life with you as we once were. I am sorry for not trying as hard as I should have before, but I won't let that happen again." Her eyes were pleading. She believed it was still possible. She was deluding herself.

"Was what he said true?" Cruor's eyes left mine at that point. "Did you have a chance to get us out of there alive?"

"I always had to choose between you two," she explained, grabbed my hand without looking at me. Her eyes were locked on my fingers as we spoke; she rubbed her thumb across each of them. "There was never a moment where I could have saved both of you, and I knew that if I saved you and not Spiris, he would die. If I saved him and not you, you would... not quite die, but you understand what would have happened." She shuddered softly.

"I don't believe that there was no other way. Ash, Claire, Callum, Felix, even Fluvis could have helped." Her hand squeezed mine, she refused to look at me.

"The possibility of them dying was too high, I couldn't lead my people to that." I gritted my teeth and pulled my hand away from her harshly.

"Instead, you had two innocent people killed," I hissed at her and started walking toward the door. She did not stop me. Before I left, I turned my head to the side so she could hear me. "You're a fucking coward," I spat and walked down the dark hallway towards my room.

The door was already there waiting for me. I could feel its power radiating out into the hallway before I even opened the door. I sighed and went in to face it—it was already open.

*It's time...*

The same voice floated through the room as I entered, I paid no mind to it and laid on the bed. The door stayed in the same spot.

"What is your goal?" I asked towards it.

*Make you remember, make you feel, make you strong.*

"Making me remember how my mate left me to die is not the way to do that," I grumbled and spared a glance towards the door. The black tendrils were reaching out to me again. I felt the pull but ignored it.

*You made your choice because of these feelings, don't underestimate them.*

I snorted. "My choice was only to get that psychopath away from me, don't get your hopes up."

*Are you sure about that? I can feel your resolve.*

I turned toward the window in this room and stared at the stars shining in the black sky. The door was right, unfortunately. I decided to live this life how I wanted to, doing the things that I wanted to do, and the curiosity I had about life beyond the door was too strong for me to stay here.

"I am not leaving yet."

*Stupid girl. While some emotions make you strong, others make you weak. It would be a disappointment if the weak ones won.*

The door was gone in an instant.

# Chapter Forty-Eight

## Iniq

My next few nights were filled with images of Baecos killing Spiris and Flayke over and over again. Sometimes Vitos was there to help, other times he was just stood at the side, watching. Each time seemed to get more gruesome than the last; it went from simple killing to straight-out torture that I had to watch. And each night I awoke in a cold sweat from these dreams, the door always there waiting for me. It refrained from speaking to me, but it just stood there wide open, inviting me to just walk inside.

Sometimes I stared at the door when I couldn't sleep. I watched as the shadows moved inside it and the tendril reach out to caress my skin. At times it was hard to tell if the shadows behind there were figments of my imagination making shapes through the darkness, or if it was a person walking through the darkness. I had yet to decide when I was going to venture to the other side. If I was being honest with myself, even though my heart still pounded with excitement, I felt a sliver of fear rise in me. What if going through the door was a trap? What if I was still being lied to? What if this was just another way to sacrifice myself for this world?

*It would be a disappointment if the weak ones won.*

I shivered and got out of my bed to start the day.

The last few days I have been carefully avoiding Cruor, but she still tried her best to strike up conversations with me and get close to me again. She promised to take me anywhere I wanted, each time she promised it to be more exciting than the last.

"Cave diving."

"No"

"Wendigo hunting."

"No."

"What if I told you that Fluvis could help us breathe underwater?"

"No."

She was trying to appeal to my better nature, the one that got excited. She knew that I couldn't resist the unknown, couldn't resist the excitement I got from danger.

"There is a mirror that shows your future," Cruor said excitedly at breakfast that morning.

"Cruor," Fluvis warned her. I raised an eyebrow at him, but he gave me a pointed look.

"I know where it is," she continued, brushing off Fluvis's warnings.

"Ya, in a sea cave filled with magical creatures waiting to chomp your head off," Felix interjected, biting off a piece of his breakfast roll. I wondered briefly if that is how his scars came to be.

"Sounds fun, right?" Cruor's eyes sparkled as she waited for my reaction.

It did actually. Really fun.

"It was charmed by the High Kings when they were back in this realm," Ash spoke. "They liked to leave hidden gems across this realm for only the extraordinary to find. Kind of like a test."

At the mention of the High Kings, my mood dampened significantly.

"No, I don't want my face to look like Felix's," I responded, and I heard a collective sigh of relief come from those around me and a few giggles at Felix's expense.

"Your walks with Ash can't be *that* entertaining," Claire's hard voice cut through the air. She and Callum were still pissed at what I had done to them and how I treated Cruor.

"You could come next time," I purred and made my magic reach out to her just enough for her to feel it caress her face. "I can show you how entertaining it could be." Felix let out a growl and I chuckled. I retracted my magic and waved him off. Claire's face was left considerably paler than before.

Cruor refused to speak; she just silently ate her food.

Ash and I did take to going on walks but that's not all we did, he turned out to be a proficient enough sparring partner that meant days were not filled with boredom. It also helped me blow off some steam. Many days after the nightmares and goading from the door, I felt as though I would have burst.

"You should just talk to her." Ash ducked as my leg came soaring towards his face.

"I refuse." His hand darted out and snapped it towards him making me lose balance and fall on my back. The air was knocked out of me, but I was able to roll away from his fist before it came down to crush my face. I let out a laugh and landed a kick right on his face. He let out a string of curses and traveled away leaving a small wisp of smoke in his wake.

"Did you have another nightmare last night?" His voice came from behind me. I let a smile show on my face, I was getting used to his signature. The first time he traveled I couldn't figure where he would show, but now I was getting the hang of it.

I threw my elbow back but he caught it with his hand.

"No," I lied through gritted teeth. Instead of hitting me like I assumed he would, his strong arm wrapped around my waist and rested his chin on top of my head. He was hugging me I realized.

"You don't have to keep it from me." I relaxed slightly in his grip and allowed the gesture but did not return it. "Even if I couldn't see the obvious bags under your eyes… we hear your screams."

I sighed and patted his arm as he detangled himself from me. "It's not something for you to worry about." I didn't return to fight. Instead, I sat down on the grass in the middle of the clearing we were in. I tried not to let familiar memories pop up to pain me, instead, I focused on the clouds above and the breeze that flowed through the trees.

"I have nightmares too sometimes," he admitted, folding his hands behind his head and laying down beside me. I remained silent. "We were in the war together, it was gruesome."

"I don't remember any of it." There was no pain when I said this, just cold hard truth.

He nodded. "That's probably for the best." His eyes lazily caught mine and he gave me a sad smile. "You were ruthless back then." He closed his eyes like he was imagining it again.

"I hope it's not me that fills your nightmares." His eyes didn't open nor did he stir.

"My nightmares are filled with people crying and begging for me to spare them. I do not regret the killing I had to do for my kingdom," *and you*—he didn't say it, but I heard it. "But the ones that begged me… those hurt."

I nodded at him. I urged to reach my magic out to his mind; I wanted to see what plagued him, I wanted to understand more. And there was a small amount of hope that ran through me, hope that maybe his nightmares were so horrible that if I saw them, I would forget my own.

"It's Spiris and Flayke… dying, over and over again." I

laid down on the grass beside him, still watching the clouds float across the sky. "I never get a chance to save them and the nightmares are getting more and more horrible. They scream my name and scream for me to save them but every time I can't."

He didn't speak as the words tumbled out of me. I couldn't stop myself nor could I stay calm as I spoke. My heart sped up and my chest felt heavy; it became harder to breathe. "I wish for just a small break from seeing their faces, any other nightmare is welcome at this point. I am so close to begging the door to just reside in my dreams. I would face whatever lies in the darkness there if I could just get away from their faces. I don't care if I must relive everything else that I went through, even if it was Baecos. It's not fair." My voice broke and I felt on the verge of tears. "It's not fair that I get to live so many lives and because they believed in me, they could only live one very short one. Because of me, their lives were cut short. All Spiris wanted to do is live a life away from the Light Kingdom, live a normal life. He didn't want anything else, he just wanted to be happy."

"It's not your fault," he said softly. I wiped my eyes as I felt tears fall down my face.

"Everything broken in this world is my fault," I pushed back. "If I had gone through the door in my previous life, none of this would happen."

"The door refused you last time." His hand brushed across mine. "The High Kings did not allow you through last time, so even if you wanted to you couldn't."

"Why?"

"No one knows, it's not like they ever explained it to us." He snorted but his hand made soothing patterns in my palm.

*It would be a disappointment if the weak ones won.*

"I will leave soon." I felt him look at me, but I didn't

meet his stare. "You have been… nicer to me, I thought you deserved a heads up."

"What's stopping you from leaving right now?" His hand squeezed mine, I did not pull away.

"Fear," I admitted.

My chest felt lighter after talking to Ash, while he was in Cruor's guard, I knew that he was the closest to me in the last life.

Dinner was uneventful, at least no one tried to fight anyone, but Cruor was uncharacteristically quiet. There were no promises of mysterious adventures, no side glances, she didn't even talk to anyone. She just sat there and silently finished her food. She was the first to dismiss herself, mumbling something about not feeling well.

"You should go talk to her," Claire spoke up after a moment of silence. Ash shot her a look, but she ignored him.

"You should go if you are so worried about her." I pushed my plate away and made my way up to my own room.

When I opened my door, I was surprised to see a figure sitting on my bed.

"I thought you were not feeling well," I remarked and closed the door behind me, but I made no move to move further into the room.

"I wanted to talk." Cruor's voice was soft as she spoke. She walked towards me slowly as if she were afraid to scare me off. She stopped only a few feet away from me.

"There is nothing to talk about." My hand was still on the doorknob. I turned it, prepared to open the door, but she put her hand next to my head effectively pushing the door back and making it so the door couldn't open. The move brought her face closer to mine. Her breath wafted across my face I could smell the alcohol from dinner on her breath.

"I'm sorry," she whispered, her eyes trailing down my

face to rest on my lips. "I can't explain how sorry I am and how regretful I am for the choices I've made. You're right, I am a coward. The biggest one I have ever seen. I don't deserve to be with you."

I swallowed loudly; I may have been mad at her but looking at her now, I felt emotion stir inside me. Maybe it was the weakness that the door was talking about but there was no denying how beautiful she was.

"As you should be." My voice was rougher than I expected.

"I know you feel for me somewhere in there." Her hand gripped my chin and she tilted my face back up to meet her gaze. "Am I wrong?" She leaned down, her lips close enough to mine that I felt them brush across my own.

"You are." She met my eyes again, her eyes darkened slightly.

"Then let me at least show you how sorry I am." Her lips met mine finally. It was light like a feather as she was waiting for me to pull back. Her hand moved from my chin to grip my throat softly. I felt my heart skip a beat as she did so, and her lips quirked against mine. She knew what that small gesture made me feel. "Will you let me?" She spoke against my lips and her body closed the rest of the space between us—there was no backing away now. I nodded weakly.

She attacked my mouth more forcefully now, using the grip on my neck to pull me harder against her. I met her kiss with little hesitation, her fangs nipped at my lips and her tongue found mine. One hand found its way to her waist and the other gripped her hair roughly. She let out a hiss of pain when I pulled too tightly, but instead of pulling away, her hands moved to my thighs and she picked me up in one motion and brought me to the bed.

Her lips left mine only to pause at the necklace that was still around my neck. It was the one she gifted me previously… even after the fight I had not taken it off. She paused but did not say anything, just moved her lips to the side of my neck and bit down softly, licking the same area. I shuddered as she did and grabbed onto her hair even tighter. She took that as a signal and bit down again but harder, I let out a small noise and she smiled against my neck. Her lips found my ear.

"Some things never change." Her voice was husky and left chills down my spine, and her fangs grazed my ear softly as she spoke. Her hands lifted my shirt and I helped her get it over my head. I heard her intake of breath when she was met with my bare chest, I didn't wear a bra today—the shirt and vest I wore while fighting were tight and thick enough to go without one. "As soon as you came downstairs tonight, I could not take my eyes off of these." Her face came down to my erect nipple and I watched as her tongue slowly reached out to flick it softly. I arched up for more contact, but she pulled back slightly.

"I thought you would show me how sorry you are," I growled at her, and she sent me a smile.

"I didn't know you were that impatient, but I guess if you would like to go faster, I can accommodate that." Her mouth found my nipple, biting softly and running her tongue across the sensitive flesh. I let out a moan and kicked off my shoes as I felt her play with the buttons on my pants. My pants were off in no time but instead of going straight in between my legs, her mouth left my nipple and she sat me up and kneeled between my legs.

Her hands teased my inner thighs, and she caught my eyes as she lowered her mouth back down to my other nipple. I tangled my hand in her hair and arched into her, her hands wandered and lit a fire under my skin as they did. Her hand easily found my aching core and I felt one long finger slide against the slick fold teasingly. I threw my head back at the feeling.

"You're already so wet," she growled against me and

pushed one finger slowly inside me. Her mouth was no longer on my nipple, but she was watching me as she entered me. Her eyes were hooded, and her breath was coming out uneven. She pulled out slowly and entered again; I shuddered but held her gaze. She gave me a devious smile and added another finger inside me, starting to pick up the pace.

I could no longer look at her as I felt my head spin at the feeling. I threw my head back and she used this to slam her hand back into me. I cried out and bucked against her hand. With her movements getting harder and faster, I fought to keep my composure. Her fingers were delicate but with every thrust, I felt myself tighten around her. Her mouth found my nipples again and it was not long before I felt myself go over the edge.

As she withdrew her fingers, she tried to push me back to the bed but I stopped her. "That's enough for tonight, you've proven your point." Her eyebrows pushed together and she met my gaze.

"There was no point to be proven," she said, but let me get up to put a nightgown on. "You seemed to enjoy it. I am not sure what the problem is." She got up and followed me to the closet but kept her distance.

"I don't have a problem," I lied and threw the silk cloth over my head. I turned to go back to the bed, but she stood in front of me. She grabbed my face and brought her lips roughly down to mine. I bit her bottom lip, but she just pushed me against the closet and deepened the kiss. Against my better judgment, I gripped her hips and pulled them closer to mine. Her fingers found my nipples again, playing with them and pinching them through the soft fabric.

"Why must you be so distant?" She pulled away from the kiss but now both hands were teasing my nipples and eliciting another moan out of me.

"You know why," I hissed. She lowered herself to her

knees and forced my leg over her shoulder. Her head disappeared under my nightgown but I soon felt her tongue against my aching wetness, already begging to be touched. She sucked softly on the bundle of nerves and her fingers entered me again. I threw my head back against the closet, ignoring the pain it caused. Just before I lost myself again, she pulled back and her face reappeared below me. The only difference now was the gleam of wetness against her lips.

"Give me a chance," she growled and entered another finger slowly. "Even if it is just to be a bed warmer. Let me give you that at least." The second one followed but didn't move, she was waiting for an answer.

"Don't expect much out of it," I hissed back, but my answer seemed to satiate her at that moment because her face disappeared back between my legs.

Needless to say, I didn't get much sleep that night.

# Chapter Forty-Nine

### Iniq

I am not sure if Ash had told Cruor my plans to leave, but she was back to her clingy self the next morning. In another lifetime I may have loved the attention, but in this one, with the door breathing down my neck, I only felt on edge.

I luckily did not dream last night, but the door was already waiting for me when I woke up.

*It would be a disappointment if the weak ones won.*

I wondered if the emotions they spoke of were my feelings for Cruor or my feelings of fear. I would not deny to myself that I did feel things towards Cruor, but they only went as deep as lust for right now. I still harbored a decent amount of anger towards her.

"What will you do today?" Cruor asked as she handed me my coffee over breakfast.

"I will be joining her and Ash on their walk," Claire spoke up, and the rest looked at her as if she were crazy. I only shrugged.

"I did say she could," I said and took a sip of my coffee allowing the warmth to spread across my body. Cruor's hand lingered on my thigh sending chills across my body.

***

True to her word, Claire joined us today. We refrained from taking her to the sparring area and instead went for an actual walk throughout the town. Ash was wary but he jumped into his normal cheerful mode and almost skipped down the streets.

"There is a lot of magic here," I stated as I felt the flowers that lined the river in the middle of the city. It had felt like so much more than compared to when I was in the Light Kingdom.

"Demon magic is not affected, and the king here is a demon, so it is much easier to keep the kingdom well," Ash spoke, plucking a flower and sliding it to rest on my ear. He ruffled my hair and sent me a smile. The familiar gesture made my mind go to a place I did not want it to go, and before I could stop it, I saw Spiris's lifeless head in my mind. I gritted my teeth against the feeling of regret that plowed into me.

"You need to decide what you want from Cruor," Claire spoke from behind me. I sighed. I knew she had a motive to come today.

"Don't start," Ash warned, giving her a small growl.

"It has to be said!" I turned to face her, and I saw her arms crossed against her chest. "Cruor has been bending over backward to make sure you are happy, but you are just using that to get what you want..." I looked down at the floor unable to meet her accusing gaze.

"What does it seem like I want?" I asked her. I let the venom seep through my voice and I saw her eyes widen. I stepped closer to her and I watched as she shrunk.

"We saw her leave your room this morning," she pushed, regaining some of her misplaced courage. "You need to stay away from her, someone like you doesn't deserve her."

I sent a smile towards her and she flinched. "What do you mean *someone like me?*"

"You're a cruel, cold-hearted murder. We all saw you on the battlefield before and I can see the same gleam in your eyes when you get excited. Cruor ignores it and only sees your pain, but we see how you act when she is not looking. Sooner or later, you will kill her as well." I flexed my hand, ready to pounce, but with a huff, she turned and stalked back towards the inn. I imagined myself running after her and finishing this fight, but Ash's voice interrupted my daydream.

"Let's go spar now that she's gone," he said abruptly as if he was also itching to let out some tension. I was still smiling when I faced him, he knew me too well.

****

The spar this afternoon was everything I needed and more, he even let me use some weapons. It lasted much longer than our other ones, but after we were done, we were both winded and I lost all urge to slam Claire's head into a wall.

After showering all the sweat and dirt off my skin, I dressed for dinner. As I walked down the hallway, I started to hear familiar voices talking in angry hushed tones. Pausing near a door I made sure to pull all my magic inward so that they would not feel it radiating off me, I made out a few voices, Claire, Callum, Felix, and I could feel Cruor's presence in the room with them.

"You have given too much to save her and this is how she repays you?" Claire's voice was hushed but angry.

"She's not the same person, Cruor." It was Callum who spoke this time. "Her time with Baecos and in the mortal world has changed her too much."

"If you went through the same thing, you would be

changed too." I was surprised to hear Felix's voice interrupting the bickering siblings.

"It doesn't matter what she went through, she does not care for us or the kingdom. She told Baecos as such, when she speaks, we should believe her," Claire pushed back. "We should just have done the same thing Baecos did, use her for the door." My heart dropped to my stomach.

"Watch your mouth," Felix growled at her.

I felt my anger rise as I felt Cruor just stand there silently. She really was a coward, I concluded.

"It's not a bad idea," Callum said, supporting his sister. "Let her open it, give her some use. Have her go beg for our world, all our problems would be solved the biggest one being what to do with her."

I couldn't stomach the conversation any longer without going into that room and letting it out on all parties there. I walked the rest of the way down the stairs and to the dining room. I felt the door invade my mind again; it was shadowed in the darkness of my mind but its presence unmistakable. It had a knack for stoking the fire, it must like these emotions.

*For this is your last.*

Fluvis and Ash were waiting for us, they smiled when I came down.

"How are you liking the kingdom so far?" Fluvis asked.

I forced a small smile. He did nothing wrong I reminded myself once again.

"It is beautiful and so lively. I am glad a safe haven like this still exists." Fluvis gave me a sad smile.

"Yes, not all places are as lucky as this one. The river helps a lot but there are some places in the kingdom that are void of magic."

"Iniq, there are many more places we can go," Ash spoke up and pushed some extra food onto my plate. "If you'd like, I can start taking us there."

"As long as it's not cave diving," I responded dryly. He and Fluvis both laughed at that.

The others came in not too long after. Cruor took her seat next to me and Felix, Claire, and Callum across from us. I was happy to see that Felix choose to sat directly across from me, the other glares were not lost on me and they only exacerbated my anger.

"How was your day, Iniq?" Cruor drew my attention away from the trio.

"It was nice. Ash and Claire took me to the river and then we tried some sweets. Very yummy Fluvis." I gestured to him across the table. "If I might add, it may be my favorite part of the city." He let out a laugh. It wasn't a lie… we did get sweets—after I beat the shit out of Ash. I saw him wince in the corner of my eye and knew that he was thinking along the same lines as me.

"Only you would find solace in food," he teased. I smiled and continued eating my food.

"Is that all that happened?" Cruor pried. I knew what she was getting at, and my eyes drifted up to Claire. She found her plate very interesting at that moment; I couldn't help but smile. The door's satisfaction was radiating off it. It wanted so badly for me to fight her, but I refrained.

I swallowed my food and cleared my throat. "Ash also seems to be quite the teacher, most of the time was him nonstop talking about the history of this land." Ash shifted uncomfortably. The rest were waiting for me to spill what happened. "Besides that, nothing else," I finished and pushed my half-empty plate forward indicating that I was done.

"That is not enough," Ash spoke up, but I waved my hand at him. I felt the door nag at my senses again. I looked towards the end of the dining room and saw it there in all its glory; it barely fit, and it was opening. I looked at the others and their eyes were all trained on me, they did not notice the door.

"Have you since been able to conjure the door?" Callum asked me. I shot a look over to him. Did he see it too? I watched him but his eyes never drifted towards it.

"Conjure…" I mused. "I wouldn't say conjure. It kind of just… shows up."

"Have you been to the other side?" Felix asks, his eyes sharp and unrelenting.

"I have seen inside only." My eyes trailed to Cruor's intense gaze. "Not any further. If I did, I would assure you that I would not be here by now."

"Why not?" Callum's grip on his fork was tight.

*Give her some use.*

"You have been quiet, Cruor," I remarked and drank the water in front of me.

"I am curious as well. Why did you not go to the other side?" I shifted my glance to her. She didn't speak last time because she also believed I should be of some use to them. My anger flared when she didn't try to change the subject.

"When I tried to reach the other side last time, I was bound to a stone table and having a knife dragged across my skin for hours. It's not that I didn't want to, it's that I couldn't." My voice was harsh, but their question was getting on my nerves. I tried to be nice for Fluvis, but I couldn't. Cruor reached out to touch my arm, but I slapped her hand away.

"Don't you—" Claire shot up making her chair fall back behind her. I felt my magic raise inside me; I was ready to fight her. She blanched at the change in atmosphere.

"It's 'cause you're a coward," Callum spoke up, his gaze unafraid. "I doubt that was your only chance. You didn't go through the door because you are afraid that it will not let you in anymore, just like last time. That's why you ran away… because you were rejected by the door and Cruor. You led yourself to your own death."

A growl ripped through me and I crossed the table,

grabbing Callum's neck faster than he could blink. Before anyone could stop me, I had a magical dagger to his throat and his back up against the wall. While his form towered above mine, I had the upper hand now. I pushed hateful magic towards him and watched as he paled, his eyes widened with fear.

"Don't you talk about things you don't understand."

"The only one who doesn't remember last time is you," he snarled. "It's you who has yet to understand that the only one you have to blame is yourself."

I could kill him right now; my dagger was pointed right at his neck. I watched as his pulse beat through his skin.

"You would regret killing him," Fluvis spoke, breaking the tension. "I would also hate to have to pay to clean the blood."

He almost made me laugh with his comment. I sighed and stepped away from him.

"You are all so eager to see me leave, I might as well obey. Tomorrow." I threw my dagger down on the table close to Claire's hand, she jumped with a yelp. "I was planning on staying a few more days, but if you insist, I will leave tomorrow. But do not expect me to beg for any of your pathetic people." My eyes drifted to Ash and Fluvis, they were not angered or surprised. Fluvis sent me a quick nod and Ash forced a smile towards me.

I left without another glance towards the others. The door did not follow me as I made my way out into the town. Fluvis seemed to love his inn and the last thing that I wanted to do is destroy it and some of the innocent people in it.

# Chapter Fifty

### Iniq

A cold hand clamped down on my mouth to stop the scream that was bubbling in my throat. Another one snaked around my waist and pulled me closer to them; the form was unmistakably male.

"Don't scream if you know what's good for you," Callum's voice rung out through the quiet night. My mind flashed to when Baecos's arms would hold onto me. I felt sour liquid fill my mouth and panic rise within me. I focused on covering my body in magic and pushing it out in spikes. Callum cursed and jumped away from my body. I turned quickly and readied my stance.

Callum did the same. He was in the same clothes as earlier meaning that he had to have followed me shortly after my outburst.

"What do you think you are doing?" I spat and conjured my bow and arrow. The weight was familiar in my hands, but it had been a while since I felt the urge to use it so strongly.

*You will regret killing him.*

At least I could say that I wouldn't ruin the inn now.

"You really didn't think he had people on the inside?" Callum gave out a humorless laugh.

"Cruor will not be happy to hear this." I fired an arrow

at him, but he dodged it easily. Even though this body was slightly healed, I still felt the effects of the torture Baecos had put me through.

"We are doing this for her. To save her from you. She is not as strong as she once was because of *you*."

I felt a magical signature behind me too late, I was hit with magic so strong that I flew forward, and my shaky hands failed to catch me as I went down.

"Let's hurry this up," Claire spoke up.

I shouldn't be surprised really. It was obvious they both hated me. A laugh bubbled up in my chest and before I could stop it, it came out of my mouth. Even without looking at them, I knew they froze. I pushed myself up on shaking arms and pooled my magic within me. Instead of the small tingling sensation, I was left with previously, this new one felt like it was vibrating violently beneath my skin. It was begging to be let out, trying to claw itself to the surface.

"You fucking freak." Callum came close to my form to try and wind his leg out to kick me, but my magic blasted out to catch the offending limb. This magic was no longer the dark sparkly magic that I had been so in awe of, no… this one was pure black, and I had a feeling it hurt like a bitch. With the flick of my wrist, I heard a sickening crack and Callum fell back onto his back, his leg now bent at an odd angle. I felt his and Claire's magic grow but I knew it was minuscule to what was filling me.

"Baecos really picked the fucking weak ones huh?" I asked and turned towards Claire; she was scared now, shaking like a leaf.

Claire shifted into her hound form and suddenly lunged at me. Instead of running away, I opened my arms as if I were to hug her and gave her a winning smile. My magic wrapped around her form and stopped her from moving, the darkness seemingly wrapping around her like a blanket,

She yelped, and her brother screamed for her. I came up to her and wrapped my arms around her neck feeling her soft fur around her face. My magic purred around us; it loved what I was doing. Her attitude towards me earlier flashed through my mind. I guess I could finish the fight now and leaving her alive would guarantee me a one-way ticket back to Baecos. I imagined Cruor's face if I told her they betrayed her. I wondered who she would believe.

"You know I have to kill you, right?" I hummed. Her brother tried to throw magic at me, but it didn't break my shield, "I would have no guilt about it. I have been holding back, you know. I dream about killing people like you." I squeezed tightly and heard some small pops in her neck.

"Please stop, I'll do anything!" Callum's voice was but a small annoying fly.

I felt the magical signatures of the others come towards us. I sighed, there was no pretending now.

"Let her go, Iniq," Cruor's voice rang out. I refused to look up at them.

"For both our sakes, I hope you do not get reincarnated." I forced my magic to crush the rest of her neck and spine. The only sound she made was an exhalation of the scream that was caught in her throat, and by then it was nothing more than a whisper. I let her dead body drop to the ground with a thud.

It took all but a second for Felix to launch at me, and I let him… but that was a mistake. I was too close to the barrier and in a second I was thrown out of it with his hound form still on top of me, baring his teeth at me. This one was smart. I didn't want to kill him, so instead, I forced my magic out and sent him flying back into the border.

"Maybe letting them take you was a good thing." Baecos's voice was behind me suddenly. I scrambled up and sent my magic flying at him, but he was much stronger than the others. Instead of pushing him away like it did with Felix, he just smiled at my attempts.

The high that my magic gave me while I was killing Claire was not gone. From my toes to my head, I felt an icy panic slowly make its way through me and made the magic I was using again Baecos falter.

"Don't you fucking touch me," I hissed and conjured another bow and arrow and fired straight at his chest. He easily sidestepped it and it hit the tree behind him. He took a step forward showing me that my magic had nothing on him.

I looked back inside the barrier. Felix and Callum were over Claire's dead body and the others stood still. Cruor met my eyes, and, at that moment, I knew that I was screwed. Her face showed how hurt she was by what I had just done. No matter what she had done to my past self, she would not hold a candle to what I had just done to her. Whatever feelings she held for my previous self were gone. Or at least now she had finally realized that I was just an imposter. A shell of what Iniq had been. My eyes moved to Ash and then Fluvis. Fluvis stepped around the others as if he were to come to my aid but Cruor's growl stopped him.

"If you go to her, our kingdoms will be at war." She was armed as well but I knew that it wasn't for Baecos.

"Cruor, that's too rash." Fluvis voice was appalled but I didn't miss how his eyes drifted towards Claire's body.

"She killed one of my guards," she hissed back at him. "She deserves whatever is coming."

No one deserved what Baecos would do. My own eyes drifted towards Claire's body. There was no regret when I looked at her, instead just numbness. At least I did not prolong her suffering, it was a clean and quick death. I was still angry at her words and actions, and if anyone seriously challenged me, it should be my right to do what I pleased to them. Now Baecos on the other hand, his magic was too strong. Even if I wanted to fight him, I knew that I would lose. Maybe my senses were just so dulled before because of the shield. However, standing so close to him, it was like his magic was a bomb waiting to explode.

"They were going to hand me over to him," I explained while trying to step closer to the border.

"You were always a manipulative liar," Cruor spit at me.

Baecos was behind me then, his hand caressing my shoulder, his lips behind my ear.

"No one will care to save you," he whispered. "I have been dreaming about this moment." His arm wrapped around my waist just like Callum had done and his hand made his way under my shirt. "Been dreaming about what I would make them watch. I was so excited to see the look on Cruor's face as I took you from behind while she screamed for you. But it looks like now she may even cheer me on."

Fear pooled in the pit of my stomach and I felt it leave a sour trail at the back of my throat. I promised myself that I would be strong enough to never experience this again. I promised that I would make them remember, make them cower in fear, but it is still I who is cowering. I swallowed my fear and lifted my hand up as if I were to cup his face. I would show them that I was more than what he made me.

"That's right, if you behave, this will be much more pleasant for you." He leaned into my hand and I watched as Cruor's eyes widened. Fluvis looked as if he were about to commit murder… and Ash wouldn't even look at me. I wondered what I looked like to them now. Were they disgusted by how easily I killed someone? Or was it that maybe they finally saw that the Iniq that they once knew was nowhere to be found. His other hand caressed the side of my hip and tried to bring me closer to him.

As quick as I could, I made a burst of magic shoot out from my palm and impale the side of his face, leaving a bleeding hole where his check should have been. Baecos cursed and his grip loosened just enough so that I could wiggle my way out of it and put some distance between us. I ran parallel to the barrier while throwing magic behind me trying to slow him as much as I could. I heard the shouts of the others, but I could not spare them even a second place.

I felt the door and it appeared in front of me in the distance. I raced towards it, all too aware of Baecos's magic flailing behind me. I felt his fingers graze my shirt, but I was just a second too fast.

As I neared, I reached out to the door and watched as it swung open violently.

"Watch out!" It was Ash who spoke this time, but before I could turn to him, there was a flash of light near my foot and my whole left leg exploded in pain. I fell to the floor and white started to cloud my vision.

"No." My voice was grainy, and pain clouded my judgment.

My leg must have been charred but I tried not to look at it. I forced myself to pitifully crawl the rest of the way to the door, clawing at the dirt beneath me, not caring what it made me look like. It was only about ten feet away now, I reached out my hand and watched as the black tendrils snaked their way towards me.

"Please," I begged it. It hesitated.

I felt Baecos's full weight on top of me, so he must have been straddling my back. His hand weaved itself through my hair and he yanked back so hard I heard some tear from my skull. I let out a guttural moan at the pain.

"I told you to behave, did you really think you could outrun me?" His face was getting closer to mine and when I tried to turn away, he just pulled my hair even harder.

I whimpered and tried to stretch my arms to meet the tendrils, but they did not move forward.

"Fucking move!" I commanded, but they did not listen.

"You want to give up." His voice was like thick honey again, he was trying to use his power. I felt the overwhelming urge to relax my body but instead, I tried to focus on the urge I had to live more. I tugged at the feeling, but I felt myself losing the battle quickly. I was tired.

*This is your last.*

I gritted my teeth trying to remember anything that would help me in this situation.

"You want to give up," he repeated, but this time he also poured that sickening magic in me again. I felt my body heat up against my will. I felt tears prick my eyes.

"Please," I begged to the door, but still nothing.

*Does it work on everyone?*

*No, just those who have more darkness than light.*

I silently begged for someone to get him off me. I knew I had messed up, but this could not be what was planned for me. I had to be destined for more. The power that exploded within me just moments ago was just a taste of what I could do, just a preview of what I could do if I could just unclaw his fingers from my hair.

I really would love to just lay my head down on the ground. All this fighting was tiring. I've been tired not just in my body, but my soul. It predates this body's life span by hundreds of years, I carried it in my magic and in my memories. I was just so tired.

*My power has… limitations, yours goes not.*

The dark tendrils of the door started to retreat then; panic bubbled up inside me. I focused on whatever light I could find within myself.

"Fight." My voice was not my own when it came out. It was guttural and detached. "Fight," I repeated, and instead of Baecos's voice that filled my head, it was now my own.

*Fight. Fight. Fight.*

My voice chanted over and over again through my head. I felt the adrenaline course through my veins, readying me.

I could do it.

Baecos's laughed cut through my thoughts, and he

tugged my hair so tight that my face was now turned upward. I stared right into his violet crazed eyes. I felt my lips form into a grimaced smile and his eyes widened in response. I knew what I had to do; I would learn from the best.

"You will regret this one day," I spoke as loud as I could, my voice was not nearly as smooth as Baecos's but it made the air vibrate and cackle between us.

"That's cute that you would think that." Baecos leaned towards my lips with a sick smile on his face. Just as his lips brushed across mine, I imagined my target in my mind. His smile, his smell, the way he comforted me, his magic.

"You still have a chance to stop this." I prayed that the vibrations would reach their intended target. I felt his magic nearby spike suddenly. Baecos did not pull away from my lips and instead bit down hard on them. He only moved away when he felt the blood pool out of them.

Baecos started to laugh but it was cut short when I felt a heavy force collide with him. I tumbled with them but tried to sink my fingers into the hard ground so I would not be crushed to death. Baecos's legs finally detached from me after I tumbled in the dirt, and I was able to detach myself from him and catch the familiar hound with a white patch on his head. Ash had his large jaws clamped around Baecos upper chest and violently shook him around like a rag doll.

I pushed myself up onto my injured leg and limped forward towards the door. When Ash let out a whimper, I dared to look back and saw Baecos holding open his jaw with his hands—he was going to break it. I looked to the door and then back to Baecos. I gathered another bow and arrow and aimed it towards his head.

"Stop fucking shaking," I hissed towards my fingers. I couldn't get a clear shot and Ash's face was so close to Baecos that I could easily kill him. Baecos sent me a wild smile but it was wiped clean off his face when Fluvis and

Cruor both came running at him. Baecos dropped Ash to protect himself.

"Run!" Fluvis screamed at me while blocking Baecos's path. I spared only a small glance at Ash and turned back around to the door.

My heart stopped when I saw Vitos leaning against one of the trees beside the door, but instead of stopping me, he merely looked behind me and started slowly walking towards Baecos.

"I regret what I allowed to happen to Spiris," he spoke as he passed me. "This is my gift to him. If I see you again, I will bring you back to Baecos without hesitation."

I nodded but stayed silent and pushed myself forward as fast as my injured leg would take me, catching myself on the door frame. The darkness was not as scary as I once believed. It was now comforting.

I took one step forward and held my head high.

My life up until now had been a series of motions set forth by other people, other forces. These steps are the first steps in taking back my fate. No, it was the first step to utterly destroying them and watching as others gawked, screamed, and ran with terror as they watched me rip their heads off. I would not be tied down ever again; I would not be underestimated ever again.

With each step, I consciously took back control over my life, prying it from the cold, dead grip of the fates.

# Epilogue

I don't know how long I stayed in the dark. As soon as my whole body was through the door, I felt the darkness swirl around me, and the hand that pulled me in was attached to a body that seemed to be embracing me. Even in the dark, the body was warm and comforting. This was the type of darkness that I would strive for.

*You are home.*

*Yes.* I did not need to open my mouth to speak. The words floated around me like they were plucked right from my head. The figure that was embracing me smoothed my hair down. I felt soothing emotions fill me and relaxed my body against theirs. I felt my body heal with each stroke of their hand.

*Forget those you left behind for they will only slow down your journey.*

*They are already forgotten.* It was true. The names and the faces on the other side of the door left me then, and in their place were fuzzy memories that did not seem important.

*Good.* The voice hissed as if right in my ear. I let the figure caress me and whisper to me. I felt so tired and their arms were so tight and welcoming. I buried my head in their chest and soaked in the warmth. I don't know how long I was held against them, but I didn't care. I hadn't felt this relaxed in years.

The body was gone without warning and so was the comforting aura it left. Now, while still surrounded by darkness, I felt a chill run through me. My teeth began to chatter, and my knees felt weak. I saw a shimmer of light in front of me, and I had to shield my eyes as they adjusted.

*You have been here too long. Leave NOW.*

I felt my heart start to race as the voice turned angry. I ran towards the light as I felt cold chill me to my bones and the aura in the air changed to malice. I had to get out. It was not long before I reached the light. I prayed that my legs could last just a few steps longer. Thankfully, they did, but I felt the clawed hand that gripped at my ankle try to force me back.

I tumbled through the rip in the darkness and into the light.

I quickly looked around, but I found that I was no longer inside the door. My eyes adjusted and I found myself in a field of spider lilies. From my position on the ground, some came as high up as my head. They each had a unique magical signature attached to them and made them glow. Looking up, I realized that there was no light coming from the sky. It was pitch black and painted with red clouds, but that did not dull my eyesight. I could still see everything around me with stunning clarity. I stood up slowly and brushed off the dirt that was on my pants. My whole body was healed now and all the phantom pains and shakes that ailed me had disappeared.

It became obvious to me that this world was in fact no type of heaven; the others were right when they said there were devils here.

"You look better than the last time I saw you."

I turned at the familiar voice and my heart plummeted. He was standing with his hand rubbing the back of his neck and he gave me a sheepish look. His black curls had grown even longer, and they now formed a mane around his head that came down to his collar bones. He was wearing a black open chest tunic and black riding pants with knee-high boots. I had never seen him dressed like his before, but the black suited him.

"The High Kings are playing me," I said as I slowly walked towards the figure. I half expected him to vanish before my eyes. He reached out his hand to me and I took it, feeling the now smooth skin, and it was solid. He was real.

"I told you, wherever you go, I would follow," Spiris chuckled and brought me in for a hug. "They may not have been gods, but they sure did favor me."

I lifted my face to look into his eyes—same as before. I moved his hair out of his face and noticed his elongated ears. I traced them lightly with my fingers.

"You're a..." I stopped and watched his face; he gave me a big smile showing off his fangs.

"Demon, yes. Everyone here is." He brought my hand up into his curls, and I found small horns poking out of his head. He was watching me closely as I ran my hands through his hair and face. I still couldn't believe he was really here. His light tattoos were attached to this body as well, but I saw more that framed the sides of his face barely visible by his hair. I traced the new tattoos and felt him smile as I did.

"Everyone? Wait… why do you have horns?"

"Yes, you have a lot to learn, and now that's my job to help you. But first…" He held me at arm's length and smiled even wider before getting on one knee, one arm across his chest, the other behind his back, and bowed his head. "Let me be the first to welcome you home, High King Iniq. I will be here to serve as your right-hand and advisor. I pledge my loyalty to you and promise to protect and serve you for as long as I shall live."

"High King?" I felt dread fill me. This was not the power I wanted.

Spiris's only response was to meet my eyes and give me a big toothy grin, flashing me his new fangs.

# Acknowledgements

This one goes out to my partner. She has been the sole person who has pushed me hard enough so that I can make my dream a reality. Thank you for everything that you have done and all the patience and care you have given me. This is the start to a very long but exciting journey ahead of us.

Also, for all of those along the way who have helped me with beta reading and editing, thank you for your support and your love. Without your kind words, I would have given up on this story after the first read through.

For anyone out there reading this and wanting to start their own writing journey… do it! The only one holding you back is yourself. There is a huge community out there willing and ready to help at a moment's notice. Make it count and put your story out there!

# Cover Design

I would like to give a special shoutout to Madli for designing this beautiful cover. Working with her has been an absolute pleasure and I can't wait to work with her again. If you would like to commission her, go to www.madli.eu. You can also reach her on her social media at https://www.instagram.com/madliart/

## Elle Mae

Elle is a native Californian who has lived in Los Angeles for
most of her life. From the very start, she has been in love
with all things fantasy and reading. As soon as Elle found
out that writing books was someone's career, she started
writing stories. While the first ones were about scorned love
and missed opportunities of lunchtime love, she has grown
to love the fantasy genre and looks forward to making a
difference in the world with her stories.
Loved this book? Please leave a review!
For more books like this visit ellemaebooks.com.

Instagram: itselissamae Twitter: mae_books

Need Your LGBTQ Vampire Fix?

Check out

Contract Bound: A Lesbian Vampire Romance

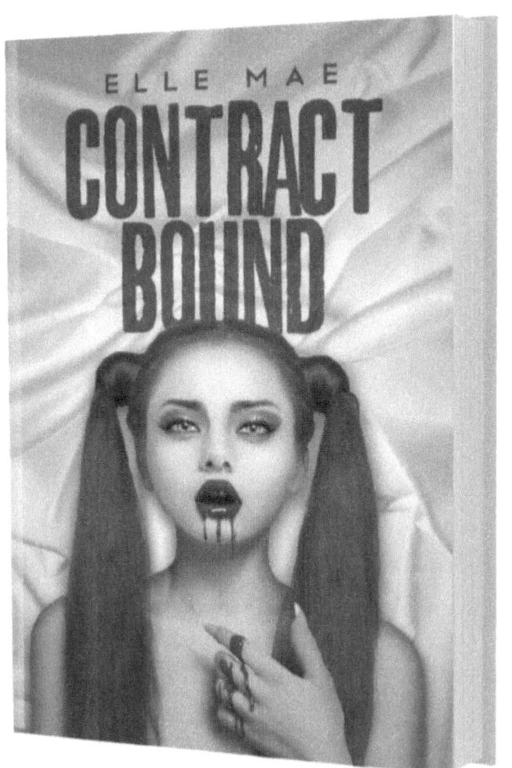